IF EVER I FIND YOU...
IF I *EVER* FIND YOU!

Robert Karp

Disclaimer

All characters appearing in this work are fictitious. Any resemblance to real persons, living or dead, is purely coincidental. Many places and institutions named in this book do exist. However there has been no attempt to accurately portray, describe, or define how they work, how they function, or their mission. This book is fiction.

ISBN 978-0-9980344-6-1

For Bob Erickson and the others (you know who you are) who have read and supported my literary efforts. Thank You.

ALSO BY ROBERT KARP

THE TED VALLAN MYSTERIES TRILOGY

STRANGER IN MY LAKE   2017

ONE ROTTEN APPLE   2018

MORE THAN MURDER   2019

- 1 -

He turned off the two lane blacktop and continued his run, on the dirt road now. The cold, bright late fall morning weather was energizing. Brown pastures flanked both sides of the road, fenced off by poles and wires. The long, challenging hill was ahead and he began to anticipate it. Initially he pushed into it, but it didn't take long for him to recognize his pace was slowing. About thirty yards from the steep crest he became aware, even through his headphones, a vehicle was coming up behind him. In response, as he always did, he moved to the edge of the road and continued to trudge up those last yards to the height of the hill.

As he reached the summit the vehicle pulled alongside him. He saw the pistol and just before it flashed he managed to yell in anger.

"Fucker! Why not before the damn hill?"

Trooper down.

———

Around noon Jorge Gonzales left to return to the City. The filthy, beat up white Outback left a plume of dust behind as it tore along the dirt roads, navigating them like a mouse in a maze well aware of the path to the cheese. This was the usual route Jorge used to come and go from Vermont for his deliveries. Avoiding main roads was an occupational decision that had served him well, so far, on his business trips.

By the time he was on his way the bright morning had turned to overcast skies and a biting, chilly wind. It was cold and getting nasty outside but he was warm and comfortable in the reliable old car. Money was safely stitched in the left side of the passenger seat and he was feeling as safe as he was going to be, thinking about when he could light up one of the three sizable joints in a small box in his door cup holder. They were located so they could be quickly tossed if he was about to be pulled over.

There was always a subtle sense of exhilaration when he began the journey home. The transfers overnight had been a breeze. Soon he'd be back with Laurinda. They celebrated his returns like a long anticipated homecoming after his success; a sexually charged setting they each enjoyed: a quick dinner out and then back to his apartment to make passionate love. Six hours to go but he was already excited. He pounded his palms on the wheel keeping cadence with his singing.

Goin' home…home…home…
to see my baby…see my baby…
make me feel so good…feel so good…so good…

'Fuck Vermont and its brown fields and brown trees with no leaves now,' he thought. Vermont was empty and quiet. He was on his way back to the City. The City was alive; always active. He had some deals in the works that would get him out of this shitty business. Something had to pop soon. More soberly, he thought, something *better* happen soon. Doing mule work was diminishing returns. Especially for a bright guy like him. Not likely too many college kids did what he was doing during some school breaks. Recently he had been thinking school might not be the place for a guy like him.

Gonzales always enjoyed cresting the steep hill he was approaching. Whenever he accomplished that and then began to drop down he sensed he was truly on his way back home. It was too steep to go up fast, but after he drove over the top he liked to pick up speed, at least not use the brakes going down, for as long as he could. He felt himself relaxing and, for the first time that day, remembered he had not yet turned on the CD player.

Leaning over to the glove box for a CD wasn't so easy as the Subaru was close to the peak of the hill. At first his eyes kept bouncing from the road to the glove box and back. Nearing the top that was too dangerous and he gave up. Good thing. At the peak, just as he was summoning his courage to stay off the brakes for as long as he safely could on the way down, he had to make a sudden swerve to avoid something in the road.

Maneuvering over the very top of the hill required him to go slowly, so the long, motionless body was obvious to him. He drove ten feet past and stopped, fixing his gaze on the object through his rear view mirror.

"Holy shit," he yelled out loud. He sat there for a minute. Jorge wasn't sure what to do. His six previous trips had all gone so well he had been very relaxed. Maybe he was too relaxed; so used to his routine that his reaction was what it would be for most anyone who came on an emergency in the middle of nowhere. He thought he should see if someone needed help. There didn't appear to be anyone else around; not even cows or horses in the pastures. He wondered what might have happened? But then he also thought it might be best for him to keep going.

'Wait a minute. Did that guy just move?' He slipped the gears into reverse and slowly backed up until he was parallel to the body in the road. He looked around. No one or anything else in his view; darkening and desolate. A barren landscape with wind whipping. Cold. Anyway, too cold to just lay down in the road.

"Hey! You okay over there? …You aw right?"

Nothing. If he had seen movement before there was nothing now as Jorge sat in his car looking through his open passenger window at what looked like a man, appearing lifeless, on the ground.

After sitting there a few minutes he left his engine running and slowly, cautiously opened his door and walked around the car and over to the immobile object. He thought, 'Man, wouldn't do this in the City. Who knows what shit could be goin' on?' It was cold standing on the top of that hill. Gusts of even colder wind were blowing around him under the darkening clouds. Totally quiet beyond the soft hum and occasional hiccup of the old car's engine.

The body of a man on his side didn't respond, in any way, to Jorge's words, even after he bent over him and raised his voice. Then he saw the small pool of blood under his chest. But the thing was, he couldn't tell, for sure, if he was breathing. How would he know if he was dead?

Probably dead. Nothing he could do for him. He stood up, confused by what lay before him.

"Oh Shit!" A slight shudder of the body. He was sure. 'The fucker's alive. Can't leave him out here.'

———

Jorge Gonzales, a drug running mule from the City, spent surprisingly little time debating with himself pros and cons of doing something about the body in the road. He was working; doing a job. He was expected. Going on his way would have been the smart thing to do. But he didn't.

Gonzales ran back to the Outback and opened the rear hatch. There was an old pastel blue blanket lying on the floor. He took it from the back and returned to where the man was. He laid it out parallel to the possibly alive or dead body. Jorge talked to the body and told it what he was about to do then rolled the body over onto the blanket. Maybe there was some response; he couldn't be sure. What there was was a lot of blood. And, as the body collapsed on the blanket, clipped to the inside of running pants, he saw it possessed a thick, black nylon holster with a small pistol.

The pistol startled Jorge but it didn't help him with any ideas about who this person might be. His immediate reaction was to recall once telling Laurinda he thought he should have a gun with this job he was doing to get money. She told him it was a silly idea because he was going to stop doing this work very soon. Too dangerous and not the kind of thing he should be doing. And the same for a gun. But there was one. Just sitting there, in the middle of nowhere.

He took it. He left the body to go back to the car and put the pistol on the seat. Back at the body he rolled it loosely in the blanket leaving the head out. Supporting the head he dragged the blanket to the hatch and hoisted it in. He didn't think the man was breathing. No vehicle or person passed by. The area was deserted.

Jorge had a rough idea of how to drive to a small hospital he had once passed on the fringe of what he heard was called the Kingdom area, still going south, more east than west, but not hugely out of his way. Until he was very close he actually didn't dwell much on what he was doing or potential risks or pitfalls. Once on the outskirts of the town, a few blocks from the hospital, he became acutely anxious about what he should do when he and his body arrived.

Quickly the entire business now no longer made any sense to him. What was he doing? Why was he doing this? Being questioned about a body at an emergency room was crazy. All kinds of questions and he'd have to stay for the cops. The cops! No that wouldn't do. This was a bad idea… But the guy might be breathing.

Jorge Gonzales panicked.

He drove to a side of the ER and quickly jumped out, leaving the engine running. By now Jorge was sweating and he could feel his heart racing. He had come this far so he had to leave the body. He ran through the automatic sliding doors. A wheelchair was in the entrance and he snatched it, on the run, and raced back to the car. He unloaded the probably dead man and pushed the wheelchair as far as the sliding door and locked the brakes, something he knew from helping with his grandmother.

Back in the Subaru he returned to the road, going west. His head ached and his mind was a mess. What the hell had he done? Why did he do this? A disaster. Did he see someone coming out of the ER after him as he drove away? What if he did? 'Oh shit...what a mistake!' He was fucked now. He knew that old blanket could never be traced to anyone. But what if someone really did see him driving away? His car? His plates? 'Oh shit.'

He was frantic now. His panic continued. How fucking dumb and stupid could he be? 'Have to get away. Fuck the cash,' he thought. If they came after him he was finished. He pulled his folding knife from the center console and unfolded it as he continued to drive. With one hand on the wheel and the knife in his right he carefully un-stitched the defect in the seat next to him, eventually pulling out the envelopes with cash and placed them on the seat, next to the pistol.

"Shit! The gun," he shouted out loud. Another mistake. 'I must be a real asshole. Why did I take that?'

Jorge was sweating and totally beside himself. He willed himself to calm down. The contingency plans; he had to remember what he was supposed to do if he was in trouble. Get rid of everything; the money, the grass, and yes, the fucking pistol. Where?

After driving for about five minutes he began to feel a little better. Maybe he should just continue on. Go home and do nothing else. His brain wasn't exploding anymore. He had done a stupid thing. Who cared if that body was dead or alive. He never should have touched it. Seemed like everything was okay now.

————

Moments later a state police cruiser passed Jorge going in the opposite direction. He stiffened. A quarter mile past him the trooper slowed and his brake lights lit up the Subaru's rear view mirror. This was no good. Instantly, panic consumed him again. Jorge was about to go over the Winooski River. He pulled to the road's edge and quickly tossed the pistol, then the money, and, finally, the box with the three joints, high and far, well over the guard rail, into the wide, deep, and rapidly flowing muddy river way below. He took his foot off the brake and started a slow roll forward.

What else was he supposed to do? What did he forget?... 'Ah shit... the phone!' He pulled his cell from the center console and with his right hand prepared to flip it through his window. But this was not his phone. This pre-paid cell was only for emergencies and Jorge thought he never used it this trip. Had to get going. Better keep it. Then he began to accelerate. The road curved to the right with the river and Jorge sighed in relief as he followed the bend in the road.

As he completed the curve and the road opened up again there was another state police cruiser just ahead, lights flashing, blocking the road...waiting for him. In a moment another flashing cruiser pulled up behind him.

———

- 2 -

Leaving the blacktop for the dirt road he recalled his own very early time on the force. At the beginning, just like the dead trooper, Ed Clark, he worked Narcotics. Trooper Clark was on the force for what turned out to be the last eight months of his life. Vermont State Police Major Crime Investigator Lieutenant Donald Dark was on the Narcotics Investigation Unit for about his first eight months also. It was not a good time for him.

He did well enough but he never liked being there. He couldn't get along with many of the other troopers. He felt they disparaged the people in the community their job touched. It didn't matter if it was a dealer or a user to them; they hated them all and treated all of them poorly. At the least, they made fun of them and their fucked up lives. The Lieutenant felt law officers who couldn't respect or try to understand something of the lives of the folks they spent their days working with weren't in the right spot.

Sometime later, reflecting about that time, he had to admit, since his views made him the odd man out, maybe the attitudes that guided their actions were the only way to stay sane and do that kind of job. Who knew? Tough job; tough set of troopers. But

Dark got out and was glad he did. What about this young guy, Clark? Dark wondered how Clark adapted to the way Narcotics ran? Short life. Sad. Probably dead, in some way, because of time on Narcotics. Definitely a dangerous job. Not that any police job wasn't dangerous; but maybe more dangerous than most.

Last seven, eight years doing major criminal investigations were much better for Dark. He guessed he had been lucky. Moving into Major Crime Investigation at a time when the force was down a few in the division so he could move up more quickly worked out great for him. Might be the youngest at his level in the state right now. Not a problem. He had worked hard at it. Studied. The work suited him.

This was going to be a down day no matter what happened. A trooper was dead; murdered. Nothing much worse than that for the force.

When he was called yesterday, late in the afternoon, a while after the body showed up at the hospital, it was already getting too dark to do much outside. So the road on the hill was blocked off and the field team and everyone else planned to show up at first meaningful light. This morning was bright and cold, a slight dusting in the fields, not the first flurries of the season, but still early. If the weather and early afternoon darkness had impeded investigating the area the day before Dark didn't know what else could have been done. Everything was brown; a stark early winter landscape, he thought.

In addition to the increasing grade of the hill small rocks and gravel noisily pinged his cruiser's under carriage, also tending to cause him to slow his speed. The road at the very top of the hill was obstructed by a pick-up parked almost perpendicular to the road. A few troopers were in the fields close by the few barbed wire strands which acted as a fence and blocked off each side of the fields from the dirt road. Looking for a bullet; unlikely, but maybe a revolver. Or any sign of recent human presence.

He parked his cruiser on an angle also, fearing the hill was so steep putting his emergency brake on and being in park might not be enough to keep the cruiser from sliding down the hill. That's how steep it was. No way for the mobile major crime investigation vehicle to get anywhere near there. A trooper had been murdered. No greater disaster, but even fifty troopers and all kinds of equipment wouldn't likely have added anything to investigating that sparse area.

"Hey Lieutenant. Not coming up with too much. This is sure a road less traveled, so my good guess is this is what it looked like up here since the shooting. Good chance this is at least the spot where poor kid was before he was brought to Central…Tell ya why."

The others in the fields stopped sifting through the grass and dirt on the ground and walked over to the thin wire fences by the road to listen. Tall and chubby, Sergeant Len Slauson was bundled up for winter and was even wearing a leather hat with insulated ear flaps drooping over his ears; a questionable item for a trooper in regulation uniform.

"Fucker kid moved his car back and forth coupla' times. Really no one else's tread pattern obvious. Then look here Lieutenant. Pretty obvious again."

Slauson stood in the middle of the narrow road and pointed down and east.

"That's where the vehicle was."

Then he turned to the west and nodded at the ground.

"There's poor Clark's blood."

Dark started to walk by the Sergeant but was quickly stopped by a wave of Slauson's hand.

"Careful Lieutenant. Look at what's in the road."

Indeed, a two, two and a half foot wide area was disrupted by a lightly grooved pattern running from the splash of dried blood on the ground to the tire tracks on the other side of the road.

"Guess is kid rolled him up in the blanket he was found in at the hospital and pulled the body across the road; then hoisted him in his vehicle."

Lieutenant Dark wasn't the kind of person who thought out loud. He tended to mull things over to himself. He only spoke words he wanted others to hear. Today his initial response to the scene and Slauson's comments left him with no reason to share his fledgling reactions.

Dark was puzzled by what he was looking at and had heard. For a time he stood by himself at the edge of the dirt road, listening to the soft whistle of the cold wind, surveying the desolate and lonely place. The location might as well have been on the moon. Possibly a spot for a meeting, but not too likely. Something undercover maybe? Everything about Clark's body suggested he was out for a run…except maybe his holster. But even that was consistent with an off-duty weapon, something all troopers were encouraged to carry. The revolver was gone and could have been the weapon that killed him.

If this was the site of a meeting how did the trooper get to it? Maybe Clark was in the kid's Subaru and was shot right here, or shot before and brought here. His place was only about four miles away. Not too far for a run. But who would choose to run up this hill, Dark thought?

He caught himself. He was drifting. None of this made a whole lot of sense since whoever the kid in custody was he was the one who brought Clark to the hospital and later, after his arrest, directed troopers to this location, where he said he found Clark's body. He said he brought Clark to the hospital because he thought he might be alive. Not what you'd expect to hear with some form of a drug deal or interdiction gone bad.

As if he thought he might be able to know what the Lieutenant was going over in his mind, Slauson continued.

"Trooper in the first cruiser heading to the hospital spotted the kid's car from his rearview. Believes he saw the kid toss some things in the Winooski. Nothing up here. Bet he tossed Clark's weapon and other shit in the river. This time of year, and after the heavy fall rains, not very likely divers will be able to find much; probably nothing…at least not till late summer; or maybe ever.

"This drug shit is getting to be too much, Lieutenant, don' ya think? No place is safe from these murderous bastards. Invading Vermont, and everywhere. Like fucking cockroaches!"

Dark was still trying to think of a way, or a few ways, to fit together what was known. He realized Slauson's last comment was meant to be answered and that diverted him from his thoughts. His glance to Slauson reminded him there were a few others within earshot and they seemed to be waiting for the Lieutenant to say something also. He looked to the ground and lightly kicked some loose stones with his shoe.

"Always been a bad business…even here in Vermont. Getting worse everywhere I guess."

To Dark, it was obvious from his job what was worse about drugs was the way they were tearing families apart, and especially destroying the lives of so many young people; if not just outright killing them. The Lieutenant knew Slauson was talking about crime associated with gangs and dealers who supply the stuff. The violence and occasional homicides that came from them probably hadn't changed much in years but most cops focused on them as the drug problem kept growing bigger.

Slauson wanted everyone there to know where he stood. "Hear that kid's a spic; not likely local. The blacks and spics really stand out up here. Burns my ass the balls they have to act like it's okay for them to be here and act like this. And now this… Shit!"

Nobody responded. Everyone there was tense. No one appeared inclined to add to Slauson's comments or attempt to soften them. The troopers returned to the areas they were searching and the

Lieutenant and Slauson slowly walked the road a short distance north and then south of what had been seen in the dirt. It was a discouraging time, and place, for all of them.

"Okay, nothing much else here. Why don't you take your team over to that river spot, Len, and see if you can find anything there. That kid's in a holding cell in Williston and I'm gonna go talk to him."

———

Donald Dark was angry also. This was a devastating plague and all kinds of awful shit came from it. Too many weapons helped fuel the magnitude of the violence it produced. As he managed to carefully turn his cruiser around on the steep hill without it tipping over Dark slowly drove back to the blacktop, brooding about the scope of an equally big problem for him. What the hell is policing all about, he wondered? What are you really supposed to put your life on the line for in this fucked-up world anyway? Good or bad people getting shot wasn't ever going to make a difference one way or another in the grand scheme of dealing with this disaster fueled by drugs.

His dark thoughts did not really echo the Lieutenant's usual personality or outlook. He was, by nature, a friendly guy who generally liked to see the lighter side of things; known for his often funny and clever take on the world around him. Dark shivered, just slightly, as he proceeded on his way. He felt he was almost second guessing himself for having such thoughts. Sure, it was a grim setting but why was he reacting like he was being pressured by it? Thinking if it was such a good idea for him to remain a cop was no longer a new thought. Maybe this kind of world view reflected a growing estrangement with the idea of putting your life on the line without qualification.

The idea of dying on a bleak frozen hilltop because of drugs, an unsolvable problem, created a palpable tightness in his chest; almost a fear. Even contemplating trying to weigh the good and importance of his job with its risks was un-nerving in a way. Could these kinds of thoughts cause him to lose the edge he needed to be successful as a law officer? Any sense of adventure was long gone. Donald Dark was stuck on mulling over the apparent senselessness of Ed Clark's homicide. Of course it could have been him. Why not? Guns against guns. Too much money involved for anyone to back off. Too many acts of violence while on drugs or alcohol.

———————

For so long the Lieutenant's job seemed like the most important part of his life. He tacitly accepted that as the reason his personal life was so limited and poorly developed. Indeed, his personal life wasn't exactly the highlight reel he hoped but he was young enough to assume, in his mid-thirties, there was still a chance he'd meet a woman for him. Dark's failures on that front were a constant source of needling from his few good buddies and an annoying family topic.

At times, lately, he thought what was the point of any of that anyway if he couldn't assure a life companion he would always be there for her or a family? Sure, Dark had flashes of these thoughts over the last year but it never hit him nearly this hard before he stood that morning on that desolate hilltop.

Tall and more fit than Sergeant Slauson, Dark's height made it difficult for him to leave his hat on when in his cruiser. Somehow the Lieutenant's body and his movements never seemed to have lost a certain awkwardness commonly associated with teenagers when they have a growth spurt. The more recent dour turn in his personality seemed to amplify his awkward appearance.

Consciously, he turned his attention to chatter on the radio, hoping it would divert his train of thought. Then there was a call for him.

"Hey Donald D, it's Fleury. Where the hell are you? This f-ing Mexican kid is causing big trouble here."

Dark's distracted mind reacted like a wrench had been thrown at him from across a room. For some time he had been uncertain about the usefulness and risks of his career, some of which may have been quickly re-kindled by his first thoughts at that crime scene. But the kid he heard about sounded like no obvious murderer. Now the Barracks Commander at Williston seemed to be suggesting the fucker was raising hell in a place he should know to keep his mouth shut. Dark's glimmer of any possible empathy for this kid faded fast. And his brief reverie about the larger picture of his career in law enforcement also seemed to fade with it. 'If this asshole killed one of ours, or anyone, he needs to be finished; forever,' he thought. He was getting upset but still managed to toss something back at his friend, Lieutenant Edmund Fleury.

"Come on Fleur, can't you handle a City boy? Find someone who can speak Spanish; the University is just down the road, you know. You…"

"Just get down here DD. Waiting for you to waddle on in. Bastard seems to speak English, but Spanish too. Imagine. Turns out this kid managed to call people in the City and there's a lawyer here now who wants the kid out of custody immediately. Imagine; a cop killer walking out of here? Burlington attorney? Don't know the lawyer; maybe you do. Anyway I made it clear no one's going anywhere until you get here."

Dark was surprised again about the kid. Details so far had all the signs of a drug transporting mule. Knowing the kind of perps sent from the big cities to peddle shit up here this was not what he was expecting. Who figured out to get him a lawyer; and so quickly?

"Tell the asshole lawyer we generally keep suspected cop killers locked up for a bit but I'll be glad to talk when I'm ready…an proly won't be ready for quite a while. Up to him if he wants to hang around. ETA 'bout ten minutes."

"Will pass it on, bud. Oh by the way…" Fleury's last words were lost in static.

Dark was back to ruminating about the case unfolding that morning. His brief drift into thoughts of frustration and some fear were tamped down by that odd report from Williston. Many of the questions in the Lieutenant's head remained unanswered. But then he thought this part of the case still might not turn out to be all that complicated.

———

- 3 -

Laurinda Alvarez was in a panic.

She was exhausted. She worried through the night and wasn't sure she slept at all. She thought she loved Jorge but wondered if he was too wild for her. Like all young men he insisted on living more on the edge. He took chances she thought were too risky, although that may have been part of what attracted her to him. They were young, maybe too young, to feel so committed to each other. Now it had suddenly all come crashing down on them. The whole idea of doing this had been crazy for someone like Jorge. Laurinda had told him it was reckless.

Eighteen months younger than Jorge Laurinda was about as directed as a twenty year old could be. In high school she was lauded for her math ability so she was studying accounting in college. It didn't come to her nearly as easily as she had assumed it would. She second guessed the quality of her high school background but that only motivated her to work harder at succeeding. Jorge might not share her resolve and motivation to succeed in college and that was a concern. If Laurinda had known Jorge was considering dropping out of school she would have been upset, perhaps even to the point of re-evaluating their relationship.

Jorge insisted the money was too good and the risks too small not to do occasional mule trips. Accepting that for the moment, Laurinda worked with him to minimize his risks and come up with plans for contingencies if things did not go well. A significant part of her exhaustion this morning related to her constant efforts to remember and try to implement the strategies they had talked about if one of his trips went sour.

When they did their planning it was always done in a light vein, as though neither truly believed anything would ever be needed. They joked about the possibilities as much as they wrote down some ideas of what to do if he was in trouble. In bed together they laughed uproariously as they acted out some scenarios, inevitably winding up arm in arm, channeling their fear of the potential awfulness of a glitch into an intensity of their love for each other as they had ardent sex.

Today Laurinda wondered how much, if any, of what they planned Jorge would remember, or even attempt. His call to her late in the afternoon yesterday exposed his complete panic and fear. She was amazed she hadn't gone completely to pieces also. She remembered a few of the contingencies. On reflection today she also thought maybe she might be holding together a bit better than Jorge because Jorge seemed so terrified and lost. One of them had to stay in control. She felt some anger that he had put her in that position. There was no time to think about that now. Laurinda had to help him. The call was frightening.

"Oh my God baby, why are you in jail?"

His upset and fear were telegraphed in his voice.

"Very bad babe, very bad. They say I killed someone; a cop babe! Maybe a Narc babe! Jesus babe a Narcotics cop! I didn't do anything to anyone babe. I didn't kill anyone. What is going to happen to me? Oh shit babe, worse than anything I could ever have imagined. Oh shit!"

He was almost sobbing. Laurinda started to cry, but then caught hold of herself. Her strength was essential at that moment. She wasn't at all sure what had happened but she did know they had talked about how Jorge must behave if he was arrested.

"Baby!..Baby, the accent. Accent babe."

Mexican immigrants, documented and undocumented, made up a large component of the labor force on very rural Vermont's numerous farms as younger people abandoned the area for more urban opportunities in Vermont, or left the state entirely.

Jorge Gonzales was brought to the US when he was two. His English and Spanish were flawless. For his work in Vermont they decided his English needed to be pigeon with as close to a Mexican accent as he could manage. It would complement the thick semicircle Pancho Villa moustache he had grown for the trips to Vermont. The effort created a stereotype they knew might only fool an Anglo, especially since Jorge's roots were in Puerto Rico and he was far taller than the average Mexican. But it was on the list they developed and everything had worked well…until now.

"Please try to remember baby. Okay?"

"Si" he responded, dragging the word out and adding a nasal tone to his inflection. He remembered and would try.

"I'll call the farm workers legal aid number we have. Have no idea how complicated it will be to talk to someone. If I can reach them will only tell them you're in trouble baby. If you really are in big trouble you may have to tell them everything, you know. Maybe not. Wait and see. But Jorge, until I can find a lawyer for you, remember, try to tell the cops nothing. Remember?"

"Oh it's so bad, I think. A while ago they brought me some soup, you know. This guy opened the cell and walked in with a tray. He started coughing and spilled it all over me. Said 'so sorry cop killer.'" He sniffed back a sob. His voice became desolate. "I already told them where I found the dead guy. They don't believe anything I've told them."

Her voice was more firm. His treatment angered her. "Baby try not to say or tell them anything. Say you want a lawyer and wait for that."

―――――――

Hoping it wasn't too late in the day she found a notebook with the number she needed and proceeded to call the migrant legal aid number but could only leave a message. She looked up Williston, Vermont and called the number for Chittenden County legal aid where, after a brief discussion, she was advised to call the Lamoille county Public Defender's office. Since Jorge was in Williston now and she did not know exactly where any potential crime had taken place in Lamoille county the Public Defender's office there advised trying to get the Chittenden county office to represent him at least preliminarily. This time, when she called, that office told her someone would get back to her in the evening.

She sighed, and then tears rolled down her cheeks. She stayed in her chair and put her face in her hands and tried to fight a collapse. Her parents and sister would be home soon. She had to find a way to keep this from them. Laurinda then remembered everyone knew she was going to be with Jorge this evening and stay at his place. Better to be there than at her family's apartment. So she grabbed a few things and left. Classes the next day seemed an impossibility but she packed what she would need.

An hour after she arrived at Jorge's there was still no call on her cell from anyone in Vermont. Around 7:30 Manny Samuels showed up. Samuels had recruited Jorge for this business. He was a nasty, malevolent appearing young guy who she never liked at all. His arrival stoked a fear she had not thought about. He wanted to know where Jorge and his car and the money from his trip were. Jorge was late and the suppliers were concerned. With his obnoxious and mildly threatening tone Manny suggested he better get the money real soon or maybe she, Laurinda, would have to take the place of the cash. He enraged but also frightened her and Laurinda didn't know what to tell him about Jorge. She mustered the strength to act tough and ordered him out, telling him Jorge knew who to call when he returned. Laurinda was terrified again. She knew she shouldn't stay alone at Jorge's all night. She returned home, using real tears, anger, and upset as a sign to her family to leave her alone. They assumed she and Jorge had a bad fight.

———

- 4 -

Lieutenant Dark had no idea there was a disturbance in the public portion of the Barracks as he entered through the locked staff entrance in the back of the building. Once inside he walked directly through the large open room to Ed Fleury's office. It was empty.

Back in the staff area a secretary pointed to the public room a wall away. Walking over to the duty officer's desk, through some glass, he was able to see a small ruckus. Lieutenant Fleury was trying to stay patient with a man and a woman who were shouting at him. The fidgeting of his stance betrayed his growing impatience. There was another couple and a young woman scattered about in the room.

Ed Fleury was older than Dark and was on the shorter side. In fact, it was likely he just barely met the height requirement to be a trooper. In a similar vein his present weight probably flirted with regulation limits also. Fleury's frequent desire to keep his trooper's hat on to cover the progression of his receding hairline was thwarted by his indoor job commanding the Williston Barracks. Donald Dark was tall and trended thin. His hair was not a concern. They were far from a matched pair, but they were good friends.

Dark assumed Fleury was dealing with people involved in the homicide case so he let himself through the locked door and started to stride toward the Lieutenant and the couple shouting at Fleury. As he noticed Dark walk over Ed's impatient facial expression morphed to confusion. Before Dark could say anything Fleury pointed to a chair where a woman was sitting with her back to them.

The Lieutenant stopped in his tracks and turned toward the figure of a woman sitting bolt upright in a chair. Her back was all hair; Reddish-brown, brilliant, shining, hair to her waist, he assumed. At her waist, flaring like very short wings the two ends of a large open notebook in front of her were visible. On the floor, at her side, Dark saw the telltale briefcase.

Somehow the woman figured out to stand as he pivoted and began to walk toward her. Dark was then further struck by the woman's striking appearance in her tailored suit and her dazzling hair. When she turned and faced him he was surprised and felt a modest disappointment that her face didn't exactly compliment her fine hair and figure. She had sharp features and appeared too serious to be beautiful. Attractive, but not what he expected (or was what he was hoping?) As quickly as he thought that was a shame he caught himself. Who was he to be judging or grading this woman? She certainly looked as though she was doing the best she could with her appearance. Dressed smartly and probably was smart since she was a lawyer. Dark tried to dismiss his quick assessment of her. A man's prerogative?

Look at him, he thought. A tall, thin guy whose body never lost the appearance of a teen's gangly years. A name approximating Donald Duck, not dressed in a sailor suit, but a uniform just the same. His early devotion to the force and his successes set him on a path he never considered remotely likely years before. And yet, in the last year, at a time when he could easily have been envisioning many years doing what he had grown to value in higher echelons of the force, thoughts challenging his entire career had begun to chip away at his resolve. He wondered what was going on with him?

A short time before Ed had complained to him on the radio, which was the reason Dark rushed into the public area to offer him support. Dark assumed Ed was still in a battle with the lawyer and maybe a relative or friend of the detainee. It wasn't Dark's intention to interact with the lawyer at all until he learned more about the kid. And he actually had planned to try to speak with the kid alone for a few minutes before letting a lawyer get involved. That wasn't likely anymore. It made this interaction awkward. The woman in front of him offered her hand and started to speak but he cut her off and left her hand in the air.

"Ma'am, I'm Lieutenant Dark and I expect to be in charge of this investigation. I just arrived here after viewing a homicide scene. I need to meet with several troopers and review records and information before I can speak with the detainee or you."

Finally, he shook her hand lightly, noting she had the stronger grip, and started to turn away to return to the locked administrative area. He took note he liked her scent. The lawyer left her papers on a chair and spoke up while following him to the door. Her speech was measured and her tone insistent.

"Lieutenant. Alice Madstern. Neither one of us can sit here all day. Your troopers locked a man up yesterday solely for being a *Good Samaritan*, hoping to help save a man's life. For that he's being held in custody, approaching twenty-four hours soon. He needs to be released immediately."

Dark stopped at the door and stared at her for a second. 'What!' he thought. Impatiently he jiggled the handle, waiting for the duty officer to press the button unlocking it. She continued to speak as he opened the unlocked door and walked away.

"Please release Mr. Gonzales immediately or tell me why it was wrong for Mr. Gonzales to have tried to help someone in dire distress."

———————

Major Harry Caruthers' left foot remained anchored to the floor while he had perched himself on the corner of a desk so he could look through the one way glass mirror. Armed with the few reports he had on the case Donald Dark nodded to the Major as he walked by him and into the interrogation room. Dark felt a greater sense of uncertainty than usual. It would have been better to have more ammunition. He thought he was being rushed by that woman and wasn't very comfortable.

The room was intentionally designed to be spartan and an uncomfortable setting for those being interrogated. Today that included the Lieutenant. As he placed his lanky form in a chair across a metal table from the detainee and Ms. Madstern Dark's expression mirrored Jorge Gonzales'. They each wore their confusion in their eyes and flat mouths. Alice Madstern's face betrayed only a fierce intensity. Lieutenant Dark mis-interpreted her *all business* appearance as a sign of self-confidence. It bothered him. He wasn't sure why but her aggressive affect encouraged Dark to want to try to find a way to remind her of the risks of *over* confidence. He seemed at risk of focusing more on Alice Madstern than Jorge Gonzales.

Introductions were brief. No one shook hands this time. Dark leaned into the small table.

"Mr. Gonzales, why are you in Vermont?"

Jorge stirred in his seat. Before he came close to saying anything Alice Madstern spoke.

"Lieutenant Dark, it's none of your business why Mr. Gonzales is in Vermont."

Dark wondered, 'who is this lady? Is she going to contest every word out of my mouth? Shit!' He spoke again.

"Mr. Gonzales, is there anything *you* would like to say about what you are doing in Vermont? I mean you don't live…" She cut him off just as Jorge had turned to look at her for direction.

"Lieutenant Dark I told you that's none of your business. I…" He interrupted her.

"No, you never told him not to answer my question, did you?"

She started to speak then stopped herself. She paused then sat back and offered a hint of a smile.

"You don't have to answer him, Mr. Gonzales."

So Jorge Gonzales didn't, but his expression amplified his continuing worry and confusion.

Dark leaned back, pushed his papers aside, and looked directly at Jorge.

"Mr. Gonzales, I have read your statement. When you came on Trooper Clark's body in the road why didn't you call 911?"

Alice Madstern looked as though she expected to be the one answering his next question but Dark's query stopped her. She sat, mouth slightly open, thinking, not speaking. It was a fair question. They both looked at Jorge. He raced to decide how to answer and also to remember to try to approximate a Mexican speaking English.

"I…I guess I never thought about that. I think I forgot I had a phone."

When it was clear that was all he intended to say Dark continued.

"So you forgot you had a phone with you, huh? Interesting phone too; pre-paid one with exactly only one call listed on it. To a Laurinda Alvarez in New York City. Not a phone you used regularly was it?"

Before he could ask any more about it Madstern started speaking. She feigned irritation.

"Lieutenant, my client told your troopers, as soon as he saw the unfortunate man's body in that road and thought he was alive, he went into action and brought him to a hospital. The very definition of a Good Samaritan. He…"

Dark interrupted her again. She was annoying and consistently aggressive. Was she succeeding in making him feel frustrated? For just a few seconds they stared, directly, at each other. The shared glance diverted Dark. There something about her. She looked so alive but now less intensely involved; a more reasonable posture than initially.

"Mr. Gonzales do you know what a *Good Samaritan* is?"

Jorge looked right at Dark, his face still showing confusion. Then he turned to Alice Madstern and quickly back to the Lieutenant. After a short hesitation, he spoke, haltingly, maintaining a nasal prolongation of some of his words. His tone was timid but direct.

"Jesus told the 'Parable of the Good Samaritan.'" He paused and looked at each of them. "A man in biblical times finds a badly injured stranger on a well-travelled road and is the only one who helps him. Jesus said to help the less fortunate in their time of need no matter who they are."

Both the Trooper and Ms. Madstern appeared surprised at the way he phrased his response so relevantly, and shared another glance. Notably, each was less wary of the other this time.

"Why'd you put the Trooper in a wheelchair and leave him at the entrance to the Emergency Department and drive away?"

Perhaps buoyed by Jorge's succinct answer just before, Ms. Madstern said nothing. Now both Gonzales and Dark were surprised. As he spoke Jorge looked towards her with uncertainty.

"I…I was very late. I…I wanted to get home before it was too dark. A long trip, you know."

This was getting ridiculous. The Lieutenant had enough. Dark's anger, at the kid…and himself, welled up in him. He had let Alice Madstern slow him down and he wasn't putting any pressure on Jorge. Dark worried the kid was gaining confidence as the interrogation was loping along. Screw the lady. Now his words expressed his anger.

"So let me understand this. You wanted to get to your home before dark and you happened on a dead or dying man in the middle of a road and figured the right thing to do was to load him in your car, take him to a hospital, then dump his body in an entrance to the hospital and run to your car so you could quickly head for home. Is that it?"

Jorge looked at her and she started to be speak but Dark continued with the same mocking tone.

"You found a man with blood all over him but figured you had done your part by bringing him to a hospital and then thought nothing about just rushing off on your way so you wouldn't get caught in the dark. Makes sense, huh?"

As Alice Madstern tried to speak he spoke over her.

"Oh…Ms. Madstern, you think this man may not have shown the best judgement by just leaving? Or maybe he just didn't understand how the law works when you bring a wounded or murdered trooper, or anyone, to a hospital? You think getting home before dark makes more sense, do you?"

Her expression exposed a disarmed look. It softened her face. Again, she looked better to him. Looking at her distracted him but he knew to keep going.

"Mr. Gonzales, you know we found evidence of marijuana in your car." Dark paused but continued to look directly at him. Madstern spoke up.

"Lieutenant you wouldn't have said 'evidence of marijuana' if it was more than a very small amount. You know possession of small amounts is barely criminal almost everywhere now."

Dark purposely never let his eyes move from Jorge.

"Did you have marijuana in the car and were you delivering grass in Vermont?"

"Oh Lieutenant…"

"I can't ask him why we found *evidence of marijuana* in his car? You sure about that Ms. Madstern?"

Despite being notably diverted by her manner and appearance he was no longer finding her as intimidating. Had he put a crack in a facade? If so it didn't give him any sense of satisfaction. But now he thought he saw a subtle sign of vulnerability in her expression. Dark didn't know what to make of it but he thought it made her more appealing.

The lieutenant figured any likelihood this kid murdered Trooper Clark was probably about as small as the traces of grass found in his car. But he was going to do everything he could to ensure Gonzales stayed in Vermont, in custody, for now.

And he sensed Madstern was also somewhat uncertain about the kid's true story. Dark relaxed. He realized he was continually re-assessing his impression of the woman sitting across from him. He decided he was a bit harsh in his initial thoughts about her appearance. Her hair was truly astonishing. Again, he thought she really did well with what she had. Not that unpleasant a person either.

Dark was undecided if now was a good time to bring up the missing weapon. He decided to wait.

"Mr. Gonzales I assume you are aware of the tear in the side of the front passenger seat and the space cut out of the seat?" Asked as a question. "Here's how it's described in the report from the crime scene evaluation team." The Lieutenant read from a paper in a folder on the table. "A surgical cut in the side of the seat back vinyl." Dark looked at Alice Madstern. It was a benign glance, but almost an early warning if she was planning to get back into the interrogation.

Jorge had relaxed a bit with the woman's interruptions but never acted as though he was especially reassured by her presence. Now, as the interview continued, he appeared increasingly anxious again. Neither seemed inclined to say anything immediately. Dark decided Alice was waiting to hear what was coming next from Jorge. Who knew how much this kid had told her, much less, the truth?

Dark's opinion of lawyers wasn't great but he was becoming convinced she might actually care about what was true. At that moment he was still far from even considering how thinking like that probably said more about him and thoughts he was having about this woman than the truth about her. Finally feeling more and more in control of the interaction, although he didn't know why, he was loosening up. The Lieutenant broke the uneasy silence.

"You know, our trained drug detecting dogs can even smell money. Isn't that something, huh?"

Dark was surprised at Alice's muted reaction to his lie, although he guessed Major Caruthers might have slipped off the desk he was sitting on with that one. He thought he had both Jorge and the lawyer rattled; off guard. Time to bring up the weapon.

"Trooper Clark's holster was empty. His revolver is missing. What do you know about that, Mr. Gonzales? We know you threw some things from your car into the Winooski river below."

Alice Madstern was back. It was as though those words snapped her out of passivity.

"Lieutenant, so what? Now are you going to cite Mr. Gonzales for littering; another inconsequential crime? None of this is enough to hold him. And what? You mean a trooper looking through his rear-view mirror could be sure what was going on some distance away?"

Dark feigned surprise.

"Yes... Yes Ms. Madstern, you should be aware of our standard trooper cruiser crime detection exercises. The force trains specifically. But that's not critical." He lied again. "Soon we'll be hearing from the divers. That location is a well-known drop spot. The divers know the currents and riverbed well. Whatever was tossed, especially something like a pistol, will be found."

Jorge Gonzales' gut was in a knot. When Alice Madstern first showed up he had relaxed significantly. He was so appreciative of her take charge behavior and her continual reassurance. She told him to admit little and look to her before he spoke to anyone. She never even asked him what he was doing in Vermont. He assumed she kind of knew, but she never let on one way or the other. Now his anguish continued to rise and his mind was reeling.

This cop made it like he had a lot on him. Jorge tried but it was difficult for him to believe the woman when she said the cops had no good reason that they could keep him in Vermont; in jail. Didn't seem possible to him. This cop was going to tie him to a bunch of crimes; drug crimes and who knew what else. He wondered if the less he told them the more likely they would assume he was the one who killed that trooper?

Dark and Madstern had taken to staying fixed on each other. Jorge's voice was dry and cracked. He startled both of them.

"When I turned the man over to roll up the blanket I saw this gun, loose, on the ground next to him. I really was trying to rush. Didn't think too much about it but didn't think I should leave it there on the ground… Put it on the seat. Later guess I freaked out when a police car passed going other way. I…I pulled over and tossed it. I'm telling you, I just found that guy. Didn't have anything to do with his dying. I mean it."

Jorge Gonzales' Mexican twang was gone long before the end of his short speech. By now he was completely terrified again. Alice Madstern was definitely caught off guard by his confession, even though it was quite limited. Lieutenant Dark realized he had enough now to hold Jorge for the immediate future; until an arraignment could be scheduled.

The tension in the room diminished considerably. At the start Alice Madstern had acted as though she thought she would be able to brashly bully her way through the legal system and intimidate the troopers to get Jorge released. At least it sure looked that way. Now she seemed to back off and appeared to accept Dark had accomplished what he needed to keep Jorge in custody. She argued but no longer in any challenging way. She offered Dark a curt but soft, almost inviting, smile and turned to Jorge.

"You hang in there kid. I'll get you out real soon." As she stood to go Dark was again struck by how she looked, and that beautiful long hair. He noted there were no rings on her fingers. Her appearance and her manner continued to grow on him. Before leaving she paused a few seconds. Standing there, suddenly she looked serious and Dark thought he noted a trace of sadness in her eyes.

"Lieutenant, this business with drugs and guns is destroying more than a few lives. Like being hit by a tsunami. It's hard to think anything can stop it, you know. Lives are being lost to the drugs, and weapons, because of it. I can imagine the sense of futility troopers like you feel trying to battle this thing. I don't know who murdered that trooper but who knows if losing your life in a never ending battle is worth it."

When she spoke Lieutenant Dark had just stood also. Her words froze him. He had never heard anyone say anything like that out loud before. Those were exactly the thoughts he was wrestling with. Amazing. Dark wasn't sure what a 'tsunami' was but assumed what she meant.

What a remarkable woman. He was genuinely startled and it showed on his face as their eyes locked. Without thinking about it, in barely above a whisper, he found himself responding to her words.

"Yes, there is a lot of reason to worry about how much of this dangerous battle is pointless, ma'am."

Still stunned, he watched her walk out. It was a memorable interrogation for the Lieutenant. Alice Madstern was in his head. More than that he felt their few words together and the way they looked at each other created a connection, and, possibly, an attraction, between them. Right away there was anticipation about crossing paths with her again. Donald Dark could not stop thinking about her.

————

Around one o'clock Dark was sitting at a desk in one of the available cubicles in the Williston Barracks, finishing a sandwich from the gas station deli next door. The duty officer walked in with a puzzled expression on his face.

"Lieutenant, there's a Roy Harmon in the public area. Here's his card. Guy says he's the lawyer called by the family to represent the kid we got for Trooper Clark's homicide. I told him to take a seat… Maybe I shoulda' told him to take a number too, huh?"

————

- 5 -

"It's hard to take, you know, Lieutenant. Eddy was a good kid, I think. You know, his parents started early; too early I guess. Me and Mary pretty much did most everything for Eddy and his sister, Jean, for a long time."

Retired Vermont State Trooper Sergeant Timothy Clark's head was down and his hands were folded in his lap. He and Dark sat in opposing parlor chairs in the poorly lighted living room of Clark's small home off route 15 in Jericho. His wife, Mary, was in the house but Dark gathered she was not planning to join them. It was late afternoon. Cold outside and warm enough in the house but nobody was feeling good.

"Me and Eddy have stayed pretty close."

He was not yet able to accept the finality of a loved one's death. Clark's expression remained grim but with his words his head shot up and he spoke with more intensity and emotion.

"My guess is that's why he was out running. Me and Eddy are signed up as a team for the marathon in Burlington this coming May."

He turned his head and looked reflective. Like other old men he wanted to tell a story he clearly liked to tell about himself.

"Yeah, I been a runner for years and years. When Eddy said we should do it I said 'I don't know.' " He turned his head back and forth slowly, marking a 'no.' "Lieutenant, running at my age, the last few years anyway, it's like the miles are getting longer and the hills are getting steeper. Never was fast but now I'm really slow, you know. Doc has had me doing a stress test every few years cause heart disease is in my family and I like to run. Well I knew it was gonna be a lot slower this last time so I decided to train for that stress test . Did sprints and stuff. Probably not so smart but I think it helped. Did okay on the time. Didn't tell Doc till after.

"Well Eddy was gonna run more than me, but we were both planning to work on doing the best we could."

The cold reality of what had happened came back to the Sergeant and it hit him hard again.

"You know, Lieutenant, guess I always tried to point Eddy to a career on the force. Worked out good for me. You know I did most of my time with the Lab. Eddy wanted to get out into policing; like you I guess… Didn't go okay for Eddy." His head dropped again.

Donald Dark had never considered this potential pathway for hurt and guilt related to the force before. He did now and his recent brooding about the risks and questionable usefulness of his job descended on him again, by now becoming like a greek chorus in the background of most everything that happened. It stayed with him as an annoyance or impediment. He could not shake it. What could he say to Sergeant Clark?

———————

- 6 -

"So Lieutenant, you wanted me to let know how the Gonzales kid's arraignment went up here in Lamoille."

"Right Dawkins, what have you got to tell me?"

Sergeant Dawkins, out of the Johnson Station, had been to Jorge Gonzales' arraignment at the Lamoille County Courthouse in the afternoon.

"Upshot is this kid had two lawyers and seemed like they tag-teamed the young guy from State's Attorney's office. They sure made it sound like the kid only happened on Clark and did the right thing bringing him to the hospital. Then he freaked out, they said, and tried to run away. I know everyone thinks the kid needs to stay in custody but the State's Attorney wasn't much of a match for the lawyers. Bottom line is judge says kid's okay to be released with conditions."

"Shit! You're right Dawkins. There's already a lot of anger on the force and now it's gonna get worse."

"Yeah, Lieutenant, I think so. Only real thing judge gave the State was that kid's Subaru needs to stay with us so it's around during the investigation. Kid was real excited when judge said he could go home but then almost freaked right there in the courtroom when judge said car had to stay.

"So, Lieutenant, he'll be brought back to Williston by early evening."

Dark was unhappy hearing Dawkins' report. Though he was aware it might have made no difference he felt he should have been there. He also still seriously doubted the Gonzales kid had much to do with Trooper Clark's murder on top of that lonely hill. But him out of custody and leaving the state wasn't going to look good for anyone; considered a minor witness, not much of a suspect.

From Dawkins' first words he was wondering who the two lawyers were who accomplished his release? "Dawkins, did you get anything about the kid's lawyers? Was an attractive young woman one of them?"

As soon as he spoke Dark was struck by the way he had described the young lawyer from the day before as 'attractive.' He guessed the fact her image kept appearing in his head was an indication his first impression of her had truly evolved. And he supposed if anyone could be persistent enough to talk a judge into releasing the kid that sounded like her. There certainly was something about that lady.

"No Lieutenant. One was a guy from legal aid, a Roy Harmon, I think. And the other was an older woman from the *Migrant Workers Legal Alliance,* Marcia Hernandez. But you know sir, after the judge gave terms for the kid's release a pretty, young lady dressed in a suit, with really killer long hair, walked up front from where she was sitting back behind all the press and said she'd be willing to take the kid, right then. I think the kid looked like he was ready to go. Obviously they told her he'll have to be released through Williston; probably tomorrow morning at the earliest."

"Thanks, Dawkins."

Dark was confused. 'What's the deal with that woman?' he thought. Odd for her to keep showing up wherever this kid was in custody. Especially if not acting as his lawyer in court. As he mulled it over he wondered, again, what was going on with her?

She stayed on his mind. Lady certainly acted like she was representing the kid when he interrogated him. But Dark knew nothing about her...or the kid, for that matter. Didn't seem like she or the kid knew each other much either. He puzzled over it for a while and decided to call Fleury, at Williston, to see what info they had on her; at least what was on her card when she signed in.

That didn't work out and the mystery about her continued to grow. Fleury's excuse for not having that woman sign anything, or even getting a card from her, was the distraction of the lengthy spat he was having with the man and woman Dark saw him with in the waiting area the day before. Dark was just as guilty. He hadn't thought to ask Fleury anything about her or even ask her anything himself; even for a card. No one still knew anything about her. Clearly a screw-up; on him.

Who was she and what was her true involvement with Gonzales and this case; the homicide actually? That worried him. Dark thought about being at Williston Barracks in the morning and confronting this lady...if she showed. There was a chance he and Dawkins were talking about different people; not the lady on his mind. But then, even if it was the same person what was there for him to confront? He guessed if he found out she misrepresented herself that might be notable, but probably nothing much he would, or could, do about it. Meeting face to face, again, how strongly could he really press her? And there was little chance anything would come out to affect the kid's agreement and desire to go with her anyway. Dark doubted there was a way he could interfere with that.

Even if she bullshitted him (again?), so what; what could he do? No way he could stop her from leaving with Gonzales, an adult, he thought. He knew it was crazy but Donald Dark also just wanted to see her and, hopefully, talk with her again. He decided he needed to use his resources to find out more about her; and probably Gonzales also.

The more he thought about it the more angry he became with himself. He should know more about that lady than what she looked like and the name she gave them. Of course, getting a card from her might have been as useless as her name if she isn't who she said she is. 'Shit.' It only got worse when he wondered if she was even really a lawyer. 'Fuck that briefcase.'

Among Dark's growing list of worries about the case was a feeling once the lady left with Gonzales he would never see or hear from her again. Which would mean her involvement might never be explained. Equally disturbing to him, he admitted to himself, was that he had been looking forward to interacting with her more as the case progressed. Was it possible, he kept wondering, that in their brief moments together they shared a mood and perceptions of their lives he had never felt with anyone else before?

Thoughts like that quickly became an annoyance, just short of embarrassment. Despite knowing he and the woman had spoken only once, for hardly more than a few minutes, she stayed fixed in his mind. He truly knew nothing about her.

What he did know was the investigation of a capital case that was his responsibility had gone virtually nowhere since Trooper Clark's body arrived at the hospital. Events of the last twenty-four hours or so seemed to add nothing.

———

"Ed, don't you think it's kind of a worry that it was probably the same lady showed up in Lamoille and volunteered to take the kid out of Vermont?"

"Guess so, Don. Sorry I never got any info on her."

"Well, me neither." Dark wondered if her appearance had contributed to Fleury messing up too.

"Don't know what we can do to stop her from picking him up or even finding anything out about who she is when, …I guess if, she shows up tomorrow. She doesn't have to tell us anything."

They each were quiet on the phone for a short while; thinking the situation over. Then Dark spoke again.

"Fleur, I can't just let them leave like that in the morning. There could be plenty of stuff going on with one or both of them."

"Yeah, but what'cha gonna' do?"

Fleury's words were more like a sigh, signaling frustration. Lieutenant Dark was beginning to sense some options.

"Okay, here's what I'm thinking. Ed, see if we've gotten anything from NYPD in the City. Make sure we find out what precinct he lives in and talk with an officer there. Maybe something will come up. Then that lady… I'm going to run her name through a couple of databases tonight. I'll let you know if I find anything. Eddie, if she shows tomorrow we've got to try to get more from her about herself.

"Play dumb. Should be easy for you. Tell her you neglected to get a card and stuff from her last time. You know. See if you can find out where her office is. If she's chatty try to find out how she got involved with this kid's case. No matter how she acts try hard to get her to tell you where she and Gonzales are going. Meantime have someone run the plates for whatever she's driving. Okay?"

Lieutenant Edmund Fleury's response was out of character for him, especially when he and Dark interacted. He regretted the error he made so, atypically, he remained serious. "Sure Don, but even if she talks to me who knows if any of it will be true. And even if she has some answers for yesterday; you know, the briefcase and all, what will you do with that? Besides, connecting her to Clark's homicide may be quite a stretch. And now guess there's a chance the kid wasn't either. But letting him go doesn't seem right."

Dark had already made up his mind. He was listening to Ed Fleury and didn't disagree with what he said…completely. He was stuck on a feeling that woman's aggressive behavior had to be significant in the investigation; because of Gonzales, or maybe, beyond some involvement with Gonzales, with the homicide. She was so different than Gonzales. Sure seemed like a lawyer. If she isn't a lawyer, he thought, then what the hell was she doing around here?

He felt he was close to exorcising how his attraction to her might have interfered with his thinking and helped get him into the mess he was in now with the closest thing he had to a witness about to leave the state.

Or maybe he wasn't done with his attraction to her.

"So Fleur, here's what I think I'm gonna do. Tonight you have to get me an unmarked. Not a clunker; a late model that won't be noticed. And have it gassed up, okay? I'll get to you in Williston early and get my gear in the vehicle and sit in the holding lot out back. You'll talk with her, have someone run her plates, and then talk to me on the radio when she leaves with the kid. Unless you come up with some answers you let me know all about her vehicle when she pulls out. I'll give her some time and I'll follow."

Fleury wasn't especially impressed with Dark's plan. His response heralded Fleury was done feeling guilty.

"DD? So you'll follow them? Okay, then what? You investigating or providing an escort, Donald? Want us to start sending you your messages to some NYPD precinct in the City? Gonna settle in and run your cases from there for a while?"

Dark had no easy answer.

"Dunno, Fleur, just don't want to see this business get any more screwed up…or screwy. Maybe if they get at least half way to the City I can figure that's where they're going and I can turn around;

one less curve then since that lady showed up. Still will have to work on what the fuck is going on with her.

"Honestly Fleur, we're nowhere on Clark's homicide. You know how I feel about Narcotics in general. Those guys are not my favorites. And I guess most of them know that. So my past rough sledding with them hasn't made the investigation any easier, that's for sure. Still may affect their cooperation for looking at what Clark was working on lately, I think. Have had Sergeant Haber handle interacting with them, mostly, so far. Also for getting any sense if there was anything goin' on between Clark and maybe someone on the force, you know."

Actually, Ed Fleury knew very little about why Lieutenant Dark and a number of members of the Narcotics Division might not get along. He had only heard Dark's side of the story about what bothered him about other troopers when he was there. He didn't know Dark had filed a few complaints when he asked to transfer. Some people could hold grudges a long time. Dark had been out of Narcotics for almost a decade.

————

- 7 -

Who would still say winter was *coming?* Cold every day now. Not bone chilling cold yet but very chilly all the time. Weather that could not be ignored in everyday activities. Before he went inside his condo that evening Dark made sure he moved his winter parka from his cruiser's trunk and placed it on the back seat with his gloves. His protective vest was already there along with a few other usual safety items. He left his warming blanket, first aid kit, and several other things in the trunk, unlikely to be needed for the trip he anticipated in the morning.

The Lieutenant wanted to be all set for an early start. He wasn't sure when that apparently unpredictable lady would arrive. He had to be certain not to miss her. He readied some soup for a thermos while he nuked his dinner.

Those who knew him well had no easy answer for why Dark's life and lifestyle seemed to drift toward a more spartan existence over the prior year. He socialized beyond the force and he interacted with family regularly but there was a subtle change. His temperament was flatter and he had become more introverted. He actually believed few on the force were aware of any of that.

Donald Dark recognized he was discouraged. He believed any changes in his relationships reflected his ongoing struggle with his perception of the apparent futility of his job. Most especially he had become stuck on the impact of the unstoppable illegal drug catastrophe on the daily dangers of being a law officer. He reacted very personally to deaths like Clark's.

Donald Dark had been highly motivated to be a state trooper for as long as he could remember. Like all dedicated law officers he accepted the potential of a violent death. Now he worried about his own death serving no real purpose. He found himself shying away from deeper contacts with others on the force, recognizing a fear of getting close to others at risk too.

The Lieutenant thought any depression he might have was a reaction to his very reasonable growing conclusion that a significant chance of a bad ending in a futile setting might mean staying on the force was a mistake. He also assumed very few other troopers had similar feelings so he kept it to himself.

Mid-thirties and on his own. He supposed each day that passed the greater chance by now he would stay that way. He was starting to look around for a new dog. The death of his last one, about four months before, was hard on him. He missed the dog. A true loss of companionship that had nothing to do with danger but certainly added fuel to his mood and outlook.

And yet, his recent observation that the more time that passed since he put the dog down the easier his daily routine had become bothered him. Whether by intent or circumstances he accepted he had become a loner. Unplanned; just happened he guessed. It was his tacit acceptance that bothered him. No long term committed female companionship had ever developed. Dark figured he was an asshole to wind up this way.

Lieutenant Dark was struck by that woman; not only her appearance but her apparent attachment to Gonzales. Or maybe it was the kid's case? Who was she and what was she trying to do yesterday…and today? Pretty aggressive lady. He was convinced he had to find out more about her. Her interest in Gonzales probably had something to do with Gonzales' situation, but maybe even more than that, Clark's murder. But how?

If she was a loose thread he needed to place her involvement in this case. But was Dark being honest with himself or was that hint of sorrow in her face and her last few words what mostly underlay all of this for him? Which were the strongest determinates of his thinking in the poorly formed plan that followed?

Following her to New York City? Unlikely to yield much. Because of his attraction, however reluctantly, he began to convince himself he probably should follow her and Gonzales all the way into the City at least to a point where he could ascertain what relationship, if any, the two of them had.

He knew that could be done better by asking local cops to take over the surveillance in the City. But it would be almost a joke to even begin to try to arrange something like that based on only his hunch and hope that lady was part of something he didn't even understand...yet. No, he thought, either let her take the kid and try to forget about her or see if he was able to find out more about her, Gonzales,...and the case.

New York was a monster city. He knew exactly one cop there but instantly discarded any fleeting thought about trying to contact that detective.

His immediate superior, Captain Ronald Bushey, reluctantly had agreed to Dark's plan to follow those two for a few hours. The Captain had no idea Dark was now thinking he might follow them all the way into the City hoping to find out where they were going to end up. Probably not what the Captain would have wanted and almost bound to break some inter-state protocols. Hard to sense any of it as a smart, well-thought out move. Dark getting lost or in trouble in the City were among the more likely results.

Dark went to bed early and contended with a restless night. Her manner and her appearance stayed in his mind. That interrogation of the kid with her there was so strange. After a time it seemed to the Lieutenant like she and he were kind of getting along. Had he smiled at her at all as they were parrying? He thought she relaxed her intensity and really softened as the kid told his story. Did she smile at him…or was it at the kid? Who knew. And why was any of that in his head? Where were leads on Clark's homicide that made any sense?

In the morning a number of troopers were going to fan out and visit farms with known or likely legal and illegal workers to try to get something about the kid's visit. There would be language challenges and not a great chance anyone would admit to buying pot from the kid; and certainly if the kid made a delivery to one person, forget it. Gonzales remained very vague about where he was on his trip before he was caught; too many places to check out?

Other troopers would continue to investigate and explore Trooper Clark's personal life and his state police activities and force relationships. The Vermont State Police was mobilized for the homicide of one of its own. They had the manpower but needed better leads. Dark might as well follow what he had for now.

Well before the anticipated arrival of the woman who was to take
Gonzales out of Vermont Lieutenant Dark was parked on one side
of the Williston Barracks. Not knowing how long he would be non-
stop in the unmarked gray late model Ford sedan he was reluctant
to even sip any of the juice, coffee, or soup he had with him. He
figured he was prepared for most anything except a pit stop. He was
hungry so he ate the roll he brought but without anything to wash
it down.

His cruiser was parked behind the building. When Dark arrived
he transferred gear to the back seat and trunk of the unmarked
and pulled to the front edge of the south wall of the Barracks.
From there he would be able to see any vehicle drive out of the
front parking area and head to the Interstate entrance, only about
a hundred yards away, to the south. Everyone assumed she would
go that way to begin her navigation to the City, or at least out
of Vermont. Dark could watch her after she drove out but his
unmarked was not visible from the public parking area.

"All right, Fleur, I'm in position. I talked to Waterbury late
yesterday and looked through some screens I was able to access

from home but I couldn't find anything connected to the name she gave us. She's not listed in any Vermont state databases as a lawyer, paralegal, or anything. Name draws a blank. Staff will contact NYPD today but I don't know if that will go anywhere. Man, we sure fucked up with her. Maybe we should hand a cup of water to people like her then try to lift some prints later. But who knew?"

Ed Fleury was not a morning person like Dark. He had a bunch of early responsibilities getting his troop going. He was interested in what was happening but not nearly as intensely as Dark. He, too, was irritated by events with that lady but had mostly moved on.

"DD, hope you closed your eyes last night. So we almost got screwed by that lady." Fleury paused. His ability to flavor most of his conversations with salty words and phrases even caught him for a second after he said that. "What I mean is, looks like she tried to scam us in our own house. Know what I mean? Her game? Get the kid out of custody? Failed two days ago but today seems to be heading where she wanted to be then. What else?"

———

In Vermont it's frowned on to let your engine idle while sitting in a stationary vehicle. Dark wondered if it might actually be illegal in Williston. He knew it was in Burlington, a place where individual freedom was prized yet everything that could possibly be regulated was. But it was cold! Dark's motor was softly humming when Lieutenant Fleury's excited voice came over the radio.

"Donald! Holy shit, you're not gonna believe this! Soon as lady we're waiting for drives up I got a guy lookin' out and nabbing her car's make, model, and plates; which, by the way, are Vermont green… I watch her get out of the car and start to walk in. So get this. She's got no hat or hood on and I don't see that lady's famous hair."

"What? …A wig? You think that was a wig yesterday?" Dark was shocked and the disappointment reflected in the tone of his response, was obvious.

"Nah, don't think so, DD... Yeah, so I watch her come in and I can see her through the small one way to the waiting area. She opens her coat an goes with her hands up in the air behind her head, like to fluff out her hair. You know, like she's done it a million times, but there's no fucking hair there to shake out! Her hair stops just below her neck now. What's still there got that same striking shine and color. Must have cut it. She looks good today, DD; proly better than last time. Dressed casual; for the road. But she's got some low heels on. And forget getting any prints, Einstein. Lady's got mittens on and kept them on even when using that really fat pen we gave her to do the paperwork. Cute mittens."

"But..."

"Wait, there's more Donald. I hang back and listen while she talks to the desk. It gets worse... Gives different name DD! What the fuck?"

Dark no longer needed any stimulant to keep him alert. What was going on? He knew he'd have to make some quick decisions.

"Ed, hope you put the right glasses on this morning. You sure this is the same lady? You're gonna have to go out there and challenge her, Ed. This doesn't fucking add up. If you're wrong or even if it's her and she gets pissed we still gotta try to get answers. Can't imagine what she can do to us anyway if we're fucked up.

"So Fleur go out front and quiz her. Play dumb; remember, always easy for you. Tell her you see she's cut her hair. Watch her reaction. If things get hot, what the hell, tell her she used a different name a few days ago. You still have to try to get info about where they're going, and stuff like that. Hey, and then watch her closely when she comes face to face with Gonzales. See how the kid, and she also, I guess, react when they meet.

"Shit! What is going on?" More thinking out loud than asking Fleury a question.

"Something, DD. Something."

He sat quietly. Waiting. He killed the engine. Cooling down inside the car seemed like a good idea now. Mulling over his thoughts about this lady and what on earth she was doing kept his brain more than active. Information from Fleury kept on coming.

"Donald. So her Vermont plates are local, registered to a rental agency near the airport. I'll get someone over there to look at the rental agreement she signed and whatever they have on her, but you'll be on your way by then. Wonder what bullshit that will be? Gonna go out an talk with her and then get the kid. Don't think I'll be too long though."

Ed Fleury was a good guy. *Nose to the grindstone.* Hardworking. Not the person you'd go to for deep reflection or expect to play chess with. Reliable and dedicated to his job and the force. Four kids and a gossipy wife. Dark figured Ed had his hands full both at home and on the job. Fleury dropped comments from time to time that left Dark thinking Ed kind of envied Dark's independence; lack of family encumbrances. Dark played along to an extent. He didn't long for four kids but his life at home was missing plenty. He knew that, and felt it. In fact, lately, almost all the time.

Time on his hands in the car, sitting there for a while, he also thought about himself. Not new thoughts. He wondered if anyone sensed his discontent; and maybe worse than that his growing disaffection from what his job was supposed to be. Were his thoughts making any sense even to him? Was this some depression or was his apparent growing preoccupation with feelings of the futility and risks of trying to enforce the law at his level, with the drugs disaster anyway, a warning for him. It was continuing to haunt him more and more: dying as a trooper because of drugs might be pointless. He did worry if his relatively new found tentativeness about his job might show. He decided it probably did not.

Sitting in that cold car pondering these recurring thoughts again it struck Dark this whole business right now might not be so unique for him. He remembered his time in Narcotics when he first joined the force almost ten years before. There was futility and a hundred other things, along with danger, doing that job. At least *Dark* sensed futility in that never-ending struggle even then. He was surprised he didn't recall ever reacting then the way he was feeling currently. Maybe he *was* depressed now; whatever that means, he thought?

When the radio suddenly crackled to life Dark was relieved. He needed other things to think about.

"Bullshiter, DD. That lady's got balls, I'm telling you. Who knows who the fuck she is? Denies she was ever here! Do you believe that? Holy shit, what a slinger. Gonzales kid don't know her before his arrest but said he did. Think he'd leave with Charlie Manson just to get out. This has potential to be some mess, Don. Shit!

"Did say she's going to the City. I said 'in a rental' an she said 'none of your business.' Tough, tough lady, DD. Your plan gonna keep you on her tail all the way to the City, I think. Still not sure how much good that will do. She's leaving now.

"Say man, stay in touch while you're doing this, okay? Will need your cell."

"Yeah, okay Fleur. Go eat some brain food and let this craziness percolate. Call if you can make any sense of this. GPS on in the car and dispatch knows my cell and that's got GPS too. Hope you'll call me with what you get from the rental agency."

Dark was trying to think if he had anything else to say to Fleury when he saw his lady's car practically fly out of the parking area onto 2A heading toward the highway. His engine was on and he was ready.

"See you in bit Fleur. Hold down the fort or at least find someone who knows how to, bud."

With that he pulled ahead and was also on his way. Took his time exiting onto 2A and then immediately moved to the right lane and signaled his intention to turn right for the ramp to the Interstate. He was convinced there would be some value in what he was doing.

But was it going to be worth devoting an entire day? He had no idea. His thoughts were abruptly interrupted.

"Oh shit!. That's her…entering the Interstate *going the other direction!*"

Indeed, just as Dark was committed to the on ramp to get to the southwest, his eye caught her leaving the underpass under the highway and turning to go in the opposite direction from him. Did that make any sense?

He sped up and briefly put his flashers on. He had to rush a half mile to a restricted turn around. Had to hope no one in a marked cruiser would see him and think about going after him. The Lieutenant raced around to get on the highway in her direction. He kept his speed up and called Fleury.

"Shit, Fleur, with all your whining you never told me this might happen. Where you think she's heading now?"

"DD, you better waddle on quickly or you'll lose her before she's barely started on her way. And try not to get pulled over for speeding, pal." He paused a short time. "You know, maybe she's heading for 91 and plans to go through Massachusetts to get to 95 to New York. Gonna need directions, DD? Not in your memory bank, I bet. Course if you can find her and keep up with her all you gotta do is follow her. I thought you could figure that out. Shaky start though, eh bud?"

"Fuck you, pal." Dark was worried about how he'd be able to monitor her when they hit real traffic, closer to the City. Not this soon.

Just two interstate highways course through the rural state of Vermont. Those roads cut through wide swathes of fields, farm lands, and forests. Sparsely populated towns bordering the rarely busy roads helped to account for the tendency for locals to drive fast. The frequent sense of isolation on these roads also made the very excessive speeding of lots of out-of-staters who were passing through a significant activity occupying Vermont State Troopers.

Vermont roads and highways are generally a succession of hills (yes, bordering fields and farm lands) and curves, not many long, flat straightaways. Shortly, Dark glimpsed her car cresting a hill up ahead as he was at the peak of one also. He determined the distance he planned to keep between them, took a deep breath, and started to settle in.

Another gray day. Overcast, blustery, and cold. Still quite a while before true winter in Vermont (or *Burrmont*) but more days seemed nasty than not lately. He wondered what else might be about to blow in with the strong northwest wind shaking his car? He kicked himself for not checking the weather going south, especially for later in the day when he presumed he'd be returning.

What had he gotten himself into? Already he was feeling a bit dumb, not ever having considered she might head south this way. Did it really make any difference? Maybe only to the Captain. From the start he wasn't especially keen on Dark's idea of possibly devoting an entire day to tracking the lady and the kid without a more solid plan.

Well the die was cast and Dark was on his way. Her initial curve really wasn't an unheard of way to go to New York. Dark just hoped that would be it and her likely destination would remain as expected. But hell, that's why he was doing this: to find out where the two of them were going to end up. Some bumps in the road shouldn't be that surprising. He felt some of the tension ease up. He took a few more deep breaths and tried to relax. Eyes riveted to the road and careful to shadow at a safe distance, his mind wandered to the murder of Ed Clark.

The Lieutenant realized the flow of the case was likely to go through something involving narcotics; not a kid finding a body on a barren hill. What he really needed to do was eliminate the kid and, hopefully, this strange lady, from prime concern. Then he would have to find a way to join his deputy in working with the Narcotics Investigations Division. That staff and their activities in the community were where the clues would be, he knew.

It was time for him to learn to work with them again, especially those Dark knew from years ago who were now officers running the Division. They never got along well. It was unlikely Clark's death was tied to something like volunteering with the Boy Scouts or marathon training. Still, Dark hoped there wasn't anything within the Division. That would be sad for everyone: Narcotics, the force, and of course, Clark. Dark wondered if he got involved and it looked like they were locking him out whether that might be a sign of something going on inside?

"What? Now what's she doing?" he exclaimed out loud "Damn." Suddenly the Lieutenant exited the Interstate and reached for the radio handset. "Yeah, Francine, see if you can get me Lieutenant Fleury, okay? Yeah, Williston Barracks." Dark hadn't set up any contact or support plans for his journey. Now he realized that might have been a mistake.

"Hell, Fleur, I better stay in touch with someone cause this surveillance may be getting crazy. She barely signaled and pulled off the Interstate at Montpelier. Seems to be sticking with Route 2; going northeast now. Unless she's lost she sure ain't plannin' goin' south now."

"Really, DD? Not what anyone thought, eh? Christ, DD, now you may really have something going on: you know, a police action, eh? So you may not have time to sulk about your career for a while. That should be good for a change. This just ducky, eh Donald?"

Dark was stunned. How did Fleury know anything about any of that? On quick reflection he was sure there was no one on the force he had ever talked with about his doubts or frustrations with police work. 'Huh.' That diverted him for a minute. Did it show on his face or in his actions? Dark had to accept that possibility. But it still shocked and bothered him. He had no idea he was seen as withdrawn or a brooder lately. Would not be a great presentation for career advancement if he decided to stay on the force.

"Shit." Out loud. He was distracted. Fortunately his finger was not on the mic.

"Still there DD? Where's she off to now?"

Dark decided this was not the time to blow off Fleury or even try to talk with him about any of the things he was wrestling with lately. So he ignored the jab. He struggled to let that comment go and get back to his immediate problem.

"Well, she's still on 2. This lady might be lost but I doubt it. She's a mystery but she hasn't acted like she's dumb at all, you know. So my guess she's heading somewhere she wants to go. Lots of missing pieces here maybe, Fleur."

As he followed along Dark thought some more about her. No she wasn't a fool. That lady came across as pretty sharp to him. What's her deal? Unless Fleury was totally fucked up and it's the wrong woman this lady had a plan. Imagine. Cut all that hair off so suddenly? Not likely completely impulsive. So what could be going on? Something relating to Clark's homicide? The kid? Sure still going to great lengths to get him and now take him somewhere. The idea of her taking the kid somewhere became a prime focus of his thinking.

When the Lieutenant next sought out Lieutenant Fleury it was about a half hour later and he was just about positive she wasn't lost. It was obvious she was on her way north; clearly heading some place other than New York City. She found another Interstate. Yes, it was 91, but that entrance was far north of the way to get on for going to New York. And she kept heading directly north now.

"Well Donald you better get plugged into Newport station. They should keep an ear out for you, okay?"

Fleury's words and tone suggested concern and maybe some worry. Dark was heading toward a sparsely inhabited region and who knew what was ahead? He toyed with requesting some sort of back-up. But for what? No, his only goal for this trip was to do exactly what he was doing: find out where that lady was taking the kid. And besides, time was passing but it no longer appeared he'd be in his car for hours and hours traveling to other states. The Canadian border was less than an hour ahead. Couldn't imagine she would try to cross the border.

Just to be safe, when he connected with a sergeant in Newport, Dark gave him her plates and asked they be forwarded to border crossings near 91. She'd have to be a magician to get into Canada now.

Abruptly, she pulled off the Interstate into a rest area. As Dark approached he could see the small parking area had two portable outhouses and that was about it. It was almost deserted. Only one other vehicle. He decided he better not pull in. A quarter of a mile farther along he moved to the shoulder and quickly contacted the Newport station, requesting any nearby patrols ignore his illegal stop. Her car was visible enough that he was pretty sure he could tell no one got out. Two minutes later she headed back to the highway and passed him. When Dark followed she was driving more slowly. It was obvious to him something was about to happen. He wondered if her stop was to study a map since everything east or west of them was mostly farms or forest, often unlikely to contain roads known to google maps or whoever.

He was right. Five minutes later she exited the Interstate, turning off into a totally wooded area, heading west, about ten miles south of Newport. Dark was nervous he would lose her on the winding, hilly roads. Staying closer was his only option. If she noticed or was already aware of him they would each have to take their chances. Still, he was alert and worried. He wasn't sure why he never considered the possibility she would head north, going somewhere in the area where the kid might have been before. Never had occurred to him. Small consolation his deputy or Fleury never raised the possibility either. He and the others were jerks; all of them were the fools; not this lady.

Even before he began tailing her he knew she was smart and decided she had some kind of deeper involvement in recent events. But he was surprised. He had pegged the kid, Gonzales, as an almost peripheral part of all this; an unfortunate mule who stumbled into trouble. Maybe not. Willing to go with the lady? Of course. Maybe willing to go with anyone to get out of custody. Her driving into the Northeast Kingdom region appeared to be a strong sign of more than that to Dark.

Local roads were largely untraveled as they made their way north and northwest. Some sun now, lower on the horizon this time of year, but still breezy and cold outside. Most leaves were down and, despite the state's nickname, the surrounding woods contained only sparse green pines. No open areas or fields. She pulled over again.

"Shit."

Within a minute she moved forward, then slowed briefly at each of the infrequent intersections. She found one she wanted and turned, heading west. The road was paved but barely two lanes. Dark asked the Newport station to try to ping his cell and advise him where he was and what might be ahead. They couldn't really help. But it was good they knew he was out there.

After a few minutes along a winding road it straightened and Dark could see an open intersection ahead. Getting closer a country store with a gas pump was visible straight ahead, meaning this road was ending. He slowed considerably knowing her options would be limited when she reached the stop sign. He only had to determine if she turned left or right.

She went right; pretty directly north again. The border could not be much more than fifteen or twenty minutes away.

Dark picked up speed, intending to slow again after his right turn. As he was arriving at the intersection he saw a dark green sedan accelerate hastily from a side of the tiny store's parking area and drive off north. He was unable to catch a glimpse of the plates. Now what?

"Oh man. What the fuck?" He turned north and felt his heart rate pick up when he wasn't positive but was pretty sure the vehicle up ahead had no plates, or the plates were covered. There was absolutely nothing he would be able to do to ensure he could get behind the woman again unless he sped up and tried to pass the green car. It didn't seem wise. Dark quickly decided, or assumed, the green car was also following the lady's white vehicle. Nothing more to go on than the way that car rapidly pulled out at the country store, but the action seemed to fit that possibility.

Was this planned or a sign of trouble? *'Damsel in distress?'* popped into his head. Again, but to himself, 'what the fuck?' as he immediately challenged how his brain could come up with something like that. Obviously he wasn't completely finished with his attraction to her.

Newport station's reception was spotty. He hoped they understood his instruction they keep trying to locate him and it was time to send some back-up...if they could find him. Dark was confused and surprised about the entire day. He didn't want to quit now even though he really didn't know where he was and wasn't at all sure what was going on...or about to happen. His gut told him the green car had surprised the lady's but how would he know that?

Going faster than he wanted Dark stayed at least a hundred yards behind the second car. It kept increasing its speed, which implied the lady was driving faster up ahead. The two lane road continued to be bordered by forest and the area remained completely isolated. When they hit a straightaway, for a few seconds, he could see her car up ahead and he relaxed slightly. But it quickly became clear the green car was getting closer to the speeding white car.

Just then, still at some speed, the woman must have jerked her steering wheel abruptly, maneuvering her car into a sharp left turn. It looked to Dark like she entered a dirt road into the woods. The green vehicle made a similar hurried turn and followed her. Dark reached the area soon after and he could see plumes of dust kicked up from each of the cars as they appeared to move deeper into the forest. As he arrived at the turn Dark realized the dirt road they were traversing ahead was actually barely wider than a logging road.

Her speed stayed way too fast for what was essentially a single lane road. She had to be in trouble. Dark kept trying to hail Newport but had no idea if he was being heard. Driving on the narrow, rutted road while attempting to manipulate his cell to make a call was a challenge. Dark doubted any reception anyway. He continued on but moved slowly convinced there would be greater risk and little benefit from attempting to keep up with those cars now. Looking into the woods he thought he could still follow some of the stirred up dust.

The situation had deteriorated into danger so quickly the Lieutenant was astonished when he realized he might be in more trouble than any one of them if he continued ahead and the two cars were intentionally travelling together. Still, more likely she was in peril, he thought. Dark was sweating.

Then he saw nothing. The road was barely improved beyond a typical beat up logging path, but not by much. He wasn't sure what to do. He stopped to look and listen. He opened both front windows and played with the radio and his phone but heard nothing. Everything was quiet. Losing the car he had followed for several hours was tremendously discouraging. Were she and the other car running from him or was she running from the green car? Maybe she was running from him *and* them? He felt bad. Should he quit now and work his way to Newport station to look at their maps and talk over this unanticipated development? He wasn't sure what he wanted to do. Daylight was still assured for several more hours.

He sat in the quiet a few minutes; frustrated, displeased, and uncertain.

"Pop…Pop, Pop."

Obvious gunshots. Not too close.

———

- 9 -

There was no response from Newport to his efforts to call in an emergency. Dark slipped the unmarked into gear and maneuvered it close to perpendicular to the road so no vehicle trying to leave the area could get by. He jumped out quickly and went to the back seat to get his vest and heavy jacket. Not finding the vest there dismayed him, but then he recalled he had left it in the trunk. He took the jacket, slammed the door, and moved to the trunk and opened it. After getting the protective vest on he picked up the jacket and began to put it on.

Before he could get his coat completely on he heard an engine sound from the road ahead coming closer to his location. The Lieutenant looked up to see dust from a rapidly moving vehicle heading his way. It would reach him momentarily. He doubted the way he parked the unmarked made it a safe place to rush to get back in to deal with a racing, oncoming car and, probably, at least one weapon. There really was no time to think. Dark dashed toward the woods, practically diving to the rough forest floor. Crawling about five feet he lodged himself, low, behind a sizable trunk, wide enough he hoped, to shield him from being seen from the road.

The green car roared up that road at a fast clip and suddenly slammed its brakes less than twenty yards from Dark's car. Dust settled and it was all quiet again. Completely still, he lay flat on a blanket of newly dead leaves covering branches, dirt, and dying moss on rocks. The green car sat there for at least two minutes. Dark was glad he didn't have his hat on so his ability to peek from his spot was not highlighted. Then he recalled his hat was on the back seat and that could be a problem.

He felt his heart beating fast and his breathing was increased. Where he was, out in the middle of nowhere, he suspected his ability to manage this situation based on society's respect or, hopefully, at least fear of law enforcement, might not come into play. Fleetingly, he thought of Trooper Ed Clark, gunned down on a barren landscape in the middle of nowhere with no one else around. Kind of similar setting.

No, not the best way to use the force to maximize personal safety. How did he wind up out here in this position? He reminded himself someone probably just got shot; good chance by someone in that green car. Quietly he unholstered his revolver and waited.

'Shit!' His engine was still on! They could move…or take his car. 'Shit!'

Both of the green car's front doors slowly opened. Dark was dismayed to know there were at least two inside. Haltingly, two men got out. From his distance he couldn't make out much about either. They had on coats and hats appropriate for the season. Locals? As they headed toward his vehicle…and him, they each stayed to a side of the road. Unfortunately, they both had a pistol in one hand. They came forward slowly, almost in a crouch, obviously quite wary of what was ahead.

They stopped. One started to speak but immediately was waved off by the other and they resumed moving forward. By now Dark could determine the one on Dark's side of the road, who had called for silence, was older; not a young man. But the other was young. Eight or ten feet from the unmarked they stopped again and the older one began to look around the area. Dark had no feeling of safety or good protection in his location. He wasn't at all sure they would not see him. He worked to keep his breathing shallow.

Was this the way it was going to end for him? Had he had a death wish? Or was there going to be a gun battle and if he survived would bureaucracy rule his life for a long time as the scene, setting, and gun play was reviewed and dissected forever? And, of course, he had that sick feeling reminding him of the danger, violence, and, yes, death that his job seemed to encourage…and for what? Drugs again? 'Shit.' He wondered if the woman and Gonzales were dead and he was next.

With a slight tip of his head the older man barely motioned and they began walking forward, getting closer to the unmarked… and Dark. They seemed to relax a little when they were very close; close enough to presume a good chance there was no one in the vehicle. The front windows were still open. Once they reached the car, inside they would find custom electronic gear fitted to the front dash and a state trooper's hat sitting on the back seat.

Cautiously, the older one started to initiate a step to the front passenger door. Dark held his breathe and began to think about a possible position he could draw back to, if necessary.

Sudden loud static, followed by *"Lieutenant this is Trooper Star, assigned to improve our connection…"* Another burst of loud interference. *"Copy your location now, sir."*

The older one probably never heard the second scratchy, distorted words. He, literally, jumped back and began to quickly backpedal, maintaining his face to the car. His eyes darted around the area, including right where Dark was positioned. But he was rattled and wasn't concentrating at all on what was there. He was spooked.

They both drew back, shouting under their breathe at each other. Static sang from the radio periodically and then died again.

These two likely had no idea what the vehicle blocking the road was doing there until the radio shook them. They had known that vehicle was compounding their obvious goal of getting out of the woods on this road. Now they knew police were involved; a major distraction and probable confounding of their plans.

While they seemed to be arguing, Donald Dark, lying flat on the damp forest floor, made what he considered a major decision: He was not going to let them take his vehicle without a fight. His best chance for being found required the vehicle stay where it was. And if one of those guys (or both) took the unmarked he worried about danger to any trooper who happened on the car, assuming it was Dark in it, rather than possible murderers.

He worried about the recipient or recipients of the recent gunshots too. They needed help…he hoped. He felt pressured to try to wait until the next actions of these fellows were clear. He would try not to initiate the gunfire. But he was unsure how vigorously he would demand their surrender before going ahead.

So the Lieutenant tried to prepare himself mentally for the challenge of a life and death battle; something he had grown to believe, in the war on drugs, was usually a futile exercise in the name of law and order. His immediate reasoning to stay and fight made sense to him in the heat of the moment and he determined he would do what the situation required.

Despite his view of law enforcement that literally had been haunting him for some time Dark's conclusion about what his job required of him at that moment was not immediately upsetting. He considered whether this was what was called fate or, in fact, his fatal moment. Then he thought about how many rounds he had, locations he could crawl toward in a firefight, and a goal of alerting the station about his situation and his concern about the occupants of the white car.

The two men stopped talking and Dark stiffened. In the distance, at the green car, a rear door opened and someone yelled at the men. There were at least three. The two men started walking back to their car. Suddenly, the younger man turned and ran back toward the unmarked. Three feet away he leveled his pistol and pumped bullets into the engine and front tires, disabling the vehicle. The engine and all power died.

Whoever these assholes were Dark instantly believed disabling the unmarked stood a very good chance of being the dumbest thing that young guy was going to do all day. With keys in and engine running they might have assumed, and might have been able, if Dark was taken out, to simply get in his car and remove it as an obstruction. Now it was dead weight; beached; a lasting obstruction to their ability to leave the way they came.

Dark couldn't tell if that guy took any heat from the others as he returned and they loaded into the car. They drove forward, just to see if there might be a way around the unmarked. After a few deep exhalations and hope their apparent withdrawal moments before meant there would be no direct confrontation Dark was incredulous seeing them come closer again and quickly resumed his wariness. Whoever was in charge rapidly determined they would not be able to get by the unmarked.

The driver literally floored it in reverse before twice slowing and both times failing to find a spot where their vehicle could even be turned around. On a third try he succeeded. The green car sped off as fast as anyone could travel on a rutted, dirt road. The Lieutenant's gaze followed their dust until no cloud was visible any longer. He had to wonder if they would be back. Good chance they knew of no other way out. To Dark it seemed highly likely the woman, realizing she was being chased by the green car, which was closing in on her, had turned onto a road she and, odds were, they knew nothing about. Less plausible after the shots that they were working together.

What was up ahead? What if those shits couldn't find another way out of the woods? Dark focused more of his thinking on the status of the folks in the white car. He had no radio and no cell service. He did figure the unmarked would eventually be found.

————

Even though he had done nothing physical Dark was tired. His uniform was covered with leaves, dirt, and burrs from his low hiding spot in the forest and sweat was cooling uncomfortably under his heavy parka and vest. At least for the moment he was alone as he stood up and clambered out of the woods to the road.

The task was ridiculously dangerous but he felt he had no choice. He grabbed two candy bars and some gear. While he ate one of the candy bars he thought about the mortally wounded unmarked. He decided to leave the keys in it. Maybe that would facilitate its removal in some way. Tired as he was the Lieutenant set out on a tense journey up the road, farther into the forest.

Rays of fading sun filtered through trees as he walked slowly, trying to keep all his senses as alert as possible. He thought listening was key. But his mind did wander a little. His steps along the isolated road brought to mind a memorable old World War II movie he had watched twice: *"A Walk In The Sun."* Some survived; some didn't.

Looking and listening, he determined he would walk the road for as long as it would take to find them. If Dark had the situation wrong and the white car and its occupants survived a shooting he might have an awfully long hike and find nothing. Just didn't seem likely. There was some daylight and he had a flashlight. A trooper had to make every effort to find potentially injured or harmed. He never questioned this effort.

The road did a lot of winding as he walked and that was worrisome for what he could be walking into. Dark hadn't realized there also was a gradual, then steeper elevation to the direction he was travelling. Might be good for cell reception as it got higher. *Reception* stayed in his mind as he tried to look ahead and to his sides, considering the very real potential for some sort of ambush. He was calm, but there was an unavoidable nervousness. Moving more uphill and rounding a bend he definitely thought he saw something reflecting the sun in the distance. He slowed.

Dark hugged the edge of the forest as he, cautiously, moved forward. His movements caused the patch of light to come and go but he was sure it was from a reflection of something foreign to the forest. Getting much closer he saw the white car up ahead, crashed in the woods a few feet from the road, a rear signal light inexplicably and feebly blinking.

His cell had one fleeting bar and he was ecstatic to reach 911 and have them ping his position and alert Newport again. He needed support immediately. What he found when he reached the car was worse than he anticipated.

The engine was off. The wind had picked up and rustled in the tall tree branches, but there were no distinct sounds as he approached the car. At the rear of the vehicle he stopped, unsnapped his holster, and slowly looked around the area before going to the passenger door. Nothing. He crouched down and cautiously opened the door.

Jorge Gonzales' limp body slid off his seat and into Dark. No seatbelt. Dark pushed him back and propped him up on the seat. Blood was all over his right chest and shoulder and he was as pale as a ghost. But he was breathing…barely. Next to Gonzales, in the driver's seat, were the remnants of an airbag. It had been punctured to deflate it and was draped over the seat. White powder dusted the area but none of that attracted Dark's attention. There were streaks of blood on the seat. The driver's door was open a few inches and, notably, the door handle was bloodstained.

He walked around the car and blood was immediately visible on the ground. Crouching down he looked to see if there was a trail of blood but he saw none. Still crouching he looked into the woods ahead then stood and cautiously walked a few feet farther. For just a second he thought he heard some rustling in the woods. He stopped, looked, and listened.

"This is Lieutenant Dark of the Vermont State Police. If there is anyone out there you need to tell me. If you are injured I can help you."

Soft rustling in the woods, otherwise nothing. He wasn't anxious to go into the forest but he would have to check it out…in a few minutes.

Dark secured his weapon and returned to the car to offer attention to Gonzales. Jorge barely responded to his name and was unable to converse with him. Sitting up was probably not the best idea for someone losing blood so he opened the back door and then carefully picked the kid up and moved him to the back seat. He positioned him so his legs were elevated against the opposite door. He knew that might boost his blood pressure, if he wasn't totally in shock by now. The Lieutenant was aware Gonzales was in terrible shape. And yet the effects of blood loss, anyway, could be readily reversed in a healthy young man…if he could get to treatment. Soon.

It was a terrible situation and Dark had no idea when any help would arrive. Brief, soft stirring in the nearby woods again. From the sounds he was hearing he thought there was a good chance someone, most likely the lady he set out to follow in the morning, was lying close by on the forest floor; clearly injured also.

He decided there was little more he could do for Gonzales at that moment. The crashed white car was probably not drivable. What about the woman?

Dark closed all the doors and started to walk along the edge of the road, peering intently into the darkening forest, looking mostly close to the ground. Walking directly into the forest made no sense unless he could fix on that sound if he heard it again. Just six feet up the road he noticed more blood. He stayed on the road and continued to slowly walk and look.

Then he stopped and pulled out his cell. He should try to call and report his latest situation to whoever he could reach. His phone said it was almost 4 o'clock. Getting late and starting to get dark. 'Shit.' He began to tap on the phone. There was a sound. Behind him?

A crushing pain in the back of his head and a brief sense of floating. Then everything went black.

———————

- 10 -

Vermont is a small state with a small population. Remember, about as many cows as people and not too many of either. Hospitals that are designated Level 1 Trauma Centers are required to satisfy stringent regulations for 24/7 availability of staffing, care, and support, primarily in surgical specialties. The only Level 1 facility in Vermont is in Burlington, by far the largest populated city and region. It's located northwest, flanking the state's west border on Lake Champlain. Dartmouth Hospital in New Hampshire, located southeast, just over the eastern border from Vermont is also a Level 1 Trauma Center. There are many reasons some Vermonters choose one hospital over the other for their care…if there is time to make a choice. However, most troopers have a natural tendency to want to stay in their own state and choose Burlington if it is practical to get there.

Jorge Gonzales had lost a great deal of blood and was thought to be barely alive when troopers arrived in the dark and found the Lieutenant and the dramatic scene in the middle of a forest. Gonzales was transferred to Burlington by air-vac, no mean feat in the hilly foothills of Jay Peak that early evening in the dark.

Lieutenant Dark seemed to converse with his rescuers but he made little sense and later claimed no memory after the sudden intense head pain. He left the scene in a rig. In the emergency department he woke up enough to be aware he was being worked on. He was in Kingdom Hospital in Newport. Turns out that was a suitable hospital for someone who had a whopping headache and significant concussion but no skull fracture. Over the next few days Dark and his visitors wore out every variation of expressing how troopers tended to be too hard headed to crack a skull.

Close to midnight, about three hours after the Lieutenant had arrived at the hospital, Sergeant Dennis Haber, from Dark's investigative unit, walked into the room where Dark was admitted. All the initial evaluations and diagnostic testing were completed and the doctor's plan for Dark was for him to rest for the night. Sergeant Haber had been cautioned to keep his visit brief and more like a sick call rather than trying to understand what happened and advance the case. He tried to do that…at least at first.

The Sergeant was a young man; a three year veteran of the force. He looked tired but he was alert and appeared quite concerned about the Lieutenant. Dark seemed exhausted and distracted so Haber tried to reassure him.

"Your parents have your dog, sir. Had no idea you got a new one Lieutenant. When we found you the pooch was sitting on the ground right next to you. Growled so fiercely some of the guys were a little worried about getting to you. I thought it was kinda strange to see them so cautious around a little yip yip like that. Zipped right up into the rig with you so we decided, what the hell, why risk getting bit. As long as she was next to you she was manageable. Went okay with your Dad, though. Guess they're friends, huh?"

Dark's brain was worn out from effects of his physical beating and also his efforts to re-integrate and think about all that happened that long, frightening day. Much of it was a puzzle. The dog was no exception.

"But I don't have a dog, Haber."

They both were startled. Haber quickly reviewed that scene in his mind but Dark's words didn't lead him to any different conclusion.

"Really? If you had been there…Oh, I guess you were. But you know what I mean. That dog sure behaved like she was yours. We wondered about you bringing your dog with you and all but no one spoke up with any other ideas. And we wanted to get you out of there quickly. As quick as we could, you know. Huh. That's something.

"Strange looking dog, Lieutenant, but stuck to you like glue. I mean it." At this point the Sergeant actually felt a bit unclear about the whole business with the dog and decided it wasn't a good time to try to joke about the pooch's rhinestone collar…and that she had no tags. Something didn't add up. That was clear now.

His head hurt and was still ringing but thinking about what the Sergeant said actually helped Dark improve his alertness and focus. He remembered he was carefully moving up the road after hearing some sounds in the woods and seeing blood nearby. It was quiet. Maybe he heard rushing footsteps; he wasn't sure. The next instant he felt himself going down and that was it. Nothing after until the rig was unloading him at the hospital. Must have been out a while, he realized.

'A dog? Was that the rustling in the woods? Shit, what happened to that lady?' he was thinking. That's who he assumed he was close to. He was sure no satisfactory search of that area was conducted in the dark. Something would have to be done in the morning. Was she okay, or dead, or in bad shape somewhere in the woods? Why was that so important to him? He'd go back there with the Sergeant early in the morning and look again.

At least that's what he was thinking as he fell off to sleep. A nurse disturbed him frequently through the night, doing what she called *neuro checks*. Naturally, that medically important maneuver meant he barely had any sleep. Bright sunlight and a persisting, pounding, bad headache finally truly woke him in the morning. He felt awful and wasn't sure where he would get the energy to get dressed and resume his activity on the case. Attempting to sit up made the throbbing pain worse and he felt nauseous. Dark didn't drink much but assumed that was what a hangover felt like.

Of course, he wasn't going anywhere. Certainly not to continue to search for that mystery woman. No one, the doctors or the state police, had any intention of allowing the Lieutenant back out into the field just yet. Then it got worse.

Dark was given the stark option of staying in the hospital or going to stay with his parents. Which was worse? Both were an embarrassment. A single man not yet safe to be on his own. Not too subtly he was being pushed to stay with his parents. In his thirties and returning to his old bedroom? A further ignominious development in a case that wasn't going well.

A trooper who had been part of his rescue popped his head in while a woman from social service was querying Dark for his thoughts about what he might do. Without being asked anything the trooper rolled his eyes a bit, showed a sly smirk, and suggested the Lieutenant would probably be more comfortable at home with his dog. 'What about that dog?' Dark thought.

The social worker's face brightened at the mention of a dog. "Of course you'll be do better with your dog with you. What's the dog's name and what is it?"

Dark had no answer. He looked at the Trooper so she did also. The Trooper looked down and slid his left foot back and forth a little. The smirk returned and it was clear he was taking some time to measure his words.

"Well sir, never did get a name from you last night. But you sure got an unusual looking pooch, sir." He looked like he hoped to leave it at that but his words only intensified the gaze of the other two. So he continued. "Guess I just think I never saw a pooch that small before, and any dog who's ears were almost as big as the rest of her." Looking at the confused stares on their faces this trooper also decided this was not a time to comment on the very small dog's rhinestone collar.

Beyond the optics of a grown man being taken home by his parents it was the obvious lesser of evils for Dark. And so that's what he did. He went home. To his mother, who spent his lifetime telling him she wasn't ashamed he was named *Donald*, after her father. And home to his father, a high school social studies teacher who believed being a state trooper was actually a calling and Donald had been called.

Driven from Newport by his deputy, with no dread or apprehension, but with more of a sense of resignation (perhaps part of the story of his life), he walked, a bit unsteadily, into the home he grew up in, in rural Jericho. There he was greeted more like a child than the modestly weak, injured trooper he was. He expected that.

And it turned out he also went home to a Papillon. Not fully re-integrated, initially Dark thought that was the small dog's name. How and from where he had no idea. The little dog had ears that went forever and an instantly annoying high-pitched bark that sounded off easily and frequently. And what was with that ridiculous rhinestone collar?

After a short time Dark tried to name his new dog 'Dimwit,' after his own perception of how poorly he was managing his capital case. But it couldn't stick. The dog was way too smart. She managed her own affairs quite reasonably and spent the remainder of her time monitoring whatever Dark was up to. Frequent slight twists of her head in response to Dark's words or actions quickly convinced him the dog might be substantially smarter than he. His parents didn't disagree.

But it wasn't his dog. So giving it a name wasn't right and probably disturbing to the dog, although she seemed to readily accept him calling her 'Alice.' Alice Madstern surely wasn't the real name of that woman he met a few days before, but she had once answered to Alice so why not the dog? He was sure this unusual dog was hers, but he really had no way to know.

He slept most of the first twenty-four hours he was home. That challenged his mother's instincts (and probably her desire) to nurture her boy back to health. Sleeping didn't seem right to her although it is a frequent natural consequence of a concussion. After that first day he woke feeling markedly improved. He spoke on the phone with his older sister and niece and nephew in Massachusetts. His sister wondered why he was home. He sounded fine to her. As only a sibling could he wondered if she was jealous?

Dark's superiors stayed away but Haber came and reviewed all they had with him. The word from his deputy was the Captain was thinking about re-assigning the case. But it was unclear how long Dark would be out and the Major Crime Unit was stretched too thin already. They needed him.

Greatly disturbing his parents, Dark stayed in his bedroom most of the day except when Sergeant Haber or another trooper occasionally stopped over. His buzzed brain was trying to do more than just reconcile the effects of sudden trauma. The pace of his activities made the movement of molasses seem speedy. The impact on the case of what happened that long day puzzled Dark and others. And his own brewing personal odyssey, attempting to understand whether he should or wanted to remain a trooper, affected his thoughts again also. In what way he wasn't sure though. His behavior and actions while in danger actually surprised him somewhat.

On balance he thought he reacted and handled the events correctly and showed proper regard for his own safety and the safety of others. He found himself realizing that thinking about the way he functioned was important to him. But he wasn't completely sure how he did. Should he have challenged the men who shot up his vehicle? Should he have known to work harder to get back-up sooner, when he had better communications?

Mostly he accepted that now more days had passed and Ed Clark's homicide remained unsolved. Dark's efforts, so far, seemed to add nothing to its resolution. His apparent obsession with finding out more about a woman he barely ever met had gone nowhere. Not helpful; possibly only putting his and other people's lives in jeopardy.

———

Haber came in the morning to update him. The day Dark slept through Haber and three others from the crime investigation field team walked and searched the area where Dark's action took place. They came up with nothing of consequence. In particular, nothing more was found that might be associated with the missing woman. With some difficulty the unmarked and the white car were placed on flatbeds and taken to Waterbury. After the Lieutenant's review of Haber's report they agreed the Sergeant should now go to Burlington to interview Jorge Gonzales in the hospital.

Like most everything, Gonzales' situation confused Dark. Whoever shot the kid later hit Dark on his head, he assumed. But did the shooter, or shooters, know the kid was still alive then? Did that mean whatever was happening didn't involve the kid? Or was he left alone, presuming he would die there? Dark really wanted to interrogate the kid. He asked Haber to go easy for now, only finding out his condition and trying to get a brief review of the kid's response to the events of that day.

By the time Haber was getting ready to leave Dark was actually feeling substantially better. He knew more about the kid than his deputy. The kid wasn't going anywhere. The Lieutenant asked Sergeant Haber to try today to only get those few blanks filled in about the kid and that lady and then pick him up mid-morning the next day and they would go to see Gonzales again, together.

Haber made a modest effort to challenge Dark working, reminding him he was on temporary leave. Dark said that was why he would have Haber take him to the hospital and they could talk to the kid together. Dark would be along unofficially. Throughout history most subordinates have recognized their limited ability to disagree or argue with a superior. There would be little upside in Haber challenging the Lieutenant. So he didn't.

———

- 11 -

Laurinda Alverez wasn't sure what she should do. Emanuel Samuel followed her the next day. Knowing he was doing that terrified her. When she challenged him he threatened her about the money and the Subaru. Menacingly, he shouted that his people would not let their investment go. She didn't understand all that he ranted but she realized Jorge was in big trouble with whoever he was working for. Every day for three days everything seemed to get worse. Then Jorge called to say he was coming home and Laurinda convinced herself the whole frightening episode was about to end. The next thing she heard Jorge was in intensive care in the Burlington hospital.

At first she was so caught up in trying to arrange legal support for Jorge she gave little thought to how his actions affected her feelings about him. Contacting legal agencies in Vermont, and then the hospital, it was impossible for her to keep Jorge's problems from her family. Her parent's longstanding suspicions about what kind of a person he was blossomed during this time and they made Laurinda's efforts and thoughts that much more challenging and confused. Hearing of Jorge's foolish and dangerous behavior as a drug mule confirmed their doubts about him. They actively obstructed her efforts for Jorge. Laurinda knew she could not abandon him now but she was also furious with him…and her parents, especially for their insistence she do just that.

As soon as she learned he had been shot much of her recent growing ambivalence faded for the moment. It was devastating news to receive just as she hoped he would be coming home. Jorge's father had abandoned his family long before and his mother struggled with four children. Criminal activity and injury were far from unknown in his home. Whether his mother had any interest or not her ability to get involved in Jorge's acute problems were, at best, uncertain. He really had no one remotely able to try to support and help him beside Laurinda.

Laurinda was heart sick over the image she constructed in her mind of Jorge, barely alive in a strange hospital, upset and in pain. She pushed her doubts away. Her parents argued with her, telling her to let the people in Vermont take care of him and straighten out his problems. The tension in her mother's voice was obvious.

"Laur, you got to move on. You can't keep missing your schoolwork. Will you fail your classes and then what happens? That Jorge is so far away all you are doing is sitting here and worrying. And what else can you do? Popi is sick to see you skipping your school."

Laurinda was wrestling with that problem, along with others. However, once she heard Jorge was shot everything else became secondary. Her mother, and especially her father, continued on from their initial attacks on Jorge's actions and behavior. Their words made some sense and that bothered her. But after he was shot her mother's persistent warnings and worries no longer affected her.

How she could help Jorge was predominant in her thoughts. Vermont might as well have been Labrador or Timbuktu to her; far off in the distance, not a location she could relate to in any way. He was all alone. The police arrested him again in the hospital so he told her he was cuffed to his bed. He had no one to talk to about his problems. Even his legal troubles were on hold until his health improved so his lawyer had been advised to stay away for now.

It was a maturing experience for Laurinda. She had a helpless feeling. That was unusual for her take charge personality and actually enhanced her uncertainty. She sensed the passivity she was forced into as an unwanted weakness. So unlike her. She didn't know what to do.

Sitting in the kitchen after dinner Laurinda motioned with her eyes for her fourteen year old sister, Madrana, to leave the table. Her father had been planning to get up and leave but stopped when he saw his eldest child signal her sister. Madrana dutifully left and her mother looked at Laurinda. Her father stared at his empty dinner plate. Everyone appeared somber, the dinner having passed quickly and quietly as they all tried to avoid allowing their simmering upset from rising up and destroying another meal. All three were apprehensive as Laurinda cleared her throat and spoke.

"Mommi; Poppi; I have decided to go to Vermont."

Neither parent moved or showed any immediate visible reaction. In many ways it was a statement they were expecting. They feared it but were not surprised to hear it by now.

"Jorge has no one. No one he knows to help him or even talk to him. That's not right. I know he was doing a stupid thing. But I really believe he was planning to stop. I really do. He's so sick and he should not be alone. I don't know what is going to happen to him. He can't just be left up there without seeing someone who cares for him. It's not right. Don't you see?"

Surprisingly, at this point her father got up, glanced disapprovingly over at her, and walked from the table to the living room where he turned on the TV. Laurinda's eyes met her mother's. There was some equanimity in her mother's stare. She had been thinking about this.

"Laur, there is very little you can do for Jorge here or in Vermont. Once he's well enough he's probably going to go to jail. He's going to be in big trouble for a long time. Too bad this has happened. Too late now for any easy way to get through all this. You do know what I mean, don't you?"

Laurinda stayed still in her chair but nodded yes. There was a firmness in her mother's tone or manner that made her think something hopeful might be coming.

"It's killing me and Poppi to see school going down the drain. I been thinking. Remember my brother Ramon's sister-in-law is married to a man who used to be a cop? I don't know him well but he always seemed like a nice guy. I was thinking you should talk with him. And Poppi and I been talking…maybe, depending on what he says, you and he could fly to Vermont for a day or two to see Jorge and find out what's going to be, you know? Maybe a lawyer would be better but we don't know any.

"But Laur, you got to go to school. Sitting here is crazy and making us all angry and upset. No good. I'll call Ramon if you'll promise to go back to school tomorrow and until we can talk to this guy and decide what to do."

It was not a bargain Laurinda was happy about but it made some sense, and was the first time in days she and her mother had spoken without winding up shouting at each other. She knew finding money to go to Vermont was a sign of their great concern for her; more than a simple gesture. Going to Vermont on her own or with one of her parents was a much more daunting prospect.

"Yes, mommi, please call uncle Ramon and see if I can talk to that man. Do you know his name, Mommi?

"I think so. Pretty sure it's James Wiley; an Anglo."

Seemingly removed from the conversation her father's voice arrived from the living room.

"Yes, Jim Wiley."

———————

- 12 -

A series of hard knocks on his bedroom door woke Dark from an after lunch nap. His mother barely paused after knocking and she and the dog, Alice, walked in briskly.

"Donald, are you awake? You have a visitor."

The abrupt disruption of his enjoyable nap caused his head to pound annoyingly. He was in his underwear, under the covers, and as he was remembering where he was he was not sure how he could have agreed to get undressed for a daytime nap. His mother was putting a lot of pressure on him. He was trying to be agreeable but he was not comfortable. On the other hand, he noticed she was very comfortable playing nurturing mother. It was about to get worse.

"Donald, guess who's here to see you?"

Was she trying to be ironic? He was not up for a game; twenty questions? He said nothing, but propped himself up a little on his elbows.

Lying in his childhood bed in his underwear, looking at the twisted, cocked head of a very small animal who appeared to be staring intensely, as though it was trying to understand something, Dark watched his long time, on-again-off-again, girlfriend and sometime lover for the last few years, Susan Spahn, enter the room. Would he have felt any less awkward if he had pj's on like his mother encouraged before his nap? No, nothing could be more awkward than laying in his childhood bed with his mother and his occasional lover standing over him in that room.

Susan's concern was apparent but so was her reaction to the awkward situation. Like Donald, she tended to be introverted and reserved; on the quiet side. Elementary school teacher, Susan Spahn, was an attractive woman who also happened to be tall, which suited them as a couple. She said hello and stood by his bed. After some silence she spoke.

"Last night I baked you these cookies. I heard you were injured pretty bad but I'm glad to see you look good. You're probably ready for some cookies, huh?"

Donald looked at his mother while he thanked Susan. Ms. Dark argued with herself, only slowly accepting she had to leave them alone. She liked Susan although she realized, after all the time Susan and Donald had been friends, it was probably too late for them to have a meaningful relationship. To her *meaningful* meant getting married and having kids. Somehow what felt awkward to Ms. Dark was to leave them alone in the room.

"Well, I'll leave you two. I'm sure Susan will help cheer you up. You know, Susan, it's clear to us that whack on Donald's head didn't shake him out of the funk he's been in for a while."

"Thanks, Mom. So nice of you to see things that way."

She stalled her departure. The silence goaded her along.

"Okay then…I'll leave you folks alone…I'll leave Alice here… She can be your chaperone."

Having done her job of plumbing the depths of awkward and embarrassing, his mother paused one last strained moment, turned, and left. Susan smiled and sat on a corner of his bed for a short time then reached over and hugged him. They talked for a few minutes and she hugged more of him and he pulled her completely on the bed. She didn't resist. They had fun embracing and fooling around on his boyhood bed. Dark relaxed and felt the best he had in days, possibly even before his injury. Alice didn't make a peep.

For maybe around the fifth time in almost as many years Donald thought about a life shared with Susan. Then, as always before, his thoughts fairly quickly seemed automatically directed to wondering why it never happened. By this time he understood that whatever he now thought Susan most likely had lost her hopes for them and was no longer waiting for him to commit to her. At best, he guessed they were mutually needy friends.

Even though he liked her more as they were getting older Dark remained uncomfortable confiding in her. The thoughts and mood he was struggling with were not talked about. He guessed a certain superficial quality about Susan continued to bother him and limit any thoughts he might have had about sharing some of the things troubling him over the past months. He did agree to go for dinner at her place in a few days.

That evening he had his father drive him home.

There was concern and some excitement in the Dark household after dinner when Donald announced his intention to return to his own home. His mother worried out loud whether he was ready; if it would be safe? She obviously was enjoying having him around; being a mother. But he had made up his mind. And he was feeling much better.

Originally the plan was for the dog to stay with his parents. Somehow in the process of loading the car Alice dramatically squeezed through the front door and took a huge leap, starting far from the SUV, up into the open hatch. Donald returned to the house to get the dog's things. He had yet to accept the animal as his dog but he also was no longer as put off by many of Alice's features. The extent of her intelligence still wasn't clear to him but he was at the point of wondering just how smart a dog could be.

An hour after he arrived home Dark felt substantially better and more comfortable. Getting back to the environment he was used to and the continued lessening of the buzzing in his head were reassuring. It was good to be home. Outside Alice appeared to have an immediate, innate ability to know to stay within the boundaries of his property. It took Dark a year to train his prior dog to respect them. They went to bed early.

Up in the morning while it was still dark Alice went out, was fed, and Dark took a long, hot shower. A few minutes later he was feeling really good, vastly improved over several days before and wondered if the buzzing was gone. Still didn't eat too much but was anxious to get his uniform on and try to resume some semblance of his professional responsibilities.

While dressing he found himself thinking about a few subtle similarities he thought he sensed the day before common to Susan and the woman he had followed. Today, even that observation, much less any actual similarities, seemed poorly defined and silly to him. But he still couldn't shake his obvious fixation on that lady. Why? As he contemplated the pending interview with Jorge Gonzales his questions really only focused on that woman.

With the brilliance of the early morning sun, feeling so much better, he was able to take all that more lightly. He reminded himself there was a homicide and associated mayhem and danger to deal with. But that lady was a part of that story; he could not forget.

Putting his uniform on was an action symbolic of his return to a world he knew, albeit it was quickly clear to Dark that his doubts remained. He had an almost paranoid response when he realized he had no idea where his service revolver was. He couldn't recall if it was holstered or in his hand when he was knocked out. No one had asked him anything about it that he could recall either. He became anxious worrying about what happened to it; where it might be and his apparent neglect of his responsibility to have brought up that it was missing. Maybe he still wasn't as sharp as he needed to be if he never even thought about the weapon until now.

The lieutenant didn't remember his pistol was holstered when he was found, quickly removed by troopers on the scene, and now locked up in Waterbury. Dark also didn't recall there was a protocol after illness or injury to determine when to return a firearm. He still wasn't active duty again yet.

His deputy, Dennis Haber, arrived around nine. Dark and Haber knew it was best to be at the hospital no earlier than mid-morning since the earliest part of the day was usually the more active time for the many pieces that made up hospital care. Those included managing routine personal care, doctor visits, wound care, various other treatments and sometimes also tests, although diagnostic tests often occurred throughout the day.

Haber commented on how well the Lieutenant looked and smiled at Alice while she growled and barked at him. His assumption was that for such a small dog the odds were her bark was worse than her bite. Dark was ready to go and reached for his hat. Haber raised one hand slightly, modestly signaling him to wait.

"Lieutenant, not sure if you will still want to go to the hospital after you hear the news."

Dark had no idea what Haber was about to say. Despite the nonchalant way Haber presented his pause Dark immediately sensed it was something important. He acknowledged Haber's caution by nodding and waited for the Sergeant to continue.

"Well, there's lots of excitement this morning, sir. Seems the force believes we have Trooper Clark's killer."

Dark reacted with a startled expression. Haber continued.

"Yeah, kind of a surprise. Turns out it was a good friend of Clark's.

Something about a woman, I guess. Heard this morning that everyone is being pulled back, sir. Not sure what that means for us." Haber finished his words stating the obvious: "And everyone was just sure Clark's homicide had to be because of working Narcotics. Something, huh?"

Well, yes that really was something. From the start the Lieutenant presumed some phase of the narcotics calamity was involved in Clark's death also. Yet Dark's immediate reaction to Haber's words included more than a tinge of disappointment. He felt his short absence left him out of the loop, which bothered him as a senior officer. But for some reason he also immediately thought about the kid and the lady. Whatever happened with them now there was a chance Dark would no longer be involved. There was a shooting: Gonzales'. Dark, a law officer, was assaulted. And that lady. She did a bunch of bullshit, much of it illegal but, just like Gonzales' mule work, not especially major crimes.

"Damn! That is something Haber. You're probably right; not exactly sure where that leaves us anymore…Shit! There's still stuff to know. And maybe some important things are still going on. You know, all that mystery stuff with that lady driving into the woods and the kid getting shot and me assaulted. Something's going on with all that crap… Damn! Is all that's gonna come out of all this is me winding up with some freaky dog? Closer to petty crimes… or something bigger? I don't know."

Then Donald Dark reset. He felt a chill on his neck recalling risking his life, maybe almost close to losing his life, going after them. For nothing? 'Oh shit!' He was playing life and death games. For what? Just what he was worrying about. When he was in the forest facing men with weapons and then taking *a walk in the woods* in a potential war zone he didn't even think about it. Was that what was crazy? Or his growing obsession with the futility of the risks required in his job; was *that* what was crazy? To have died chasing them? It might have been pointless.

Dark didn't dwell at all on the way his obvious attraction to that woman was also very probably complicit in him winding up out cold, face down, in a freezing forest in the middle of nowhere. If he had he might have seen that episode and its consequences actually as an outlier compared to his recent thoughts about the risks of police work. Or, maybe his similar reaction now to the experiences of that day might have allowed him to recognize just how low his mood had become. More was going on than his view of the futility of police work.

"No, Dennis, I still want to talk to that kid anyway. I've got nothin' else to do right now so might as well talk to him and see if I can find out what was goin' on out there any better, you know."

The obvious puzzled look on Haber's face projecting his immediate reaction to Dark's words bothered the Lieutenant. He didn't want to appear overly interested in questioning Gonzales and Haber's expression made him feel defensive.

"Yeah, got to do it. At least to tie up some loose ends before movin' on. But you're right; not as big a deal anymore. Why don't we go to Williston so I can get my cruiser and head to Burlington on my own and you can work on what's left of the homicide. I feel really good, Haber. Ready to get back on the job today."

Haber frowned. "Lieutenant, I got from the Captain to stay with you today. He said at least until you see the Doc tomorrow. Said you need to be officially cleared before going out on your own. I'm sorry."

Dark then frowned also. He saw no need to share his questions about what had happened and his focus on that woman with Haber and, frankly, didn't even want Haber to know much about any of that. He did assume, at some point, he would bounce some of his thoughts about all this off Fleury. Fleury had been fairly directly involved in some of it and probably would still be interested in what happened.

Any real persisting buzz in his head was uncertain. Was there still very subtle ringing or, by now, was he just imagining a sound was still there? He did feel good; stronger; certainly fit for duty. But no sense arguing with Haber.

"Okay. Then let's go."

'Go' seemed to be a signal for the dog. She stood up, shook herself off and went to stand by the door. Both Dark and Haber were surprised and impressed. The dog had been laying on the edge of the carpet where it joined with kitchen tile, close to it's food and water bowls. The Lieutenant told Alice she couldn't go but it was a struggle to get out the door without her squeezing through.

Dark verbalized his worry about what a scorned dog might do to his empty house. More notably Haber commented on Alice's apparent expectation to always be with her master. Renting a car and driving into the woods with a dog certainly seemed to echo Haber's words in Dark's mind. Quite an attachment, he thought. Then he reminded himself confirming that dog's presence in the car with the lady and the kid was one of his questions for Gonzales.

———

- 13 -

Jorge Gonzales was shot and apparently thought to be dead or was left to die in the middle of nowhere when Dark last saw him. The Lieutenant was startled at first and then disappointed as he and Haber walked into the private room where Gonzales was tethered with a shackle to his bed. The last time Dark saw Jorge he was lying across the back seat of the crashed white car with legs elevated, pale as a ghost; definitely close to death. Today Dark's most immediate reaction was disbelief that the kid already looked a whole lot better than he did; a rapid reminder he was getting older.

The return of vitality didn't do anything for Jorge's somber, down expression. His face displayed his discouragement. When the Lieutenant entered the room Jorge remembered him and shades of anxiety and fear further colored his appearance. It was unclear if Gonzales was aware he almost certainly owed his life to the Lieutenant.

Sergeant Haber drifted to the far end of the room and leaned against a wall, probably assuming this would be a brief interview. The Lieutenant nodded to Gonzales and pulled a chair away from another corner, placing it next to the bed. Before he sat he stood at the bedrail intentionally trying to ensure he projected his dominance to the kid. He didn't want any bullshit.

"Gonzales, you look hell of a lot better than the last time I saw you, eh? Gonna be all right I'm told. That's good. Guess maybe we're both lucky to be here." Not much reaction from Gonzales, who mostly kept his eyes down. The depth of the trouble he was in had overwhelmed him. "Don't care how many times you've gone over all this with the other investigators, Jorge, now you have to tell me everything I ask you. You and me been through some shit now and I want to know what almost got both of us killed. You got it?"

Gonzales looked a little puzzled but did, barely, raise his head and offered a nod to the Lieutenant. For some reason it made Dark a little angry; maybe a reaction to his own acute recall of events; the risks and the dangers.

"So, Jorge, no more fake Mexican accent. Tell me why you were in Vermont."

By now Gonzales appeared to have told anyone who asked everything he knew, including any names he was aware of. Only the locations of his drop-offs were of any immediate interest to the Lieutenant. Contrary to what he said when initially interrogated Jorge now reported he made stops at only two farms. Then he slept a few hours in a bunk area at the last place before beginning to return to the City mid-morning the next day. The kid described finding his way to the drop-offs as a series of turn offs from a secondary road to dirt roads that seemed to pass by a large number of farms. He insisted the only way he knew which roads he was after was finding small blue flags placed at intersecting roads and then, down a road, another blue flag at each farm entrance.

The region he seemed to be describing was, broadly, not that far from where Gonzales and Dark ended up, a bit more south, in hilly woods. Still not very far from the border also, but then the Canadian border ran in about a hundred mile straight line across the top of the state, so everything up north was close to the border.

It was obvious Gonzales was trying to be helpful. He understood how much trouble he was in. Any vestige or veneer of bravado appeared to be gone.

"What about that lady who said she was your lawyer and you drove away with? What was the deal with her?"

His tone remained flat and his words came slowly. "I don't know very much about her, officer. In the beginning she started right in telling me what to do and say. She said like 'here's what we're going to do,' you know. I just assumed my girl, Laurinda, had contacted her and so I never asked her anything. Now everybody's been asking me all these questions and I don't think, that first time, she ever said she was a lawyer or who she was. Then she showed up again in that court room and I didn't know what to make of her. But I was glad to be able to go with her the next morning."

Dark interrupted him.

"You never heard about her in New York or saw her before the Williston Barracks or in Vermont?"

"No. And Laurinda told me she knows nothing about her either. She said she checked with the places she called to help me and they didn't know anything about her."

"Then tell me what she said after she picked you up in Williston?"

"She asked if I was okay. Then she said we had to get out there, and out of Vermont, quickly. Man, I thought everything was going to be okay, and she looks really worried and tells me both of us are in deep shit. Said we had to get out of there before they could find us. I still don't know what to make of it all, officer. I had guessed it was good I was out of jail and getting out of the state. Then she said I might be dead if I went back to the City. I freaked out.

"She barely talked until she got really scared and said we were being followed. Was that you? She started going ape-shit and I think she was lost. Then she thought more cops, I guess. She started screaming and was driving way too fast for that beat up road. Told her she should let me drive. She looked at me then floored it and a minute later I think she clipped something; a tree or a rock or something and the car spun around and smashed into a tree and I went out for a while." Jorge's head lurched forward in his bed and he briefly became more animated as he relived those moments.

"I guess I kind of woke up because I remember the pain of being shot but I don't remember seeing anyone; maybe heard some voices, not sure. Looked over but the door slammed and she was gone. Not sure if she shot me or not. Lots of screaming."

"Jorge, Did the lady have a dog with her?"

Gonzales lay back in the bed. Dark's question was followed by the kid deeply inhaling and then exhaling, projecting his confusion and uncertainty again. His words and tone reflected his frustration. Nothing was going to surprise Jorge Gonzales anymore.

"Yeah, she had a little dog with her. I don't like dogs and I just looked at it in the back seat. But she scared me when she said she had to take the dog because she was leaving. But she never told me where we were going and by the time she said we weren't heading to the City she started to scream like crazy."

So the dog was hers. It wasn't lost on Dark that his actions may have played a role in the woman and kid winding up crashed in the forest; and worse. But he reminded himself that other car with those men were waiting for them anyway. Weren't they? Sounded like she was trying to protect more than just the kid.

The Lieutenant realized he could stay there and ask the kid a hundred more questions about that lady but Gonzales didn't learn anything more about her during their ride beyond the idea she was running away and feared for both their lives.

Back to drugs? If all this had nothing to do with Trooper Clark's homicide then what else was left to explain why she showed up from out of nowhere and wound up in a brazen attempt to get him out of custody that first day? Could it only be related to his mule activity? Something else?

Haber was shuffling his feet, obviously more than ready to move on. Driving down, in Haber's cruiser, the lieutenant already had said he wanted to make a quick stop at the car rental agency the lady used. He told Haber after that he could drop him at the Williston Barracks to see Ed Fleury. Dark's cruiser was there and it was unspoken but they each knew Lieutenant Fleury would let Dark take his own cruiser home.

As the Lieutenant was finishing up with Gonzales and preparing to leave, the kid propped himself up on his shackled right arm and reached across with his left to the bedside table. He opened a drawer and removed a piece of paper.

"Officer, my girl and her family are really worried about me. I don't know what's gonna happen to me. I didn't shoot anyone but the lawyer they got for me was here late yesterday and says I'm still in big trouble. My girl, Laurinda, and her uncle, I think, are flying here tomorrow to try to help me. Her uncle, he's an ex-cop. Officer, can I give you his name because I think he's going to try to call the lawyers and police involved with my problems?"

Sounded to Dark like an annoyance he wasn't sure he would respond to. The Lieutenant looked unsympathetically at Gonzales but his reaction was softened by the fear he saw in the kid and he was struck by Jorge saying 'thank you' as Dark took the piece of paper. He did think the kid surely wound up in much more shit and trouble than he ever intended and he always thought, right from the start, it was unlikely Jorge was involved in Trooper Clark's death. So he pulled out his small memo pad to transfer the name on the piece of paper. Immediately, the Lieutenant was absolutely stunned.

"Jorge, you got to be kidding?"

Instantly, Gonzales' face looked deflated. He couldn't get anywhere with anyone.

"Gonzales, do you know this man? What did you say your connection is to him?"

Jorge repeated what he had just said about the man whose name on the paper was James Wiley.

———————

On the short trip to the car rental office Lieutenant Dark had difficulty concealing his utter amazement that the name the kid handed him was someone he knew… Well, he *did* know James Wiley, very briefly, almost seven years before. He and Wiley were part of a case that was so notorious in Vermont even Dennis Haber, ten years younger than Dark, knew about it. Probably because it tore through the fabric of the force and the community when it happened. The Lieutenant was totally astounded that, of the more than thirty thousand police officers in New York City, the girl's uncle turned out to be the only policeman he actually did know there. Imagine.

At first Dark felt some excitement seeing Wiley's name. As that case wound down they each agreed to stay in touch, but it never happened. By the time Haber's cruiser reached the rental agency Dark was more reflective. He wondered what Wiley would expect him to do for Gonzales? And he self-consciously wondered how obvious his own personal issues might be to someone like Wiley?

Despite his progress on the force Dark had an instant of worry about what he had really achieved. Shouldn't have been any surprise to him, especially lately. He didn't think at all about Wiley, then a young NYPD detective who already had a paunch when he knew him. And, in the excitement of seeing his name, hearing Wiley was now an ex-cop never registered with him.

———————

Lieutenant Dark and Sergeant Haber hoped they would find a photocopy of a driver's license with a picture of the lady they were seeking at the rental agency. No luck. It was not a requirement. Investigators from the force had already determined the number on the New York State license she gave the company was a fake. She also guaranteed the rental with a stolen credit card with a man's name. None of the agents could describe anything useful about who was with her. By the time the agency was made aware of the stolen card the vehicle was sitting, crashed into a tree in the forest.

It was notable to the Lieutenant that the car had only been rented later in the day, the day before she picked up Gonzales. Several things stood out but nothing offered any solid information. How she got around before getting the rental, and access to a counterfeit license and stolen credit card, all seemed to further confirm it was unlikely she was acting alone.

———

- 14 -

At first Ed Fleury was defensive when Dark walked into his office at the Williston Barracks. He felt badly he hadn't found time to visit his good friend in the hospital. He hoped Dark would agree that traveling to Newport was awfully far for him. Didn't matter; he was ready for Dark.

"Gee Fleur, so nice of you to stop by the hospital after my head was almost split open driving in the middle of nowhere. You remember that day, don't you?" Dark was anxious to resume their usual, incessant attack and respond banter. He had sent Haber on his way and felt good, in familiar territory, sitting across from his friend.

"Yeah, DD, I do recall something about your insistence on following some strange female all over the state. Didn't end too well, did it? Rarely does, eh? Sorry, police business kept me here." His last words were spoken without sarcasm. He was pleased to see his buddy looked well.

"Well, gosh Fleur, my parent's place in Jericho's only 'bout a few miles from yours. Too far too, I guess."

Fleury paused and delivered the defense he prepared.

"You know, DD, actually, late in the day yesterday I was getting in my cruiser for a quick trip up that way when there was another dang emergency and by the time I cleared things up it was too late to go. Of course pal, in the evening my gal, Molly, told me she talked to Susan to find out how you were doing when Susan visited you…"

Dark turned in his chair and looked away from Ed. Maybe he never realized how close those ladies were.

"Might not have been the best time to drop by after all, eh?" Fleury wasn't naturally given to a leer, but he offered Dark his best version of one. Fleury was absolved. Dark was ready to move on.

"Well, I'm okay. I think you're gonna tell me tomorrow when the Captain says it's time to drop anything that's left of this investigation I should agree and move on; forget about that lady and whatever was going on that day in the forest." He was serious now.

Fleury knew better than to respond yet. With his head up, Dark leaned forward resting his forearms on his thighs, signaling his earnest concern.

"Hard to let go when someone's been shot, you know. Maybe not the kind of calamity like Ed Clark's homicide, but some real strange stuff was going on…and you know that too." He sat back and looked less tense.

"Think about it Fleur. A mule, a lowly, fucking mule, gets arrested and all hell breaks loose. Sure a trooper was killed. But it wasn't the kid." He tried to verbalize his confusion. "Why did that lady show up like that and do all she did to get him out of jail and then away from…away from…away from I don't know who or what? But I watched those fuckers, Fleur. Looked like cold-blooded killers… and on like a mission, you know.

"Woulda shot it out with me without a second thought. Then wopped me hard on the head, probably thinking they killed me that way. My guess is they left the kid to die and went after the lady…unless she was part of all this with those guys… But I just don't think so.

"No, there's more here. There has to be. Sure, something about that lady attracted me but it's more than that. I don't think I'm gonna get any more from the kid. He's spilled everything he knows. If that lady's dead then I guess it probably *is* over. I tell you, we find that lady alive then there will be answers." He twisted in his chair reflecting his frustration.

"Shit! Can't imagine where to begin again. But even if Captain says to close the books I'm gonna keep my ears out."

Fleury could see Dark was totally serious but he couldn't resist. "Yeah, sure DD. Good thought. And you know what's going through the force like wildfire? I hear you got your own personal little *earhound* and that should help you keep your ears out. Haber said that little thing more ears than anything else.

"Course, then might have to suspend your operation now till spring. Six pound dog out in five below may not go, DD. Unless, of course, maybe you tuck it in your parka. Head with ears like that sticking out of the middle of your chest almost guaranteed to freeze any sonofabitch coming at you. Lifesaver, maybe."

Dark almost looked like he was blushing. Fleury had him. But Fleury didn't just want to fool around.

"Don't know, pal. You sure you not stuck more on that lady than you lettin' on? Ain't gonna say any more but you spent no longer than thirty minutes with that crazy lady and she's almost all you've been thinking about. Admit it."

"Bullshit, Fleur. That's bullshit." It came out forcefully but not convincingly. If he had to Dark might have admitted he wasn't sure. No, he would never do that.

"Well, you see Fleur, you're so fucking in another world, stuck with your *nuclear* family, living with atomic explosions every day, you're so fucking shell-shocked all you dream about is stuff like that, I guess. Nothing romantic about this story pal."

The Lieutenant picked up his keys and headed home to see what Alice had wrought in his place.

On the road he wondered who the real bullshiter was? He was the one who used the word 'romantic.' 'Shit, where did that come from?' he wondered. What was going on? Dark struggled with feeling forced to confront an apparent fixation on a lady he did not know. The comfort of being with Susan flashed through his mind, but her image was gone as quickly as it had arrived. Romantic?

Was what started playing in his head two ways of saying the same thing? 'Sound like freaking song titles,' he thought. 'What the fuck? *If ever I find you?*…or is it *If I ever find you!*' But they are different, aren't they?' he thought. 'Which is it? Chasing a dream; like an imaginary person? Or, like if I catch up to you and your crooked ways you're fucked lady?' Would there ever be an answer?

Donald Dark figured his thinking was still off. Left over from the concussion, he decided.

Alice was insane. The dog wasn't only no care. When Dark returned she looked like she was in control of the household. Just cool, like glad to see him, but no big deal. Like "want to go out?" 'Sure, if you're okay with it. No rush.' Dark wondered if he had tasked Alice with doing some laundry while he was gone what would have happened? She was quite a companion. She sat beside him when he stretched out in his club chair. He looked directly at her. She twisted her head at a slight angle and was, literally, all ears.

It was late in the afternoon and Dark was exhausted. In the morning he had a nine o'clock appointment with a neurologist in Burlington and he knew he should go to bed early to be sharp for that doc so he could be cleared to return to work. The Captain wanted to see him at three later that day. In the evening, until he called in for his messages from staff, he wasn't sure how he would kill the time between appointments.

One of the clerks told him that later in the day she had a persistent man calling from New York City who wanted information about who was running the Gonzales kid's investigation. He said he was

NYPD. She told Dark at first she wasn't sure if his was the right name to give the guy, since he was on leave. No one else had taken the kid's investigation over so she told him it was him.

Before she could tell him the Lieutenant might not be able to be contacted for a few days, hearing Dark's name he got excited and started swearing and told her he knew the Lieutenant. The upshot was the guy really pressed her to let Dark know he was arriving in Burlington early in the morning and really hoped he could meet him at the hospital.

The Lieutenant had her call Jim Wiley and tell him he would find Wiley at the hospital later in the morning. 'Where is this gonna' go?' he wondered.

———

- 15 -

Instead of being examined by the contracted GP for the force in the northern half of the state Dark was asked to follow-up for clearance to return to active duty with a Neurologist at the med school in Burlington. Lately, concussions and potential long-term effects had become a big deal nationally in the sporting world. The Colonel and Captain were advised to be sure to have Lieutenant Dark carefully evaluated before returning to unrestricted duty.

Dark was unhappy with his visit, feeling the wordy Doc who examined him was more interested in trying to find problems than let him get back on duty. The Doc asked a lot of questions; maybe too personal for Dark's brittle psyche lately. After answering a few queries honestly he tried to blow off the Doc's effort to probe into any of that stuff beyond a superficial level. The Doc seemed to leave it and the actual physical exam was no problem. Dark breezed through it.

When the Doc said it was all good and sent the Lieutenant on his way with only a few words about possible minor changes he should keep an eye out for Dark figured he had passed the exam and that was the end of it.

———

Dark intentionally planned to meet with Wiley at the hospital later in the morning. That way the girlfriend and Wiley would have time with Jorge first. Dark hoped that discussion would help inform both him and Wiley when they had their chance to talk. As far as this case was concerned Dark wasn't at all sure what he would be able to offer Wiley that would help the kid or his girlfriend. The magnitude of the kid's remaining crimes didn't seem especially significant anymore but he was still in some trouble.

Dark doubted Jorge's girlfriend was likely to add anything especially useful to his own quest to find, or at least explain, the missing woman whose involvement continued to elude him. But, even after all the years that had passed, he did feel he owed it to the NYPD cop to help him out, if he could.

Their actions together in the celebrated case years before were brief but signaled a lot about each of them. Initially they interacted covertly, an effort to aid Dark in a difficult setting. Then the Lieutenant worked with Wiley to ensure the innocence of the man Wiley had wound up in Vermont hoping to assist. They never really socialized or even made much small talk during the few days their paths crossed back then. Neither ever learned virtually anything about the other's life. But in that short time they each developed a respect for the other that continued to this day.

It was good Wiley had a place to go after he and Laurinda had a chance to speak with Jorge and hospital staff. The millions of thoughts and emotions bombarding Laurinda's mind spilled out in a torrent of emotion on seeing Jorge, upset and shackled to his bed. Her ability to talk with staff was limited. Jim Wiley inserted himself into the discussion and asked the pertinent health questions. Laurinda was considering climbing onto the kid's bed when Donald Dark showed up at the doorway to the room and knocked on the partially closed door. He was dressed in his usual state trooper's uniform but had left his hat in his cruiser. Doubts and worries darted around his brain but he looked and felt well.

He would not have recognized Jim Wiley if he ran into him on the street. Probably the same for Wiley. Dark was in uniform and that helped. The last time they met Detective Wiley wore a cheap suit and had a suit on again. He was slimmer and wore a better quality suit now. He actually looked sharper than the way Dark remembered him. They both were surprised that they felt comfortable greeting each other as though they were old friends.

"Came over in a rideshare Trooper. Less likely to stir up the local PD this time than 'bout seven years ago, I hope. Good to see you again Dark." Wiley smiled as he spoke and walked across the room to shake the Lieutenant's hand. He seemed to want to direct the discussion away from the room. He wanted to leave Laurinda and the kid to themselves and closed the door behind him as he and Dark walked into the hallway.

The Lieutenant put an arm on Wiley's shoulder as they shook hands. He offered an easy smile and an expression that transmitted his recognition of Wiley's travel reference.

"Crazy time, huh, Detective." Not meant as a question. They took a few steps down the hall. Immediately, the Lieutenant was struck by Wiley's appearance. Something was wrong. Wrong with Wiley. The way he moved. Dark couldn't put his finger on it, but there was something different about Wiley. He looked good. He smiled and looked sharp and moved down the hall okay. But something wasn't right or completely natural about him. It was subtle. Dark decided whatever he sensed was none of his business and tried to move on.

But the change in Wiley wasn't meant to be a secret. Shortly it became more obvious. Wiley was prepared for it to become a topic of discussion; no surprise to him. Wiley impressed with his smile and relaxed demeanor. Whatever his story he appeared at peace with his world and quite comfortable meeting Dark again. He looked happy, actually. If Donald Dark ever presented himself similarly he didn't come across that way lately.

They walked to a small conference room the Lieutenant had requisitioned. Once inside Wiley began to remove his suit jacket. Then Dark knew what was not right. Ever so slightly Wiley struggled to remove the coat. His left arm was weak and didn't move very much.

Two men who, at best, barely knew each other years before, carried on convinced their past shared experience qualified them as more than only prior professional contacts.

"Good to see you, Jim. Sorry to see that arm doesn't look like it works too well. How far back does that go? Don't recall noticing anything like that when you were up here last time?"

"Yeah, terrible business. Happened about three, four years ago now. Changed my whole fuckin' life." He spoke without any signs of rancor.

If Donald Dark was anything he was a good listener, especially lately. It suited him to try to understand others.

With effort Wiley slowly raised his left hand above his head and glanced at his effort, monitoring his progress. Then he was able to gradually spread his fingers apart. With notable further effort he allowed his arm to drop down in a controlled fashion. It wasn't a flaccid paralysis, but he had significant weakness.

"That's it Donald; the whole story. Nothin' else wrong anywhere. Just my fuckin' left arm." He sat back in his chair.

Dark was puzzled. How could this guy still be a cop with his major disability. Apparently his confusion showed in his face. "Must be really tough for you to…"

Wiley anticipated Dark's confusion.

"No, of course you didn't know. Not NYPD anymore. Been out since it happened." He could tell Dark was, like virtually everyone he met, curious what happened to him. He tried to keep it short but he leaned back and launched into the story he often told about how he acquired his paretic extremity. He had it down. Dark listened intently.

Wiley had a slight smirk on his face. "Maybe you heard about the case; called the bastard 'The Whistling Killer.' Was making good progress as a detective, you know. Liked it. So some asshole made of nothing but steel nerves did a year long terror campaign in the City. Figured how to get into rich old ladies' apartments. Fucker started whistling in middle of the night or when lady taking a bath or shower. If his whistling, alone, didn't kill most of the old ladies from sheer fright then he stabbed them. A couple of them lived to tell the tale of his terrifying, insane whistling. Would scare the shit out of me also, you know, alone in your place in the middle of the night."

Dark was entranced. What a story. He could only imagine where this might go. 'Man, police work in a gigantic city!'

"So there was a whole team of us working this; you can imagine. Became a task force. We set up some decoy female cops around the neighborhood and he finally fell for one. Followed her home and was able to get into her building. I was inside an apartment and saw him slip a jimmy in the door as it was being closed. Then we waited hours till he decided to work his way in.

"Don, you sure you never heard about this before?" Wiley smiled.

Dark signaled no with his face. Wiley sat forward and continued.

"Fucker waited four long hours. Lady cop went about her business and off to bed with a pistol for a companion. I was stuck in the dark in a hallway corner outside her room, afraid to fuckin' move, much less breathe. Had to hear him whistle before the collar, you know.

"Started warbling in the hallway. So fuckin cocky and confident. So I step out of the dark and flip on a light. Bastard's so startled he shoots me in my left shoulder. Never used any weapon other than a knife before. Who knew? I shoot him and he lives for a week. End of story."

The Lieutenant and Wiley sat quietly for a couple of minutes. Dark was thinking over what he had just heard. Interestingly, his first thoughts were kind of clinical, thinking about how this perp, supposedly, got into the buildings and apartments.

"Something Wiley; really." Dark wasn't going to say a word. Wiley seemed to sense Dark's concern.

"So Donald, you remember from the case way back that Captain Vallan's kid? Yeah, Henry. He's an author. He and I worked on this story and he made it into a book. Made a few bucks. Never happened, but book did okay. Why I thought you might have heard about the story. Made a few bucks. Maybe a movie someday."

They both smiled. Wiley more than Dark. Wiley sat back again. Now he looked serious.

"No, no, that's it. It was nothing special Don. I was chasing an asshole, drugs I think, into an alley. I tripped over some garbage cans just as we started shooting. We each got hit. We lay there for a time an he bled out and I couldn't use my arm well after that. Nerve damage they said.

"Shit Don, I got a wife an two kids. What the fuck was I doing chasing an asshole kid over drugs and winding up in a life and death spot?

"But you know Dark, life is real fucked up. Lose lotta my arm. Go off the force on total disability in my thirties. Didn't know what was gonna happen to me; or my family. Had a really bad year. For something to do started helping Henry Vallan a little an slowly realized I still got skills; in my head. Decided there has to be a non-violent side to this business. Used some of the money I got to join with some smart young guys working on security systems. Dark, you believe this? These guys actually valued the skills of a cop. Imagine that? So I work with them and then I also set up a small investigation agency. Believe me, nothing dangerous, Donald.

"Hey, you won't believe me when I tell you what I call that business."

Dark was transfixed on Wiley and his words. Holy shit, the first part anyway was like listening to his worst fears come true. At least Wiley was still alive. It was taking Dark some time to begin to sense any other good that may have come out of it.

"Don, do you remember that New York State Police Captain back then? Regardi was his name. He told us how that Captain Vallan was known for stressing the importance of not forgetting to work the *nuts and bolts* of a case. You know, searching for basic facts and small details when putting a case together. Remember, we talked about that at the very end?"

Dark did recall his last contact with Jim Wiley. He vaguely remembered something about nuts and bolts but he guessed what it signified never impressed him enough to stay with him. Wiley's stories just amazed him. He nodded again.

"Well, that's it," Jim said.

Dark wasn't sure what he meant.

"'N&B Investigations.' You know, Nuts and Bolts. Telling you Don, whole lot of white collar shit out there you can get well paid to work on. No weapons involved. Wife and kids can sleep at night too… Course I still carry. Some nasty dudes out there even if they do their robbing with a pen, if you know what I mean?"

Dark practically forgot why he was meeting with this man. Wiley's stories, fake and true, were startling to him; more than diverting. Like a train coming down a track they spoke right to his dark outlook. His worst fears, but maybe also a story with an element of redemption or a kind of silver lining. Was Wiley a living example of a path that led to a life that might make more sense to the Lieutenant?

When they interacted many years before Wiley barely spoke. Today Wiley more than dominated their conversation. Dark worried he was so introspectively focused on himself his dark mood would be obvious to Wiley. Wiley asked him nothing about himself.

Wiley was ready to move on. He asked how much trouble the Lieutenant thought the kid was really in. And he wondered if getting shot and then spilling anything and everything he knew might help lessen what he'd be charged for. Dark thought the kid's mule work would be the extent of it. As they talked both he and

Jim were comfortable with the idea that Jorge should try to revise down the amount of weed he originally said he brought up so his crime would turn into a minor misdemeanor. That might work its way through the court system more harmlessly. The Lieutenant agreed to make some calls to the State's Attorney's office.

Dark had no problem allowing his friend to help the kid, never having had much worry, from the beginning, about Jorge's role in Trooper Clark's homicide. He did, however, want to speak with Laurinda, and Jorge (probably one last time), about the mysterious woman Dark remained stuck on.

———————

"Jim, I guess I have my own story in this business and I think somehow what Jorge was doing, in some way, has to be involved in a part of what I can't figure out. Wait till you hear it, Jim. You're gonna tell me I made it up; just like your whistler. But it happened, Jim, and I been having a real tough time figuring it out."

So now it was time for Donald Dark to tell Jim Wiley his story. But like all recollections the telling was tainted by what the spinner of the tale was willing or not willing to say. There was no one in the room to begin to complete the picture of Dark's apparent continuing strong obsession with one feature of his narrative. The Lieutenant told his story in some detail, graphically communicating some of its harrowing nature. While he focused mostly on his plan to shadow a woman and its consequences Lieutenant Dark essentially left out his imagined personal attachment to a woman he did not know.

Either Jim Wiley had been a very perceptive cop or Donald Dark's intense focus on that lady lit up his face and words like a pulsating neon light. Jim figured more was up with Dark and the woman Dark tailed into his own life and death situation. Wiley decided there was no reason for him to follow up or even begin to ask Dark any questions probing his suspicions. Wiley's business in Vermont looked like it was going to wrap up very rapidly; and favorably. His trip couldn't have gone better, to that point. He was pleased he and

Dark, with their very different lives, seemed to be hitting it off well after so many years. Wiley felt a kind of unspoken connection had lasted all that time so it wasn't such a surprise they seemed to feel comfortable with each other so quickly.

———

- 16 -

How do you explain a situation like this to a commanding officer? Armed with a superior record and clearance from the medical consultant Lieutenant Dark tried to make his case that the Major Criminal Investigation Division (actually he) had reason to continue to explore further aspects of what had happened. A homicide was solved but there still were pieces that made no sense.

Lately, Captain Bushey's confidence in the Lieutenant was on the fence; a superior who was beginning to worry about an impression that one of his best and most reliable detectives was, at the least, appearing distracted. It was obvious to Dark the Captain's demeanor and remarks reflected concern about Dark's recent mood, probably communicated to the Captain by others. Apparently there were a few colleagues on the force who interpreted and reported Dark's present mood and rare use of the word 'useless' as possible signs of a loss of nerve; a very ominous and dangerous development for a trooper.

Dark believed if his fellow troopers or the Captain recognized he was struggling with some issues they were much more nuanced in their assessment and concerns than that. He didn't exactly get it. He was very worried the Captain wouldn't buy his argument for continuing on the case, much less anything about his mystery lady. Captain Bushey had to admit, though, the Lieutenant's job performance remained fine.

Bushey clearly didn't feel he had anywhere near enough reason to limit his Lieutenant and, like everyone else, he liked him anyway. He asked Dark if he was comfortable handling the remaining threads of this case along with his other unrelated developing investigations, to which Dark responded affirmatively. The Captain then told him he hoped he could tie up loose ends within a week or two.

Donald Dark was pleased. He was still hovering at a point where he tried to assume his mood and outlook were, perhaps, more reflective of his response to *occupational hazards* than a worrisome depression.

Driving home that evening he mulled over everything, maybe for the hundredth time. But this time he was feeling buoyed after Captain Bushey's almost non-existent, superficial probing. What Dark knew was Ed Clark was killed by a rival; a love triangle. Jorge Gonzales was guilty of transporting marijuana for sale. Ah, and the lady? …Who the fuck knew.

Obviously, it was more than just figuring out where she fit into all this. Dark was smitten with her. Why? He wanted to see her again, and talk more with her. He was sure they shared an intellectual and physical attraction, just as they each had already expressed their shared view about the drug war. He couldn't…or wouldn't let it go.

For the moment everything appeared to be okay. On the other hand, if his obsession didn't fade, his career stood a good chance of fading instead.

————————

The next day Jorge appeared fine. Even behaved like some of his swagger had returned. His lawyer arranged a brief bail hearing and after that Wiley had the three of them on a flight back to the City the next morning. Hearing of the flight set Gonzales off. Somehow the kid hadn't connected that the plan to leave Vermont still meant leaving the Subaru behind. At first his disagreement with Wiley's plan seemed like a simple mis-understanding.

"Jorge, that car is evidence in a crime. They don't have to let you have it, certainly not until your case is completely resolved. And I don' know the laws here in Vermont, but there's a chance they might never give it back to you. Some places confiscate property used in crimes, you know."

Wiley and Laurinda were startled by the sudden intensity in Jorge's features and his words.

"No, no, Mr. Wiley. I have to get that car back right away. Now. I, I guess I was kind of out of it before. I didn't really get that I can't take the car back to the City. No, I have to bring it back."

Wiley felt his gut tightening. Then he was angry. He worked hard to suppress his upset with the kid.

"What's the deal here, Jorge? You makin' me some nervous now, you know? Just what's the story with that car?" Jim Wiley knew something was wrong. He had an idea but whatever the exact problem was he sensed it was about to throw a large wrench into the works of what had been, up to that moment, a seamless visit and approaching goal of getting this kid home. Wiley sighed and leaned forward in his chair toward the kid.

"Jorge, that Subaru isn't yours, is it?" He collapsed back in his seat and looked weary. "We haven't talked about who's paid you to do this. The state police didn't bring it up so I been hoping to get you and Laurinda back home without any of that complicating all this. But now you got to tell me what the deal is with that car."

Jorge was sitting in a chair, still in a hospital gown tied in the back by Laurinda, who was sitting on his bed during all this, looking confused. The kid was no longer shackled and stood up with surprising ease and strength. He walked to the window and spoke with his back to Wiley.

"No, it's not mine. Give me a fake registration with my name. Every time, those guys always made a big deal about making sure I was to get that car back to them. Said there wasn't much profit in these deals and if they lost a car the whole thing would be bad. Said if I ever came back without the car it would be big trouble… deep shit…for me. But, you know, I just never thought this would happen and I never thought about it. That lady said we had to run for our lives and forget the car for now. I was so scared. Then things went crazy so fast I didn't think about it. I got to get that car back or I can't go home."

The kid could do all the wishing he wanted and demand whatever from Wiley but now Wiley's task had just become a whole lot more complicated. Not only was he now required to inform Donald Dark, who would also immediately understand implications of the kid's rant, but he was probably also obligated to stay involved when they returned to New York. At the very least he'd have to work with, and maybe even protect, Jorge, and Laurinda, while the NYPD figured this all out… Could it get dangerous? He knew the answer as he sighed and then stood up. Never was good but had been working out well; almost too straightforward. "Shit!" Not so simple anymore.

———

The Lieutenant was at Williston and when Wiley called him about why Jorge was flipping out Dark arranged for a trooper to bring Wiley the ten or so minutes it took to get from the hospital to the Williston Barracks. Dark and Wiley thought they were done the day before. Wiley had agreed to make some inquiries in the City but Dark made it clear he wasn't expecting Jim to do more than let the NYPD know about the problem. Although he did give him a picture of Alice…the dog. Implications of doing that were upsetting but also clear to the Lieutenant.

At Williston Barracks the Lieutenant introduced Jim to Ed Fleury. Dark was continuing to feel better each day. He wondered if it was exclusively his returning health or if he was also successfully diminishing his fixation, something he, at least intellectually, knew would be good for him.

The three of them bullshitted for a while. Wiley thought Dark took a lot of shit from Ed Fleury, but sometimes gave some back, and they seemed to enjoy doing that to each other. Dark did act uncomfortable when Fleury asked Wiley if Donald had told him much about the "lovely lady who apparently couldn't keep her hair on…and Donald couldn't get out of his mind?" Wiley latched onto 'lovely' as a confirmation of the missing link Wiley had assumed when Dark told him his story two days before.

Over the phone Wiley had given Dark the gist of the news from Jorge. Now he told both Lieutenants who he planned to call in Narcotics when he returned to the City in the morning. Dark wanted to talk about that and Jorge's new found anxiety. Ed Fleury looked disappointed their banter was being interrupted by serious business. Their routine broken Fleury remembered he had something for Dark and told him there was a letter addressed to him at Williston instead of Waterbury. Wiley and Fleury chatted while Dark retrieved the letter.

Walking back in Dark opened the envelope and began to pull out a piece of paper. "Bet this will be something," he said. He held the envelope up for them. "Look no return address. Looks like it's post marked…" The Lieutenant had difficulty reading what was stamped in the small circle over a forever stamp. He squinted and said, "Post-mark could be *Akwesasne*. That's the Res, right?" Anticipating it to be a crank letter, a common phenomenon for a law officer, especially without a return address, they all smiled. Suddenly Dark's mouth dropped open, and he stared, intently, at the sheet of paper.

Fleury nodded to Wiley and joked: "See, that's what I'm talking about. Donald doesn't talk too much anymore. Has perfected that speechless, kind of clueless, look." Fleury was right, Dark was speechless. He stared a few more seconds at the paper in front of him, looked at the two men, then back at the paper and, sounding mesmerized, slowly read aloud:

"You bastard. You've got my dog." With a vacant stare he looked back up at them.

Fleury was never at a complete loss for words. "What the fuck, DD?"

Dark ran to the crime lab and carefully dropped the paper and envelope into a plastic evidence bag. He was hoping a print could be lifted. But there turned out to be nothing.

Dark was totally distracted. The discussion was over.

———

- 17 -

The morning of the their third day in Vermont, with conditions for Jorge, Wiley and Laurinda posted Jorge Gonzales' bail and all three flew home. The Subaru stayed in Vermont.

On the flight to LaGuardia Wiley directed Jorge to sit with him so Laurinda sat in the row in front of them. It was the first time he was able to be almost alone with the kid. Both were uncomfortable. Jim Wiley's boy and girl were younger than Jorge and Laurinda. Periodically on this trip, under his breath, he thanked the Lord he and Idelia had been spared such upset and dark challenges from their children, so far. He worried about Laurinda and Jorge, but felt more sorry for her. She was the innocent in this tangled mess. Jorge seemed chastened by it all but Wiley wasn't sure how much of what Jorge said could be trusted. Jorge was clearly going home to a more challenging setting.

On the plane Wiley made it clear to the kid he was going to speak with NYPD Narcotics officers about this right away. He gave Jorge a final opening to tell him anything more he knew but was told there was nothing else. Wiley wrestled with the expressed hope of Laurinda's parents that he would find a way to caution the kid to stay away from Laurinda. He doubted his effort was successful or went anywhere. He chided himself for presenting his warning in such an awkward way he felt like a jerk. For the duration of this trip, anyway, Laurinda and Jorge appeared to remain a committed couple.

They took a rideshare back to the City. Approaching city streets all three relaxed and felt better. The activity and hum, sounds of the City on a typical early afternoon, were what they knew and made them feel comfortable. The kids lived on the Eastside. First they dropped Laurinda off. The ride to Jorge's small apartment was short but Wiley used the time to remind Jorge about what had happened and cautioned him, again, about staying out of trouble…and, maybe, away from Laurinda.

Wiley lived on the Westside and went on alone to his apartment. It was, hopefully, the end of a stressful period. He guessed it would be considered a successful conclusion by Laurinda and probably the Alvarez family…and, therefore, him too. Jorge Gonzales' situation and status, beyond being out of jail, was uncertain. Wiley made sure Jorge knew how to contact him if he wanted to but doubted he would ever hear from the kid again.

———————

A day later Laurinda made no effort to hide her almost constant phone contact and planning with Jorge. Her parents had, perhaps naively, assumed the relationship was over. Her mother literally bit her lip in her effort to be patient with Laurinda. Her father became discouraged quickly and was furious.

The next day she announced she was going to spend the night at Jorge's and help him pack to move back in with his mother. That's when all hell broke loose. Her mother's effort at staying calm dissolved and her father started shouting. When Laurinda left with a small overnight bag it was very unclear if she would be welcomed home if she ever returned.

But her parents mis-read their young daughter. Laurinda's feelings about Jorge evolved significantly while they were in Vermont. She understood his fear and recent suffering and felt badly for him. However she was put off by his complete avoidance of even beginning to talk about how he was going to put this episode behind him and would avoid the contacts and activities that would insure more trouble was ahead.

In quiet moments in Vermont Jorge told her he didn't want to return to school. He said he knew some guys who were doing *legit* businesses and were willing to bring him in. He waxed on about how he thought of himself as a player. He apologized to Laurinda for what happened this time but said he would do better and make more money now. He said school just wasn't right for him anymore.

Actually, Jorge was soon to have no money and no source of income. He had to move back with his mother and the two siblings still there. It was unlikely to go well but he knew of no other option. Laurinda agreed to help him pack up that night and move his things in the morning. That was it. She saw no reason to try to convince her parents of that at that moment. She was aware Jorge may not have accepted the end of their relationship either. She would have to be strong and it would not be easy for her…or him also, she guessed.

Hearing Jorge's despair at his arrest and then seeing him recovering from his wound in the hospital was terribly upsetting. Her heart and affection went out to someone she cared about who was in such difficulty. But she was also pretty sure she was reading Jorge's words and actions, and his personality, correctly now. Maybe she was actually the one who had decided, to her own satisfaction, he wanted to go to school and ignored things he did until this.

Laurinda did not want to end up like many women in her culture, marking her years picking up after a man who didn't get it. A man who always found trouble and relied on having a strong woman, the only reliable partner in the relationship, to pick up the pieces. There was limited future for her in that.

Her parents were probably right about Jorge. And it wasn't entirely his fault he appeared to be bound to fail and find trouble again and again. Even if he finished school; so what? They were poor people in what was likely a rigged world. It was hard for Laurinda. The man she dreamed about might not exist in the strata of America that was her world. But she was nineteen and not nearly ready to give up. Ending her time with Jorge left her even more motivated to stay strong.

It was not unreasonable for Jorge to assume Laurinda remained less than resolute about ending their relationship. After all, she had agreed to stay the night at his place. But he was wrong. They had a quiet dinner nearby and then started packing things up right away when they returned to his apartment. They worked until well after midnight to get most of it done. Laurinda then crashed, in her clothes, on the bare mattress on the floor.

Jorge was tired yet all through the evening continued to hope they would make love at some point. Despite all his problems sex was foremost on his mind. He turned off the lights and delighted in lying next to her. His troubles of the last week and just now happily faded for that moment. She was on her side, at the edge of the mattress. He pulled her to his body and put his arm around her waist. Laurinda was asleep and there was no resistance. He wasn't sure what to do next. But nothing happened.

Jorge Gonzales found himself unable to decide what to do. He wanted to make love to Laurinda Alvarez. She had told him no; their time together was over. So much had gone wrong and now this. For a few minutes he became angry. He tried to tell himself a woman should not disappoint her man. How could she do this to him; practically taunt him by lying on his bed and deny him sex? Leave him? …But it wasn't enough. Then Jorge was consumed with guilt. He had fucked up…totally. What was he going to do now? Would he be okay without her? He put his head on her back shoulder, closed his moist eyes and silently cried himself to sleep.

————

They didn't get going until mid-morning the next day. In the chilly air a buddy with a small van helped them load up and then deposited them with Jorge's boxes and stuff at the curb in the middle of a busy city block high up on the eastside of Manhattan.

Laurinda stayed at the sidewalk, watching the belongings. She was pleased when Jorge returned from his first trip to the apartment and told her his mother and siblings were all out. Laurinda prepared to load him up for another drop off. As she turned to place a small box on top of one he was already holding a young man came running, charging up the sidewalk, right up to them. Each holding a box, they turned to him.

It was a young guy, same size as Jorge, and he was frightening. Wearing a gray hoodie, black pants and big white hi-top sneakers, the kid's eyes were red and almost bulging with anger or fear; it was unclear which. He was sweating and started moving all over with jerky motions, like he was high. Neither of them knew who this intense and ominous young man was. Jorge quickly glanced down the street in the direction the scary guy had come from. He thought he saw Emanuel Samuel lingering at the intersection about twenty yards away.

This looked to be trouble and Jorge wasn't sure what to do. Laurinda didn't understand what was happening. Pedestrians were all over the sidewalk and the street was bustling with mid-day traffic. The young man began to scream at both of them. At first his appearance and behavior on the street had no impact on activity around them.

"Motha fuckers, motha fuckas, you and you bitch in big trouble. You lost that money and that car and they after Manny. He sure they gonna kill him. You fuckas the ones who did this." His face was violaceous red. His pacing and herky-jerky movements and shouting finally began to attract attention from passers-by. He shouted into Jorge's face. "How you gonna fix this? How you gonna fix this?"

Laurinda yelled for the kid to go away. That infuriated him. He turned to face her.

Suddenly he stepped back, reached into a pocket, and produced a knife which quickly opened to a five inch blade that kept reflecting the bright sun as he nervously flailed it around in front of them.

Never losing eye contact with the crazed man a few steps from him, Jorge carefully placed his box on the ground. Laurinda was frozen, facing the man, still holding a box. This didn't make sense to Jorge. Was this kid put up to this to prove his commitment; like an initiation? Why was this happening? The guy got increasingly intense. He looked dangerous… like he was going to explode.

There were audible footsteps racing down the street behind Jorge. He decided he had to stay focused on the threatening man with the knife. His heart was racing. The guy began to scream again.

Jorge Gonzales was in disbelief. It seemed as though his life had devolved into a boatload of trouble and major upset in just a matter of days. So much had gone wrong so quickly. He was in trouble with the law and who knew who else; had no money, and his girl was leaving him. His mood left him a man not to be toyed with. Until he saw the screaming man's knife he considered him no more than an annoyance.

"The bitch gonna go, then you gonna tell me you can make this thing right, else you gonna go too! You get it asshole?"

With that the man simply lifted his arm and started to lunge at Laurinda with his knife. She leaned to the curb. Jorge was standing right there; next to her. Fueled by his anger at the world, perhaps spoiling for a fight, he didn't hesitate. Despite his recent gunshot injury, he used both his arms to forcefully push this homicidal fellow away from her. It was over in an instant. The young guy went off the curb into the street where his body was immediately met by the front end of a six ton produce truck that had just pulled, at speed, into the curb lane anticipating a right turn at the approaching corner. Laurinda screamed.

The footsteps behind him continued and an early middle-aged man in a topcoat ran by them heading toward the intersection where Jorge thought he had seen Manny Samuel. Samuel had started up the street to them, then quickly turned and fled in the other direction, followed by the running man.

Who had time to breathe? Laurinda and Jorge looked at each other. What had just happened? A crowd gathered at the curb. Cars and trucks not involved soon began honking, wanting to keep traffic flowing. The frightening young guy was not moving, splayed out on the street, halfway under the produce truck, dark red blood oozing from his cracked skull.

Within a minute the man in the topcoat returned. He was out of breath and *his* face was also red, but it was from running after Manny Samuel. He was a plainclothes detective shadowing Gonzales at the suggestion of James Wiley. He recognized Manny when Manny made his move up the street. But he lost him.

Soon the area was alive with sirens and flashing lights. Laurinda and Jorge sat on his boxes on the sidewalk; in shock. Laurinda would not let him touch her. The plainclothes cop stayed until more senior officers arrived and also until Jim Wiley showed up in a squad car almost thirty minutes later. Wiley was pleased but also impressed the NYPD had acted on his tip and also was willing to contact him and bring him to the site of this new development. He wondered if such immediate active interest by the NYPD meant there might be more to this business than they let on to him.

Wiley also realized this meant he was getting further involved in this case. He wasn't sure if that was good or bad, but he had to appreciate his acceptance even after his years away from the PD. There was no way he could walk away from this now, despite the inherent danger of these kinds of narcotics cases.

While Laurinda and Jorge were still sitting on the boxes Wiley and other officers spoke with them. Right there, in the middle of a city block quickly returning to its usual pace and activity, Wiley and the precinct shift commander conversed and agreed on what really seemed to stand out. Could it explain the most likely reason for this deadly episode? The lost money was unlikely to provoke such a potentially lethal attack.

There was something special about that vehicle still up in Vermont.

———

- 18 -

It was Friday afternoon in Vermont. Dark was resuming his usual routines and felt well. He was hoping the evening ahead would be special. Nevertheless, all that had happened and details of the case remained extraordinary to him, continuing to be a major distraction. Before leaving Waterbury for the day he stopped downstairs at the lab hoping there might be new information about the car and crash scene in the forest. He already knew the car was a mess; the windshield was shattered by bullets and shards of glass were everywhere inside the vehicle. What he really was hoping for was more information about the woman.

———————

"Yeah, so Lieutenant, I have a feeling we're not gonna be able to give you the answer you're looking for. No prints other than the kid's. You know that. Driver was wearing mittens or gloves. Not a surprise in this weather. Then what we've been able to do with the blood stains on the seats and door is confusing. We can confirm the blood in the passenger seat is the kid's; that was easy. And there are tiny specks of blood on the driver's airbag. But effects from the airbag's powder and tiny samples are beyond us. The driver's seat and door are the real puzzle though, Lieutenant. My guess is the kid's blood was smeared all over any blood on the driver's seat and the door. Maybe not too much of it is the driver's blood anyway. No other clear DNA, or even blood type, sir. Of course it's possible there's a special lab somewhere that might be able to sort this out, but I'm not sure.

"Well, Lieutenant, what that driver did is something, you know. That driver really didn't want to be ID'ed. To be bleeding from maybe getting shot and suddenly crashing, or even bleeding from just crashing, and still have the presence of mind to take the passenger's blood and mix it in on the driver's side to mess up any analysis. Imagine." The Sergeant's next words weren't really meant as a question. "Can you imagine someone doing that."

"Yeah, Cody, I can. I can imagine that."

————————

All day Dark looked forward eagerly to the dinner at Susan's place they had planned a few days earlier in his bedroom at his parent's home. Now alone together they each were more relaxed and it was obvious both were inclined to try to get along well. They even joked, briefly, about whether a commitment would ever be possible for the two of them. In truth, it was a more serious moment than either would openly admit. The tone of the evening up to that point encouraged Dark to speak about his most recent concerns, reflecting his job.

He tried, very briefly, to bring up his unease with his sense of the futility of parts of his work and whether that justified its danger and risks. Susan listened attentively but it appeared to Dark she either didn't understand what he meant or didn't take him seriously. As soon as he paused she changed the subject. Dark was confused and felt a letdown. Still, he willed the *lady* from his mind and tried hard to see a future for Susan and him. They gravitated to an embrace. The only committing they got close to that night was making love. Susan said that would be fine if he stayed the night. Dark happily agreed but then remembered he had the dog at his condo.

"Damn. Suze, don't see how I can stay all night. I have Alice at my place. She'll have to be put out; fed early in the morning, you know. Any chance you'd be willing to come over to my place?"

Maybe if the dog had been named anything other than Alice, surely a woman's name, his words might not have been a distraction to their closeness and Susan's mood. If he had resurrected his last dog's name, Busted, she might not have been disturbed by his concern. *Alice* interrupted her mood.

But not enough to kill the evening.

They drove the short distance to his condo. It was getting late. Alice greeted them in the way Dark was becoming used to: generally cool to anyone's arrival. Walking casually she came over to say hello; first to him then eyed the lady. Stood for a few seconds then continued calmly to Susan, clearly implying it was okay if she gave her a pet.

Dark and Susan were affectionate to each other. After hugging and kissing for a short time she took her things to the bathroom and Dark undressed, placed a condom on the night table, and got into bed. Susan returned in a nylon nightgown and nothing else but a smile. They made love.

Dark was excited just to hold her naked body tightly against his. It had been a while. He would be lying to himself if he didn't admit how much he missed nights like this. Scarcely beyond thirty, Susan's skin was soft and smooth and he felt consumed by anticipation. On their sides facing each other, barely touching her, his fingers slowly, lightly traced from her round hips to her breasts. He could feel her, just perceptibly, shiver from his touch and her excitement. They kissed long and passionately. Her smile was totally welcoming as they explored each other with pure pleasure. While he was able to relax and be entirely in the moment he felt wonderful. But his mind was always busy.

Doubt and confusion slowly drifted into his consciousness. She obviously loved him. In the life he was living Susan offered him so much. What was it, or why was he unable to make a commitment to her? He supposed making love was more exciting for him than Susan, assuming any interest in sex for her was tempered by disappointment in their only modest commitment to each other over the years. But she was into it and they each were active in stroking and movement.

At some point Susan's eye caught a glimpse of Alice, lying in a corner of the room. Alice's head, with her plumed ears, was bolt upright and staring. Susan thought about her. Who knows what goes on in a staring dog's mind? Didn't matter. It was Susan's determination that Alice's glance was one of stern disapproval. Still it turned out that was the least impact on their making love from anyone named Alice.

It had been a long time and Dark really tried to sustain his relaxation. He could tell something wasn't entirely right for Susan but he needed to divert his mind. Sure Susan loved him. Physically he thought she was amazing. She was a runner and her appearance getting into bed excited him. When their bodies coupled together they each appeared attentive and interested. But Dark's mind was stuck. Eventually his mind flashed with images of an Alice also. But his were of a woman both before and after she cut her hair. He had never seen her with shorter hair but he dreamed about her and her face, with and without long hair, while he made love to his good friend and sometimes lover, Susan Spahn. He knew it was a terrible thing to do…although not likely without precedent in the real world.

Neither was dissatisfied with the sex. Afterwards they remained on their sides again, arm in arm, staring at each other and speaking softly. With mixed emotions about bringing it up again, the bland expression on his face morphed to serious and Dark opened up to Susan more directly this time about some of what had been troubling him.

"I think I'm stuck with the way I keep thinking about whether there's really any point in a whole lot of the policing the force does. So much of it is drugs now. And I'm really stuck on me or any trooper risking a life over that. I'm not at all sure that problem will ever be solved. It's so crazy dangerous. Everyone has deadly weapons. And it seems like it's never-ending. Dying in a shoot-out just doesn't make any sense. You...."

Susan was listening but had a dreamy look. He wasn't done but she tried to interrupt. "Donald, if you don't..."

Since he had started he wasn't ready to stop yet. "No Susan, you have to understand it's not that I could get killed but the *uselessness* of it if it happens; almost pointless, I think. Who does that help?" He looked away from her face as he was thinking. "You know I watch the medical people whenever I'm at hospitals and more and more lately what they're doing looks better to me than what I'm doing. I don't know, maybe it's not too late for me to get into something else." He looked back at her.

Susan barely gave Dark time to finish. When he was obviously done she spoke, softly, but more emphatically and seriously. "Donald, you know you've really become quite a brooder, you know. You have a wonderful job. You've achieved so much and you're very respected. I think if you want to I bet you could wind up maybe even running the force some day; that is if you can get over your brooding.

"Your parents are so proud of you..." Susan leaned into Dark and gave him a firm kiss on his lips. "...and I know I am too." She offered a heartfelt but also sad smile. Whatever he was hoping to hear her say didn't happen.

Dark's disappointment was palpable but he said nothing in response and smiled also. He hugged Susan but he was done trying to have a dialog about what he was wrestling with. Dark was no less confused. He had tried hard to consider a future for him with Susan, but he had been unable to keep that *lady* out of his thoughts.

In the morning they took a short run together and, all in all, Dark felt better than he had in weeks. In the past Busted would have come on the run also. Alice stayed home and that may have been best for all of them. Donald told Susan he joined a relay team of troopers to run the marathon with Ed Clark's grandfather, to honor Ed. He planned to run more actively at least until that race was over.

They conversed little while running, concentrating on maintaining their efforts. Dark had no idea what might be occupying Susan's thoughts while she jogged. Donald Dark's mind drifted to the letter he had received. There was no return address and it was not signed. It was, however, postmarked from the Akwesasne Reservation and he thought about that. The Native American reservation was about a half day's drive away in upstate New York, straddling the Canadian border. While they ran he had no difficulty conjuring an array of potential connections to this lady, and this case.

———

- 19 -

James Wiley had Lieutenant Dark's cell number. He decided it was safe to wait to contact him in the early evening. If he was unable to reach him that night Wiley definitely planned to track him down the next day. There was a lot to talk about though he didn't believe it was an emergency.

Wiley's call came shortly after Dark finished a nuked dinner alone. He was watching the news and found most of it depressing. It had been a discouraging day. The Captain heard him out about his request to spend a day driving almost 150 miles to the Akwesasne Reservation to try to learn if the Indian Nation postmark could mean anything in the case. The Captain knew the letter was from the same woman the Lieutenant had followed barely a week before. The dramatic consequences of that trip were not lost on him. His confidence in Dark was being chipped away. Ultimately, he was non-committal about the trip.

Wiley's phone call, at least for a time, diverted the Lieutenant's thoughts away from that woman..

"Don, you were right, this story isn't over." With that intro Wiley proceeded to describe, in detail, the events from earlier that day.

He ended by telling Dark what his plan was in response to what happened. Dark's tone and words suggested he was not completely clear about that, or necessarily in agreement.

"So Don, I think I got to get these kids out of town, for at least a month, before someone tries to kill them again. Laurinda's dad has a brother in San Juan. She can stay with him and he says his brother has a nephew doing farming on the other side of the island and Jorge can work there for a time. Nobody's happy about it but I told them to 'fuck school if you want to stay alive.'"

Thinking while he was speaking, at first Dark seemed to agree or at least acquiesce to Wiley's plan. But he was quickly getting angry… at Jorge Gonzales.

"Yeah, right… That Gonzales, he must know more. And Jim he can't leave the US; he's out on bond."

That set Wiley off. "Hey, Donald. Man you better be careful 'bout sayin' stuff like that. 'Specially if you ever meet my wife, Idelia. Puerto Rico is part of the US and you should know that."

Dark was surprised but he got it. He still wasn't happy and barely responded to the correction. Would traffickers kill someone for losing a car? With developing concern about the Subaru Dark wanted more information from that kid. Trying, again, to find out where that kid and the car spent the night when Gonzales made his deliveries was a big concern. But Wiley wanted to get him out of town before he got killed. They were each angry and, for the first time, there was subtle, but obvious, friction between them.

"No Jim. No. I don't think I want to lose contact with Gonzales. Need to know more about that vehicle and the kid's times in Vermont." Dark's resolve became stronger; he didn't want to lose easy proximity to the kid. "Damn Jim, I may need to speak to that Gonzales again. And I'm gonna get some fresh eyes to examine that car again."

That put Wiley in a tough spot and they both knew it. "Shit, Don, that means if I don't ship him back then I'm responsible for anything happens to him. I don't think I signed on for something like that."

Wiley was quiet while Dark thought things over. The Lieutenant didn't disagree with Wiley, and it did bother him, thinking he could be exposing Wiley to a fluid, dangerous situation. But he hadn't asked Jim to come to Vermont and now Wiley was involved, even if this was far from his plan to be helpful to the Alvarez family.

Donald Dark would follow any lead that would make this case bigger. That might allow him to stay on it longer and meant keeping the mysterious lady *alive*, at least in his head. Yes, exposing Jim Wiley to possible harm probably did occur to him but any fretting about that occupied a place more distant in his mind.

There was a problem, though. Even if Dark and Wiley weren't sure they believed it, Jorge Gonzales had told the police everything he knew about his role. He was a mule, in every sense of that as a job description. NYPD Narcotics knew of Emanuel Samuel who was Jorge's one and only contact for what he did. Despite indications of a brewing conflict Jim Wiley and Donald Dark did agree continuing efforts by the NYPD to find Emanuel Samuel were an essential next step in the investigation in New York City.

The difficulty with that was late the following morning Samuel's body was found in a dumpster.

The Lieutenant was alerted to that news in a text left for him by Wiley. No call; only a message. Acceptable to many in the *modern era*, but quickly interpreted by Dark as a sign of a growing distance between them. Dark decided a subtle threat in his message back to Jim was okay. He wrote Wiley he was having the Subaru brought from Waterbury to Williston where he thought they might do a better job going over it again. Then, he wrote, depending on what happened with that, maybe he'd bring Gonzales back to Vermont and hold him as a material witness.

There was a problem with that plan also. By the time Wiley saw Dark's message he was getting off the plane with Laurinda and

Jorge in San Juan, Puerto Rico. Guaranteed to anger the Lieutenant, Wiley decided not to respond to the text.

A day later Wiley sent Dark an email, listed on the Lieutenant's VSP (Vermont State Police) official account, plainly stating what he had done. The Lieutenant read it but never responded.

———

- 20 -

"What's the matter, DD? Your new best bud pissing you off? Try to let it go, pal. You don' know where you're going with that case anyway. Confused…as usual."

Dark was annoyed. "You know Fleur, when you say 'DD' it's like a goddamn canary singing in a coal mine. You're fucking broadcasting that another one of your sorry efforts to spin everything that happens into clever, funny, little knife pricks is about to launch. I think you're working a bit too hard lately; on the jokes for sure." Dark was pissed but, by now, he was warming to the battle and spit back.

"Don't know what I'm doing, huh? Coming from the guy who came close…how close was it Fleur…to givin' everything you have to those wanabe swindlers for that restaurant deal you said was gonna be part of the Stowe Ski Area re-development and make you rich? Unbelievable deal, you said. At the last minute found out it was a steal because, even if it was real, it would have been in the middle of the forest on the wrong side of the mountain, at least forty minutes from anywhere to get to it. You got real close to steppin' in it, didn't you?"

Fleury's response was tongue in cheek; modestly embarrassed. "Well, didn't I figure it out when I finally got over there and realized even a plow couldn't get up there in the winter? Yeah, sure was a spot in the middle of nowhere." It was a little worse than that but Dark let it go.

That story was old history and Dark had used it before. But he was still annoyed. "Got any time off coming soon, Fleur? Boy, if you don't think you need it, I think you do. Would definitely be good for me to get a nice break from your bad jokes."

Dark stood and began to walk toward the open administration area where he could use a desk. Fleury was smiling from ear to ear.

"Oh sure, DD, that would make a lot of sense. I should take some time off because I am unbelievably right on when it comes to annoying you; whenever I want… But, of course, even you know the daily management of the Vermont State Police Barracks in Williston is dependent on my presence. At least in Chittenden County there's no one else who can handle this complex enterprise. Right?"

Progressing down the corridor Dark could be heard raising his voice, "Go to hell, Pal." About five minutes later he shouted into Fleury's office that he was leaving the Barracks.

That night Dark was angry with everyone. Being stuck on that woman was surely bringing out the worst in him. Even Alice seemed peeved with him. He thought the way she looked at him and her unusual distance was telling him to grow up and move on. He tried to rationalize his mindset to himself by telling Alice all he really wanted to do was know how that woman fit into this strange story and find out if she needed help; as unlikely as that sounded even to him as he thought about why he was so stuck. In the morning he hoped to at least find out if that Subaru was any part of the story.

———————

Later the next morning Lieutenant Dark paused, just perceptibly, then strode in as he arrived at the open door to Ed Fleury's office in the Williston Barracks. He hoped important things were happening. Fleury looked up from paperwork he was working on and sat back in his chair. For a moment he looked serious, then assumed a grin like a Cheshire cat. He was ever hopeful of opportunities to go back and forth with his friend. His smile grew and he reclined as far back as his chair would allow.

"So Donald, you here for the automobile autopsy?"

Dark stayed standing and didn't respond to Fleury's effort to make the process underway in the garage a laughing matter.

"Well you got boys over from Waterbury and here in Williston really been going at that Subaru, pal. I get the hunch you and your new NYPD *partner* are working on but I haven't heard anything from the guys so far." Fleury's intonation when he brought up Dark's involvement with Jim Wiley was meant to pacify Dark after the day before, but it really didn't. Currently Dark was far from thinking of Wiley as any kind of a partner. Fleury, very quickly, ended his pause for dramatic effect and continued.

"After what they're doing back there, if nothing gets found, best thing for you and your buddy is if no one knows who owns that vehicle. C'mon out to the garage and look at what they've done...or should I say what you're responsible for."

"He's not a cop anymore. I told you that," Dark said flatly.

Fleury could tell his effort at making this humorous was falling flat. Dark just wasn't as into engaging in any of their usual patter lately. Ed was disappointed but he moved on.

Williston Barracks was a large and sprawling structure. Parts of it looked more like a temporary metal construction with add-ons over the years than a solid building. It was due to be replaced... sometime. They wended their way from the quiet administrative section through a series of corridors to the back of the building where the garage area was. Lieutenant Dark understood Fleury's point as soon as they peered through the chicken wire patterned safety glass window of the door to the open area. They walked through the doorway and Dark just stopped and stood there, arms akimbo. It was quite a site.

The vehicle had been dis-membered. Pieces and parts were scattered, albeit neatly, all over the floor. Doors were off; the tires, including the mini spare were off; hood and rear hatch were on the floor. More of the car was outside than remained inside. All the seats, radio, virtually anything that could be removed was now arranged on the floor. He could see that inside some areas of material were cut away.

The extent of the destruction and mess strongly suggested nothing unexpected had been found. This was not the scene he hoped to see. He shot a glance at Ed Fleury, who's expression remained neutral. Fleury was right; no one was going to be able to put this vehicle back together. They both knew nobody was going to claim it anyway. Thank goodness. Dark was cognizant he was going to have to answer to his superiors for the time and expense required to do this job. And also the cost of getting the car and parts junked, he guessed. Fleury was back at him.

"So DD, think I should send a clerk out to get some big plastic bags so the fellas can pack up this mess soon? Cost a bundle just to get rid of it all. Think?"

Dark walked over to speak with the two remaining techs still working. It wasn't clear what it would take to satisfy him the vehicle didn't hold any special secrets. The way Wiley described the pressure and threats to Gonzales about the car sure seemed to raise suspicions. Lunging at Laurinda in the middle of a city street sounded awfully desperate to both him and Wiley. Gonzales knew getting that car back to the city was a big deal to his employers but Wiley didn't believe the kid knew why.

When the vehicle was first brought to Williston they had it sniffed again and the dog quickly found the seat-back location where the grass had been sewn in. That car probably had bits of marijuana all over it, not only hidden, over time. But that was it. The dog didn't lead them anywhere else and nothing the techs were doing led to the discovery of anything ominous or illegal to that point.

Probably because he knew it would bother Dark, Fleury stayed around. He walked over to where Dark was reviewing the situation with the techs and smiled.

"Lieutenant, maybe you need to bring your personal *hound* to sniff and, yeah, maybe *listen* for sounds in that vehicle the human ear cannot hear?"

"No *Lieutenant*, the guys tell me they're gonna go one more round and take apart some of the stuff on the deck here," Dark responded. He sounded deflated but he hadn't given up yet. The techs looked around and decided they would tear the tires apart next. Both Lieutenants watched as they hooked the air valves up and deflated the tires, one after the other. They pulled them off the rims and looked inside the tires. There was a strong odor of rubber, or more like tar, in two of them.

After looking inside the tires with a flashlight one tech was ready to move on but the other asked Dark if he wanted them to actually spit the tires down the middle to see the insides better. Dark was disappointed about the whole business but had no inclination to stop the techs from doing anything else they could dream up to investigate. So the smell of heated rubber permeated the garage area as they split the tires, one after another, straight down the center tread. There was still nothing obvious.

Picking up the pieces to place in a corner one tech stopped and carried one of the half tires to the table they had done some of their work on. He called the other tech over and after pointing something out to him turned to the Lieutenants.

"Sirs, you might want to look at this." Dark and Fleury walked over. The smell of burned rubber was still very pervasive. The tech directed the beam of his flashlight. "Look here, along this curve, which was the inside part of the tire. I think it's not as flat as the rest of the inside tire wall. And look at this: touching it with a rag, it's sticky. Tar?"

Indeed the entire circumference of that angle was barely, but definitely, raised and appeared to have sticky dark black tape placed firmly over it.

"It's not at all thick; probably taped there for something like performance reasons," the tech said. He looked at the three others. "Only on both rears."

But they weren't spending their day destroying a vehicle just to pass time. Anything, any finding, was worthy of suspicion. The Lieutenants stood by and the techs put on masks and gloves and looked to find a way to see if the notably tar smelling tape like material could be pulled away from the rubber. It could. One wondered if the noxious odor would have defeated any sniffing animal. Slowly and carefully they peeled the circle of tape away from the tire remnant.

Eureka! There was something under the tape wrapped in an inch and a half wide piece of thin material; probably a plastic wrap. The substance inside barely had any depth but it did go entirely around the circumference of the tire.

The techs stood up and moved back slightly to gaze at the odd finding. Dark and Fleury walked to the table for a closer look.

"I guess it's a powder or somethin', but there sure isn't much of it, is there?" Fleury said. Without saying much more he reached for the tube of material the tech had peeled from the black tape and held it up in his ungloved hand. He started to smile as he looked at the tube while he spoke to Dark: "What's that deal, DD? What do they say it's supposed to taste like after you rub some on a finger so's then you hear people say, 'yeah, that's coke?' Bitter; numbing, or something?"

With that he rolled the stuffed plastic wrap around a little in his fingers and mimicked, or did put two fingers to his tongue. In a matter of less than half a minute Fleury started to look pale. He grabbed for the edge of the table and began to sway. Everyone in the room stopped whatever they were doing and looked at him.

Distracted, less than a minute later he broke out in a drenching sweat and commenced to go down. Dark caught him but by the time he pulled Ed Fleury to a nearby chair the man was out.

One of the techs started shouting, "Holy shit! Holy shit! Is he dead? Holy shit!"

Instantly, Dark was in motion. "Smith, get his legs and let's get him to a cruiser. He's alive, but barely." They shouted into the corridor for help and he directed the other tech: "Davis close this whole garage off! Secure the outside and don't touch anything! Keep everyone out of here!"

Troopers came running down the hallway and Dark barked orders at them. They put an oxygen mask over Ed's dusky face and dialed the canister up as far as it would go. He wanted the hospital alerted and any nearby cruisers to pull over all west bound traffic on the Interstate and the roads off it on the way to the hospital in Burlington. In the back seat of a cruiser Dark pulled Ed Fleury, family man and generally good guy, on top of his lap and had others prop the Lieutenant's legs up in the air. Fleury had a weak and thready carotid pulse; nothing in his wrist. Dark thought Ed was in shock or having an anaphylactic allergic reaction. He looked very much like he was going to die. Fleury was out; unresponsive to Dark's voice.

Once on the Interstate the trooper pushed the cruiser to just short of becoming airborne. Under his breath, Donald Dark whispered to himself "faster, faster" the entire trip. Lieutenant Dark was trained for action, not moaning.

You or I would make that trip to the ER from Williston in roughly a little more than ten minutes during the day. A trooper going fast could cut a few minutes off of that. With Donald Dark periodically screaming at the young trooper behind the wheel and so many sirens blaring and drivers terrified by the excitement pulled to the shoulder (something Vermonters are good at) Ed Fleury was unloaded to a gurney at the hospital ER no more than five minutes after leaving the Barracks.

The ER staff was ready. They had hazmat garb on because no one knew what the Lieutenant had touched, inhaled, or tasted. Whatever it was didn't take much to put him out. It didn't really matter what it was at first because the man was in shock; circulatory collapse. So each team member took an extremity and attempted to find and turn a vein, any vein, into a conduit to pour intravenous fluids into him. Anticipating no success, since Fleury had no discernible blood pressure, at the same time a surgeon began a cutdown to a subclavian vein near his neck, which would offer certain access.

Treatment for anaphylaxis was started. But also, concurrently, a nurse was assigned to start injecting the Lieutenant with ampules of naloxone, know to the lay public as Narcan. Sure, there were a host of potential possibilities for some substance to put a person into shock, but the setting that powder was found in shouted out the likelihood of a drug, probably from the opioid family, even if the very suddenness of such a dramatic reaction was a little atypical for an opioid.

The staff did what they were trained to do; well. No one was going to give up on Ed Fleury. Troopers were calling the hospital asking if blood was going to be needed. Lieutenant Dark was impressed with the Doc in charge of the emergency effort. She listened carefully to him when he explained the sequence that led to this disaster. The nurse responsible for injecting repeated vials of naloxone moved back after the fourth unit and reported a lack of any objective response despite rapidly administering that large amount of the drug. The Doc running the undertaking didn't miss a beat and told her to keep at it; to give two or three more; far greater than ever routinely given, essentially, all at once.

Apparently the sixth ampule was the charm. The ability of naloxone, when it works, to reverse so many deathly threats from a narcotic in an overdosed or toxic individual is always gratifying, but also an incredibly striking sight. The reasonably dramatic actual sudden waking of an apparently comatose person always seems fairly miraculous. Ed Fleury didn't wake up and pop up off the gurney but it was clear he was becoming conscious. The pattern of his improvement was very suggestive of an effect from naloxone.

Everything else probably helped but the staff was impressed with the effects of a drug designed specifically to reverse narcotic effects. Perhaps more proof was demonstrated when, subsequently, Ed needed a few more naloxone amps over the night as prior doses wore off and he became transiently less alert. That suggested he had been exposed to a long-acting agent.

As Ed Fleury regained consciousness and some semblance of awareness Donald Dark felt his own body droop. He left his spot at the window to the room where he was observing all the action and sat down nearby. He was incredibly relieved knowing that when Ed's wife, Molly, would arrive shortly she would see a man who didn't look anything like Ed did ten minutes before; worn out but quite alive. The docs and hospital had saved Ed. Dark was envious of their work and ability to help others.

Nearly an hour later, when the Lieutenant was allowed to step into the room to see Ed, he took the slight grin on Fleur's face as a sign he was better; almost up and ready to parry.

"You bastard Fleur. Where the hell did you go today? Some trip, I bet. I told you to take some time off but this isn't what I was thinking. You and I ain't cut out any more to handle stuff these young assholes take for breakfast, you know."

"DD, what are you talking about? Why the fuck am I here? Bad joke bud. Looks like you topped yourself with this one. Okay, so I won't keep picking on your little dog…but your mysterious girlfriend is still fair game." Fleury couldn't muster a leer but he had tried to get back in the game.

Dark knew Ed was okay.

———

Lieutenant Dark stayed at the hospital until Molly arrived. He brought her into a small consult room adjacent to the ER and they sat. Don spared her the most frightening details but made her agree to make sure Fleury stayed in the hospital until the docs said he could leave. The ER physician who ran the code walked in while they were talking. She was very reassuring to Molly. After a few minutes she stood to leave, so the Lieutenant got up also. The Doctor turned to him and said:

"I can't begin to tell you, Trooper Dark, how grateful all of us are for the efforts the State Police are making to try to make a dent in this terrible plague. Sometimes, I guess all this effort can seem pointless, but every bit of this poisonous stuff that can be removed is a victory, maybe saving someone's life." Lieutenant Dark stared at her as she turned and excused herself.

———————

Dark knew an equally scary and challenging problem was waiting for him back at the Williston Barracks. As he was driven back he thought about who from Narcotics would be there working this apparent disaster? He wondered if that would still be a problem for him after all these years?

And, again he worried about how or whether he would be allowed to stay involved in the investigation. A trooper's homicide had been solved and the remaining active case had all the hallmarks of a more straight forward narcotics case. Not for certain, but probably. Had to find out what that crap was first. But Dark's over-riding interest in staying active on all this, understanding and finding a mysterious woman, was less and less likely to impress most anyone much longer; certainly not his superiors. And yet, somehow, the more important and complicated the Gonzales case became the more involved he thought that lady was.

For maybe the first time since this nasty business began Dark was forced to truly reckon there was a good chance whoever she was she probably was not working on his side. He had trouble with that and found himself flashing back to those few moments in their only time face to face when he thought he sensed some commonality and also a sadness and vulnerability in her expression. It all made her desirable even though it was very brief. And, of course, a man's fantasy: she might be in danger and need his help. Besides, he had to get Alice back to her, didn't he?

———

It was dark when he arrived at Williston Barracks. From numerous light banks that were brought in the whole place, inside and out, was lit up to approximate daylight. Two large hazmat vehicles were there, and also a fire truck and rescue squad; just in case. The entire Barracks was off-limits and the presence of a host of armed troopers planning to spend a cold night outside made that clear to anyone passing by.

Lieutenant Dark had a good idea of what type of ominous drug they were dealing with. The Doctor who ran the successful resurrection of his pal, Ed Fleury, had speculated to him what it was, although Dark had never heard of the specific agent. She seemed to know all about the possibilities. He knew her impressive knowledge had to be a reflection of the breath and magnitude of this deadly drug problem. He could just imagine his father saying, "How could such a nice, young lady know about all those kinds of terrible things?" What a disaster for society now and probably for generations to come.

The Doc guessed it would turn out to be carfentanil or something similar. Dark felt a little queasy after she started to tell him about it. He couldn't conceive there could be a drug so dangerous and deadly. And to be used in tiny amounts mixed with street drugs to enhance effects was terrifying, but also baffling. What type of human would do this to another?

While fentanyl had become the rage, carfentanil and a few of its cousins were literally a hundred times stronger and, therefore, even much more dangerous. He remembered what had just happened to Fleury after barely coming into contact with some residue on a plastic sheet. Produced for large animal vets to use on three ton mammals like elephants. Deadly for humans.

For the first time in a very long time Donald Dark felt an anger and, yes, a responsibility to battle with people who had no concern about the fates of others. There really was a job to do; a very necessary service. After his thinking the last few months his reaction surprised him. He also wasn't sure these thoughts would last. He sure was angry now.

———

- 21 -

In the never-ending struggle and need for human relationships
Donald Dark wasn't about to lose an opportunity to *one-up* his
buddy, Ed Fleury. Fleury never made it to visit Dark when he was
home after his concussion so it became a priority for Dark to find
time to stop at Fleury's place in Jeffersonville while Ed was still
on sick leave. So much of their incessant efforts to gently (and
sometimes not so gently) pick on each other actually felt like a
responsibility to each of them by now.

Were any of the constant efforts to go after each other, almost
always in an effort at levity, a reflection of the intensity and, as they
were both just recently reminded, inherent dangers of being on the
force? It was more likely mostly the natural result of a long-standing
friendship and a bond they each wished to maintain forever.

Mid-day, pulling into Ed's driveway in his cruiser, Dark was softly
reciting two lines under his breath; zingers he hoped to hit Fleury
with when he was in the house. When he entered the smile on
Dark's face quickly faded, at least for the moment. Molly was there
and that could become a bit of a hindrance. Never occurred to
Dark that a wife might take time off to be with her husband after
what just happened. Molly was often very much like Ed and joked

a lot, but Dark instantly felt inhibited. The tension and upset projected on her face was cautionary.

More striking and impacting on Dark when he first walked in was Ed Fleury's appearance. In a word, he looked like shit. And his first words to Donald indicated he felt that way. Any verbal skirmish to play around with insisting one had been sicker or more at risk than the other wasn't going to happen immediately. Dark knew to keep his powder dry.

Fleury actually looked like he had aged a few years in a couple of days. And for the first time Dark could recall Ed looked down and depressed, notably more so than the mood Dark projected recently. Ed was a little less than ten years older than Donald. He looked older than that now. It turned out he was very unhappy and discouraged because of one specific problem from the recent episode.

Fleury was sitting in his over-stuffed recliner in the living room. Dark was struck that Ed had an ancient appearing big, old, plaid flannel robe on that almost came to his ankles. As he sat he kept re-adjusting the two front flaps so his legs were completely covered.

"You look like shit Fleur." Apparently obvious things remained fair game.

Fleury's head was down. His flat expression suggested he felt overwhelmed. Dark's salutation wasn't to be challenged but Fleury took it as a reason to try to say something. Only his eyelids elevated as he lifted his eyes to gaze up at Dark.

"With powers of observation like that maybe you should look for a new career. Maybe try to become a state police detective."

It was often the case that Ed Fleury got the best of Donald Dark. This time Dark felt good about it. Even bits of poking fun at each other might be good for Ed, looking as he did and coming through his own life and death ordeal. Dark knew they were pretty evenly matched about that. Fleury's was probably worse, but only in degrees. They each had to spend only one night in the hospital.

Molly said little but actually encouraged the two of them to go after each other. It had served them well for many years. For the first time since he had been home Ed tried to joke about what was bothering him the most right then about the entire episode.

"I'll tell you what's truly shitty, DD." He looked over at his wife, who figured out what was coming. "Molly, would you please avert your eyes."

With a slight flourish, he slowly pulled apart the edge of each side of his robe. He was wearing boxers so the drama had nothing to do with exposing *private parts*. What became obvious was a clear plastic tube exiting through one leg of the boxer and it led to a bag, strapped to his lower thigh, with straw colored urine in it.

At the hospital Dark had been quickly educated about the importance of the catheter that was placed when Fleury arrived in shock. Dark noted the interest and significance the hospital team attached to monitoring the collecting bag fill with urine, a sign of returning kidney and circulatory function. He had no idea why it was still in Fleury. He quickly decided he would let Ed, not him, joke about that if he wanted. A tube pushed up the shaft of your penis seemed cruel and unusual punishment to Dark; probably continually sore at a minimum.

"Do you believe this, DD? Every time I move…oh shit, what's the use of even talking about it. It hurts. They took the fucker out in the middle of the night and I wasn't able to pee after. Shit! All I wanted to do was go home. It was stay in the hospital drinking fluids until I peed or have them put this thing back in…for a few days, I guess. *I hope.* They said it's probably a holdover effect from the fucking colossal narc I got into."

He stopped and glanced at Molly. Her expression telegraphed that Fleury really hadn't finished the story. He looked around a few seconds then started again.

"So they say I got a big prostate gland and that's probably also contributing to what happened. You know what a prostate gland is and where it's at Donny boy? Well now I do. Supposed to grow big in old men. So now I'm a fucking old fart?" His face oozed discouragement and his head drooped again. Such a golden opportunity was hard for Dark to let go but he passed on the opening Fleury offered him. Fleury had more he wished to moan about.

You know, we still got school kids livin' here. You know, *inquiring minds*. What the hell do I say to them. Now the jokes on me…and boy am I gettin' it."

Lieutenant Ed Fleury was lucky to be alive. He was entitled to be down but the degree to which he was wallowing in his despair quickly became a bit too much for Molly…and then his good friend Donald Dark.

"Don' know Ed, maybe you had that tube in there fifteen or so years ago could have saved us bundle of money those last two kids are costing us. Without them, instead of fixin' to work forever you might be retired by now, planning another trip south this winter. Wearin' that tube would have worked, huh?"

Dark spoke right up. "Fleur I'm gonna have to go. But I got a friend I can contact in the Mounties, just over the border. I'll have him ship down a pair of those riding pants they wear that balloon out up top so your pee bag will have plenty of space to fill up. But don't forget you'll have to empty it now and then or could be quite a mess, I guess, huh?"

That barrage was enough. They all sat back and no one said anything for a short while. Then Ed exhaled and spoke.

"Yeah, that was a bad one. I'm lucky to be here…even if it means taking crap from you guys. That was close. Just had no idea…" He looked up at Molly and then turned to Dark. "What a menace this drug stuff is, eh, DD? Lesson learned here."

Dark's cell trilled. He had no need to find a private spot to talk around these folks. The concerned look on his face was noted by Molly and Ed. Dark stood up. It was later in the day and he had assumed he'd be heading home after his visit. The call changed his plans.

"So guys, I've got to get to Waterbury. The guys in the lab think I need to see something right away." He headed for the front door. "Fleur, I know you want to stay in on this business and know everything. If there's something new I'll call you later. And, Moll, thanks for the invite on Saturday.

At the door Molly came over to him and in a show of obvious appreciation and affection, a small tear forming in one eye, gave Dark a peck and a tight hug. This had been an unimaginably stressful episode. And Molly never said a word to him about Susan. Usually she always found a moment to try to encourage that match, but not this visit.

Two steps outside with Molly, and with Ed standing in the doorway, Dark turned around and said: "So Fleur, just so you know, no need to invite me to the coming out party. Okay?" And he was he was on his way.

———

- 22 -

Surprisingly, sloppiness has become a defined way in the contemporary world. Fewer and fewer seem to care about that much anymore in what they do. One old wag finally gave up and proclaimed *ignorance and laziness* had won the struggle for grammar. More effort is put into crafting slang than writing by any established rules. *Functional literacy* is good enough for most it seems. And isn't there also a sense that same acceptance of general sloppiness has invaded so much of what people do?

Face it, drug smugglers, or any smugglers, would not be the most likely *professionals* to *dot all i's and cross all t's* in their business. So it shouldn't have been a surprise to the force, or for that matter the smugglers either, that someone messed up on the handling of a tire stuffed with a drug. How else to account for what was found there as well?

———

When Dark arrived at the Waterbury headquarters more cruisers than usual were in the yard for that time of day. There were four officers sitting in the room he was directed to as he walked in. Dark knew them all: Major Carruthers, Captain Bushey, and two lieutenants. He was immediately uncomfortable seeing Lieutenant

Steve Kamp among the group. Just as Dark was progressing up the leadership ranks so was Kamp. He was part of the Narcotics Investigations Division and was one of the main troopers whose actions on that unit many years before, when Dark was also there, disgusted and discouraged Dark. Since Dark left their paths only rarely crossed. On shaking hands with everyone in the room it was clear Lieutenant Kamp went out of his way to offer a friendly greeting to Dark. Kind of a surprise and Dark immediately chided himself for preparing for a degree of animosity to persist.

Dark was pleased he had been called to be part of the meeting. He took it to mean he still had a foot in the door in this case. Today had just been busy work, especially catching up on two other cases he was supervising. He fully expected and assumed the Captain would *officially* remove him very shortly. But here he was, called to work with the brain trust for a drug case that only he thought probably had several levels of complexity.

It was late in the day and the Major and everyone stayed seated. A senior crime lab technician walked in and took a seat just as Carruthers began to speak. The Major advised the assembled group this case of a drug mule was getting more complicated by the hour.

"Gentleman, here's what we know so far: A kid from New York was doing mule work bringing weed to some northern farms for distribution. On his latest trip home he stopped at the lonely site of Trooper Clark's homicide. So far thinking still is he had no role in the Trooper's death." Then, sounding like he was expressing frustration, he tossed out, "But now, who knows?"

Dark was surprised by those last words.

"Events in New York, where Don has been working the case with an NYPD detective, developed concern about the vehicle the kid was driving when he was arrested." No way Dark planned to contest the Major's error at this point.

"Don and the Detective decided we needed to have the lab go over that car again looking for maybe more than just weed." The major nodded toward the tech. "Harry's group proved, once again, they are the best. That Subaru, so sliced and diced, didn't fare very well and someday will be transported to a junk dealer where every piece will be sold for parts. Sometime take a look at the pictures when you have a chance.

"So that tear apart, with the unfortunate assistance of Ed Fleury, who I'm told is doing okay (which is really great) led the team, we think, to two long, skinny loops of a tiny amount of a drug carefully hidden in two of the tires. The official analysis report was faxed to us earlier this afternoon. It's kind of a disaster, gentlemen. It confirms that the crap is called *carfentanil*. Steve Kamp probably has heard of it and knows something about it. The rest of us, if we're lucky, have never heard of this shit before." The major spoke directly, in a conversational voice, and continued.

"Anyway, they say it's fentanyl on steroids. Understand this: if fentanyl is about a hundred time more potent than plain morphine and stuff like percs and heroin, this carfentanil is a hundred times stronger than fentanyl. So it's super deadly and it's killing lots of people when a pinch of it is mixed in with heroin or whatever to increase potency…and OD risk. Don told me it was designed for pain treatment for really big animals; like elephants. That's gonna be helpful stuff for people, isn't it?"

Most of those in the room already had a general idea about what the Major was reporting. The late day meeting and attendance needed something more to make it critical.

"Fellas, this shit is so toxic it's taken the lab till just a few hours ago to safely finish inspecting everything. So about the time we heard what the drug is Harry made a huge finding. You want to tell them Harry?"

Harry Cramer had an infectious smile and a bookish appearance. Maybe nobody ever loved his job running a crime lab more than Harry Cramer. He practiced his work and studied his field constantly. His unit was well respected across the northeast. Time meant nothing to him, which meant he and Lieutenant Dark occasionally went out late to dinner or a movie together. They each were single.

Harry was anxious to tell the troopers what he found. He stayed sitting but pulled a large piece of white cardboard to his side.

"After what happened to Lieutenant Fleury this job really tested us. Usually gloves and maybe a mask are the extent of how we prepare for most examinations. For this one we called Boston and Washington long before we had any idea what we were actually dealing with. So the last part went really slow even though we were very near the end when the Lieutenant went down. It sure looks like what we found in the first tire we looked at is also in one of the other tires. So two tires have barely perceptible, visible only on close inspection, slight bulges tucked, in a circle, into one inside angle all the way around each of those tires.

"The stuff is held there by some super sticky dark tape on the outside. Looks like nothing is there. Today we worked on pulling the tape completely off the second tire and removing the drug. The floppy plastic wrap tube was placed in a vacuum sealed, clear, leaded glass box with two leaded impermeable gloves fixed to sealed openings. So we got the gear to open up the plastic sheeting and transfer the powder to a secure container. Really not much powder in there for all the effort to hide a drug.

"While working to accomplish that I noticed something on the tube very near the spot where the two ends of the loop were attached together. Now the powder is almost a dark gray color. As we transferred the powder from the transected end of that loop I noticed it looked like there might be some markings, almost the same color as the powder, on the thin plastic sheeting. Can't even imagine how someone managed to write on that but looks like it was a felt pen; like a marker.

"So here's what we got. I was able to take a few pictures and I blew this one up." With that Harry bent over the side of his chair, picked up the large white cardboard poster and placed it, upright, on his lap so everyone could see it.

The Major already knew all this. Everyone else in the room was stunned. Maybe none in that room even knew what the writing meant. But they all recognized it was a foreign language; most likely French… Ah, the border.

After pausing for the expected reaction Harry continued, "Look at how it's written and what it says: '!!Ne Pas Toucher!!' Two exclamation marks at the beginning and end, and French for 'do not touch.' …Well I guess so."

Harry passed the blow-up around and the Major took over again.

"If we thought this case was complicated before, finding this adds another, huge layer, you know."

Just like everyone else Donald Dark was struck by the implications of what he was seeing but, very quickly, decided he wasn't all that surprised. Findings like these, he thought, helped make his confusion and uncertainty about all that he had been involved in begin to make slightly more sense. The bigger the case, certainly the more people involved, and the more serious and dangerous all this seemed the more likely there were going to be answers to what appeared so mysterious before. Later his reaction was tempered by a return of Dark's awareness he still had no firm knowledge of how that woman and events might fit into all this.

The Major wrapped up the meeting. "So the Colonel wants to talk about this case and today's findings with senior staff first thing tomorrow. But let's be clear: Don you need to alert your NYPD Narcotics contacts that it looks like there's been a big deal smuggling operation of that lethal drug going on for some time. We don't know how long.

"And the force is going to have to decide how and when to involve Customs and Border Protection, and likely the Mounties also, at some point. So, fellas, clear the decks. We're gonna move on all this and need to do it fast. Steve, I want you and Sergeant Abernathy, from your unit, to meet with Lieutenant Jen Davis from

Interagency Support and Don and his deputy, Sergeant Haber, Monday morning to talk out everything, from New York to Canada. Get organized, and make your plans; quick. Okay?"

Major Carruthers wasn't really asking a question. But Donald Dark wasn't so sure his instructions to them were okay. His inclusion in a continuing and now expanding investigation was welcomed. With Jim Wiley he would figure out how to make an NYPD Narcotics connection. However Dark wasn't sure he could work with Steve Kamp. For years just hearing Kamp's name made Dark uncomfortable; not angry, just on guard. He always thought of Steve Kamp as someone he would never trust. He assumed Kamp felt the same way about him. Even with the passing of so much time Dark continued to make an effort to avoid working with him.

————

- 23 -

The apron of the dirt driveway, just frozen from the evening drop in temperature, wasn't empty when he drove in from the road and up to the Fleury house Saturday evening. The car there wasn't a complete surprise to Dark, but he hadn't considered the possibility until he saw it. Molly insisted he come for dinner on the weekend. Perhaps one more effort at saying thank you. With Susan there also everything changed for Dark.

He was pleased. He remembered their recent lovemaking and, on seeing her car, had a not so random thought that maybe they could do that again after the evening was over. His thought, however, was unavoidably tied to a realization that was the kind of thing that *couples* did, and he had rejected that level of connection with Susan for some time. With literally no other relationship within his horizons beyond something or other with a fantasy mystery woman he battled his thoughts.

Sex with Susan was exciting. But they were different and, in particular, opening up to her had remained unsatisfactory to him. They both had been on their own for so long he wondered if they each were so settled in their ways and patterns that making the work of commitment of a couple to each other was too difficult; maybe never really possible anymore. Too late? He wasn't sure.

So then was *sharing* sex unfair if no other commitment was going to happen? Dark thought of that as unfair only to Susan. He never considered that sexual intimacy might be craved by a woman exclusive of a long term commitment; which, to Dark, meant marriage.

And what about his mysterious, possibly completely made up, *girlfriend*; the woman whose face and manner he couldn't get out of his head? There was a good chance that, like an adolescent, Dark had created her to match his desires. Plus, it was seeming more and more likely she had some ominous involvement with the serious criminal activity he was investigating. Still he was not ready to stop clinging to his notion there was something more to that woman. And what if she did need his help? He felt he had a number of reasons to continue to try to find her. Despite his real life involvement with Susan, an attractive and bright woman, it was his relationship with Susan, and its future, he chose to continue to doubt.

At the door Molly was missing her usual Irish glow, a face that often helped light up any room and everybody's spirits. Ed Fleury's serious brush with death still affected her. When she hugged Dark she, again, grabbed him more tightly and held him longer than usual. She put her hand on his shoulder and led him to the others in the small living room. Molly placed him on the couch, right next to Susan. All that was accomplished with the barking Fleury dog, Master, escorting them. The dog was a mutt of such certifiably complex lineage that Ed called him 'Mix Master.'

Susan looked especially good. After their recent night together the scent she wore had an almost magnetic effect and was a turn on for him. As he sat down she offered Dark a warm smile and they hugged and kissed, possibly longer than either intended. He was aroused and immediately wondered if he was supposed to hate himself for that? It felt good to be with her. Then he reminded himself of missing pieces in their relationship that always limited them.

Ed Fleury was in his recliner, sitting up and he looked fine. Dark had no idea if he still had a catheter but he certainly saw no obvious bulge in either leg of Fleury's pants. Before he could test the emotional strength of Fleury's recovery, alerted by the recent door bell and barking dog, two of the four Fleury kids bounded down the stairs to greet Dark. He had more like an uncle relationship, especially with these two youngest Fleury boys. They did some very abbreviated minor horseplay. When the oldest teen daughter came down she was emotional, clearly hugging Dark to thank him for his efforts. That changed the tone in the room.

Fleury wasn't happy to see his girl upset and so serious. He launched a salvo about *him* doing the real detective work and all Donald had to do was pick up some pieces (him) and deal with minor problems that developed along the way that day.

Molly wouldn't let that go. "Eddie, after our last guinea pig got into the walls and its carcass stunk up the house for weeks we decided no more little animals. Remember? So, yeah, then you go and become a large guinea pig at the Barracks. That worked out well, didn't it?"

Dark started to speak, then hesitated. "Fleur, there are kids in the room so you're spared…for a little while anyway." A dig at Fleury's disastrous, impulsive rush to pretend to play with what he assumed was cocaine would have to wait.

The kids drifted away. Susan also wanted to tell Dark how impressed she was that he helped save Ed's life. She told him it must have been a difficult and terrible time for Dark. In fact, she spoke softly while slowly stroking his arm and was able to openly communicate her distress over what he and Ed must have gone through.

With her words she travelled back to the circumstances of his concussion and the stress and worry about that episode, and more. Gradually, her words began to astound Dark. Maintaining her soft voice she added elements conveying both concern and understanding relating to his thoughts about the events of the recent weeks.

"I guess I get it now, Don. If all these terrible things are because of drugs that's a disaster. If you think there's no way to control it then I definitely don't want to see you…or Ed harmed in a struggle that has no real end."

Dark was amazed. After months trying to deal with his doubts primarily on his own here was someone, a woman he did care about, honestly empathizing with the predicament that was eating at him.

Of course, he thought then, wasn't it almost predictable Susan's thinking would just now change after these events? Kind of crazy because this was exactly the same time, with the carfentanil development, Dark was feeling re-motivated about his job. Yes, even with its inherent risks of futility, although he wasn't sure that would last. Homicide with carfentanil was too easy. Any dent in access to something as lethal as that had to save lives and should be worth fighting.

Everything about Susan almost overwhelmed him. That night, sitting next to him, looking great and speaking earnestly about challenges she knew were deeply impacting him so significantly, she wanted him to know she understood and was a kindred spirit. They leaned into each other and sat quietly for a few minutes. What had really changed Dark wondered?

Ed stayed quiet about himself, waiting until Susan, insisting on helping Molly, went off to the kitchen with her and the men were alone in the living room.

"DD, I'm back to duty on Monday. Feeling really great. F'ing tube has been out and I'm peeing okay now."

"Yeah, haven't noticed any puddles on the floor yet…but I'll be careful. If that's the worst from all this that's pretty good, eh?"

Fleury clearly had nothing he considered Ed funny to say about any of that and changed the topic. "So on the phone you told me maybe now you were gonna get a stick up yours too, having to work with that narc Kamp."

Dark didn't think Fleury would let him get away with telling him his latest contact with Kamp had gone surprisingly well. Kamp's words and attitude impressed Dark that the Lieutenant was very different than during the eight months they worked together years before. Dark wasn't ready to trust his reaction to Kamp yet but it seemed to him Kamp's view of working Narcotics now might be a whole lot closer to Dark's take when he was doing Narcotics also, years before. He liked him.

"I think Kamp actually gets it now. Can you imagine?"

"Huh. *Come to Jesus* moments even in Narcotics? That is something. Maybe the bastard is chasing a mystery lady too. Hey, maybe it's yours?"

"Fuck you, Fleur."

"Amen, brother."

Surviving their recent potentially deadly experiences the two lawmen found it difficult that night to pick on each other, themselves, or anyone else for that matter. So they bored themselves listening more to the ladies. Dark was into Susan all evening. Pleased to be with her. He was turned on and by dinner his brain was stuck on making love.

He figured he was more obvious than he should be but it was fun. They traded glances and smirks all evening. How to make it happen frustrated him. The whole thing was out of character for Dark. Not that long after dinner Molly couldn't take it anymore. They looked like two teenagers hot to make out as soon as they got to the movies.

"So Donald, guess you better get home to let that *hound* of yours out for its business, huh? Your Mom showed me pictures when

I ran into her at the grocery…" Molly regretted mentioning his mother in the midst of a sexually charged setting. But the couple wasn't affected.

"Well I'd better go too, Moll. Gonna bundle up and run in the morning."

Out the door as a couple but then walking to different cars. Dark knew he had to say something.

"Hey, it's still kind of early. Want to say hello to Alice?"

Probably the last thing Susan Spahn genuinely wanted to do was have any interaction with Alice. But as a means to an end Alice would have to do. She smiled.

"If you mean did I bring some things with me because you have responsibilities to your dog early in the morning? The answer is yes."

They embraced and then drove, in tandem, ten minutes to his place. Dark didn't think he'd known such a warm, excited feeling in forever. It was freezing but his ears were red and warm.

- 24 -

Busted was a rigid creature of routine. The hours of a Vermont State Trooper made meeting his needs difficult and led to occasional accidents. Dark loved Busted so he refused to accept that his job and solo household made it inappropriate for him to have a dog for a companion. Overall they did fine together, probably more of a challenge for the dog than Dark.

Alice was annoyingly adaptable. Eating, peeing, or pooping didn't ever seem to stress her. Busted thrived with exercise but it clearly wasn't Alice's thing. Over the short time Alice was with Dark what she did do was hang out with him when he was around. Just stayed close by. She really didn't do anything and yet she seemed to project a clear aura that she felt in some control of the household. Lately, she often slept right next to his bed. When guests were around, or this night when Susan stayed over, she remained at the small quarters Dark had arranged for her in his bedroom, close to a corner.

Dark and Susan made little acknowledgement of Alice when they walked in. They were of like minds; he was terribly excited. They decided to keep the heat down so being under the covers would be so nice. Susan moved to the bathroom while Dark advised Alice it was now or not till morning for her to go out. Modestly stand-offish about Susan's presence she complied.

Freezing, Dark stood at the open door expecting Alice would be ready to come back in very quickly. He knew he was probably in more of a hurry than she was. Time passed and nothing. He called out to her. Nothing for fifteen more seconds. Then he heard her bark; that hi-pitched howling bark that he detested. The bark of a *yip-yip*. So out of character for her personality. There was a dusting of recent snow on the ground so the low-to-the-ground white furred pooch was nowhere to be seen, especially in the dark. Fortunately, although still howling, she then came bounding into view.

In through the door and right over to her corner. At first Dark was pissed, assuming Alice was reacting to Susan's presence. Was she whimpering? Dark became concerned. He retrieved a flashlight and proceeded to examine Alice. She had no signs of an injury and she stopped making that sound.

Susan was in bed and had no reason to think this wasn't the dog's usual behavior. The time it took for Dark to join her didn't strike her as unusual. Dark was the one who was impatient; a bit peeved at Alice. She better learn to like Susan, he thought, as he brushed his teeth then ran, naked, through the chilly room and jumped under the covers with Susan.

His distraction faded rapidly as he pulled her to him. Just like last time her body briefly shuddered in anticipation and he felt it. His excitement was instantly re-kindled. Susan whispered there was no need for them to rush and he got it. Holding her he tried to relax and the moment sent him through the roof. He was alive; together with Susan. He thought, with eagerness, of the things they did last time. That's what being a couple is he realized. Knowing and relying on satisfying each other. No time limit; the entire night open and available.

Of course, nothing lasts forever, and neither did Donald Dark. That was okay. They talked softly for a while then fell off to sleep, arm in arm, back to back, or whatever, but always touching. Maybe again in the morning he wondered as he finally drifted off.

———

Dark was out, breathing softly and rhythmically. She assumed he was content. She was relaxed but there was a nagging sense of uncertainty that insisted on staying in her mind. Was this it? Was this what it was going to be; forever? Would that be good enough? The last few weeks were better than the entire year before, but what if it was going to stay this way; only occasional nights together?

Susan tried hard to push her worry away. She thought about the day turning light soon and Donald and her sitting together having breakfast and talking. That was something to really look forward to; a companion in the morning. A tear formed when she wondered why it couldn't be that way every day? It hadn't happened yet so would it ever? She turned over and grabbed onto Dark and held him. With a smile on her face she drifted back to sleep. Everything was quiet.

———

Susan never had a dog. At a hint of first light her sleep was disturbed. There was a scratching sound. She turned her head and could see through the hallway it was Alice scratching at the back door. Shortly, there was whimpering like the night before, and then a slightly louder cry. Susan assumed the dog wanted to go outside and considered getting up and letting her out. But Alice wasn't her dog. The night had been so wonderful she didn't want to do anything that might upset Donald. So she gently nudged him until he woke.

Dark gradually sensed his surroundings and smiled. When he fell asleep it had been his hope they might make love again in the morning. He assumed, with her soft touch, Susan was suggesting that now. But then he heard the scratching and crying. That was unheard of for Alice. 'Damn!' He knew Alice was his responsibility. He turned, they briefly kissed, and he began to pull the covers from his side of the bed.

Pulling on his *dress* jeans over his naked body and slipping on untied shoes he wondered if whatever the excitement was that diverted Alice last night might also have meant she forgot or didn't pee. He figured she probably was desperate to go now.

As soon as he opened the door the agitated animal raced across the yard and into the woods. She didn't stop to pee or poop. Her howling allowed Dark to know she was penetrating deeper and deeper into the still dark forest. Something was wrong.

Naked from the waist up, he started out the door but then stopped and thought about his revolver. It was locked away. For a few moments everything was quiet. The biting cold didn't seem to bother him and he stood, quietly listening, but also thinking. What was going on? More than that though, he wondered what he was doing? As the emerging daylight exposed the barely white covered ground the only sound was wind blowing through the pines. He wrestled with himself. What did he want to happen? What did he hope or want to find?

The howling started up again, close to a frenzy. He went back inside, looked around, grabbed a kitchen knife and headed back out into the freezing cold air. The sounds were disturbing: growling and barking; at first loud then somewhat muffled. He stopped at the edge of the woods and shouted.

"Alice! Come back here!" Quiet again, for a few moments. He ventured a few steps into the woods. Howling and growling again, but no longer muffled. Did he hear someone yelling in the distance? He thought so but was unsure. Shortly after, first he heard Alice, then he could see her dashing through the woods, racing toward him, barking away. When she was close to him she arced into the air and up into his frozen arms.

His face was totally red from anger, fury, and the cold. Suddenly Dark screamed, loudly. "Alice is mine now! My dog!" A pause. "Who the hell *are* you?"

Pushing farther into the woods with barely any clothes on made no sense since Alice was back and appeared okay. He would have if he was dressed and had some gear. Dark didn't know what was out there that, at least at first, attracted Alice. That she then escaped from someone or something seemed plausible but he couldn't be sure. Walking back to the condo, Alice and Dark each shivering against the other's body, he, briefly, considered arranging for a dog team to sniff this story out. Not justifiable he realized.

He did get dressed for the weather and put on useful gear, including his weapon, to go back out and search the area. Susan was sitting up in bed wearing one of his shirts. He asked her to lock the door after he went out and sit tight for a while. When Dark left she dressed and looked around his small kitchen for some food. Then she sat and had breakfast with Alice; a far cry from the scene she had dreamed about a few hours earlier.

––––––––––

Alice returned to him at night more or less along the same path she charged into the woods in the morning. Following the trail of tiny paw prints in the dusting of snow was not difficult now that it was completely light. But Dark was in no rush. He needed time to think about what had happened. He was sure it was her. Who else could attract Alice like that? She was here, he thought. Amazing.

Walking through the woods he wondered if she was waiting for him up ahead? Maybe she sent Alice back to get him, he thought. He moved ahead deliberately and carefully. He found no one. Tracks veered to the main road about a hundred yards from the entrance drive to his condo. There were signs of foot traffic, but Dark decided that area, just like the bloody seat in the smashed car, was intentionally trampled in a way so no discreet footprints could be found; an explanation the Lieutenant apparently hoped was most likely. At the road there was a pull off and a set of fresh tire tracks were obvious. Nothing more to follow.

Walking slowly out of the forest, re-tracing the path he had entered, he looked for any signs he might have missed of what happened.

Mostly he thought about her. He was sure she was trying to contact him but wasn't willing to knock on his door. Maybe she had been watching him and knew about Susan. What would he tell her about Susan?

———————

Did Donald Dark truly believe he could return from such unusual activity in the woods and barely talk with Susan about what might be going on? Perhaps only a confirmed loner might assume he could get away with behaving like that after such a striking commotion.

"I made some coffee. I'm sure it will help warm you up."

"Thanks Susan. Yeah, I'm kinda cold." He pulled his hat and heavy jacket off and hung them on a hook in a closet. He began to move to the stove but Susan waved him off and started to get up.

"Let me get it. You sit. Guess I can make you some toast if you'd like. Anything else you have to tell me where things are."

He bent forward in his chair, sipped the hot black coffee, then leaned back and exhaled deeply. He didn't respond to Susan's offer, appearing lost in thought; clearly distracted. Dark just assumed that woman had something to do with what happened. Probably her out there. What was the yelling? He couldn't make it out.

Susan sat, wrapping both her hands around her warm mug. At first she stared straight at the mug. She looked unhappy and was cool to him. Shortly she turned her head and directed her gaze at Dark. After few moments she spoke.

"Don, what was that all about?"

Still working his way through possible explanations and implications of the episode, Susan's words abruptly halted Dark's reverie. He was surprised how quickly and easily he had become consumed by thoughts of that woman again. Had he forgotten about Susan? As best he was aware Susan knew nothing about the mysterious woman and certainly nothing about his attraction, yes obsession, with her.

Only hours before they had an exciting night together and he felt so good about how they were getting along. Then this. What should he tell her? Dark quickly discarded any thought of telling Susan the whole story or anything related to his attraction to that woman.

He convinced himself to stay as superficial as possible with Susan. But Susan had already connected more than he would have suspected. The story of Alice, the dog, had never really been told. The first time she met Alice the rhinestone collar hadn't yet been replaced at Dark's insistence by his father. Even if a new collar had a circle of iron spikes Alice was not a dog someone like Dark would be likely to seek out. She queried again.

"Don, who were you yelling at out there? ...What do you think is going on?" Then the tough question: "Is Alice your dog or isn't she? Because I'm getting more used to her but Busted might have had her for dinner if he was hungry and you weren't around."

Looking straight ahead, as though speaking to no one in particular, he took a deep breath and in a quiet monotone said what he was comfortable telling her.

"Well you know they said she was sitting next to me when troopers found me when I got my concussion. And she has stayed with me ever since. We're guessing," he lied, "she was in the rental car with the drug mule that I was following. I thought they were going to New York City; but didn't. We have no idea what happened to the woman who was driving that kid but there's a good chance," he lied again, "Alice was hers. She could be dead, but maybe not.

"Lady driving that car I was following, if she's alive, might not have any idea who has her dog...if it was hers. But that lady and I interacted at Williston Barracks before...we think. So she may have figured I was a good bet to be involved with what happened near Jay that day."

Dark hadn't thought about it when he received that letter but now he did wonder how that woman knew he had the dog? Susan had a different take on the morning's incident. She was disappointed in what the morning had become but decided to make an effort to push her own immediate upset away and try to be helpful since Dark was so obviously unsettled and distracted. Her tone reflected her limited interest.

"Don, do you think it's possible whoever's dog Alice is could be from this area and has been watching and following you? Decided to come for Alice today? Maybe thought you'd be distracted." Of course Alice spent hours alone in the unit and could have been retrieved with a break-in. But perhaps it better served Susan's mind to suggest the distraction of their love-making.

Dark was startled by her words. Throughout the weeks of this case, and his persisting fixation on that woman and finding her, it never had occurred to Dark that she, that woman, might have been monitoring *him* regularly. She might know more about him than he did about her. After all this time he still knew virtually nothing about her. Quite a jolt and Susan came up with it, not him.

Her observation raised all sorts of new, potentially ominous, possibilities for Dark. If that was true forget about *lady in distress* fantasies, for sure. Perhaps one more strong strike for her to be on the corrupt side of what had been going on.

Susan asked no more questions and remained decidedly cool to him. Dark wondered if his disappointment about the episode showed on his face?

———

- 25 -

Weekends no longer meant anything during a serious investigation such as this one. Maybe they assembled a little later than usual on Sunday morning but that was about it.

On balance Dark wasn't satisfied with the way he handled speaking to Susan about the woman earlier. It was obvious to him she was less than convinced he had shared the whole story. The change in her demeanor from Saturday night and then Sunday morning was just that: almost night and day. She tried to remain friendly but affection was gone, at least for then. They barely spoke while she quickly packed her few things and then drove home. He was really down after she left.

On his way to meeting with Lieutenant Kamp and Sergeants Abernathy and Haber Dark continued to wrestle with the most obvious conclusion from the incident with Alice. If there was any chance Susan's idea was correct and the woman might be in the local area, the force needed to know that.

What, or how much, was he going to tell the others? So far only Ed Fleury really knew anything about that woman and he had quickly picked up on Dark's preoccupation with her.

Should she become an active focus of the investigation Dark worried it might become more difficult to mask his fixation from others in the force. In the beginning he had quietly lobbied to remain on the case so he could hope to find her. Now he realized efforts to find her through a more active investigation by the force would almost be bound to expose his personal feelings. Any superior who picked up on that would remove him from the case instantly. He certainly didn't fool Susan or Fleury.

———————

Dark and Sergeant Jason Abernathy were the first to arrive at Waterbury Barracks. While they were waiting for Steve Kamp and Haber Abernathy began to talk about what was important to him.

"Here's the thing, Lieutenant. That damn shit is so powerful those fuckers only need really small amounts to do all that damage, killing and OD'ing so many people. You know, maybe what we intercepted might be enough for most of the entire northeast for a few weeks. I'll tell you I bet some big boys are mighty upset and angry about what was lost. And losing that shit is gonna drive up prices, you can be sure. Lotta really pissed people because we intercepted that stuff."

Even with his career long effort to limit his involvement with the Narcotics Investigation Division Lieutenant Dark had heard about Sergeant Jason Abernathy. Maybe only two years on the force, the kid showed talent and smarts that had the brass swooning. It was already unusual just to have a Native American on the force. The Sergeant proudly identified with the Abnaki people, Native Americans long a part of Vermont and the surrounding region.

Organizational and administrative skills can usually be taught. Sergeant Abernathy was one of those people who showed innate ability in accomplishing tasks for himself and with others that stood out to all who interacted with him. Senior officers were already often deferring to his plans for an action.

Small, thin, and wiry, born in the forests of Vermont, he knew well the struggles of the indigenous people in his home state. Those he identified with had been left behind. As recently as the early years of the twentieth century Abnaki suffered terrible racial discrimination in Vermont. Victims of the pseudoscience *eugenics*, poor education and opportunity, among other forms of discrimination. Poverty and poor skills remained limiting. Early on Jason Abernathy saw the deadly impacts of drugs and alcohol on those around him.

 His intelligence was celebrated in his community and then in the state. His remarkable energy and abilities were his personal ticket to a different world. Abernathy took the assistance he was given to become better educated. With seemingly unlimited opportunity to achieve in society he chose policing. The Sergeant was very clear with everyone his personal mission was not to do law enforcement among the people. His plan was to skip users, and even local suppliers. Those running the drugs in this country were to be *his* victims. An ambitious agenda.

He was trying to be patient working his way up to be able to be closer to his goal. Lieutenant Kamp knew what he had with Abernathy and the Lieutenant and his Captain were trying to carefully advance the kid along on a fast track. Even with his apparent rapid rise it was unclear if they were aware Abernathy felt, strongly, the inherent bureaucracy in the force meant his progress was much too slow for him.

———

When they started chatting Lieutenant Dark, like so many others, was immediately impressed with Jason Abernathy. Spending time or working with Abernathy commonly led people to confide in him. He was that kind of guy. Astute and easy going in conversation; interested and came across as non-judgmental. The man's manner was an invitation to Dark, someone being persistently handicapped by his unhelpful obsession, to unburden himself. While they were waiting for the others, absent details of his personal attachment to the mystery woman, he told a great deal of his story to the Sergeant.

Abernathy listened patiently but Dark, by now, had few illusions Sergeant Abernathy, anyway, hadn't figured out what he left out. Even though Abernathy had the manner of a therapist Dark didn't feel there was anything therapeutic about their interaction. The more Dark spoke about all of it the more he, himself, reacted to its bizarre nature. But that didn't relieve its impact on him. What had happened to him? Why was he so stuck? He was ruining his life and other lives; Susan's for sure, he guessed. Then it all became alive and active for Dark again when Abernathy suggested the woman may be a person known to others.

"Sounds like a lady I've heard about; sometimes called 'Brazen Betty.'"

"What!" Dark was astounded. "You know the woman I'm talking about?"

The Sergeant continued. "No, I don't even know if she really exists for sure. But I've heard some things about someone like that and she sure would fit what you're talking about. Got that name because, whoever she is, I guess she shows up in strange spots, kinda outrageous. Has pulled off some wild stunts doing things like you say."

Dark was intensely interested and intended to get as much from Abernathy as possible. He tried to conceal his excitement, keeping his tone neutral.

"So Sergeant, tell me all you know about her."

"Well sir, not too much more. Only reason I think I ever heard of her is, months ago, an FBI agent showed up one day who had sought me out to ask about a lady like that with dark hair way down to her waist. Some jerk figured a young lady with hair like that was probably a Native American. Imagine. What bullshit.

"I wondered if had something to do with narcotics if they got to me. But maybe not. More likely her ancestry, I guess." Abernathy looked away, like he was thinking.

"Yeah, so if you've heard she cut that hair that distinguished her she might be having some troubles. Think?"

Dark remembered the postmark from the Akwesasne Reservation but the clear image of her in his memory had no features suggesting such an ethnicity. Never crossed his mind that neither did Abernathy. He was more struck and disappointed to have again arrived at what seemed to be a logical conclusion: the woman was likely a criminal. "You don't know if she's ever been charged with anything specific; any record," he asked?

"No... No. Here's the thing, Lieutenant, more than just if she really exists and who the hell she is, from the agent and some rumors I've heard about her, I don't think it's clear if she's on *any* damn side or what her deal is. I mean I wasn't sure that agent didn't know more than he said. If she does exist there's something spooky about her, you know. Maybe working both sides? Something crazy like that, you know."

Well Dark didn't know, but it did sound crazy. He readily accepted he was stuck on a woman and had been, as surreptitiously as possible, seeking out information about her while he tried to find her. Initially captivated by Abernathy's words he began to wonder if the Sergeant was intentionally trying to confuse him? 'Spooky?' His story seemed to make little sense, probably adding nothing. Abernathy seemed interested in continuing to talk but Lieutenant Kamp arrived for the meeting and Dark decided to end the conversation.

Donald Dark remained distracted but he also couldn't get over how well he and Steve Kamp got along. He had an idea they now seemed to be, as they say, *on the same page* about narcotics. Little came from the short meeting although it was interesting that both Lieutenant Dark and Sergeant Abernathy each strongly advocated for keeping US Customs and Border Protection (CBP) and the Royal Canadian Mounted Police (RCMP) out of the investigation for as long as practical. Dark wanted to maintain as much control as possible and Abernathy flat out said he didn't trust those agencies, although he never said why. They talked some strategy for the meeting on Monday with Interagency.

188   Robert Karp

- 26 -

Monday morning Donald Dark was well aware of effects this mixture of his personal and professional issues were having on him. He had not rested well. Too dark and cold to try to run himself into a more relaxed mood. Arriving at Williston half an hour before the meeting he was tense and, of course, also wary not knowing what Ed Fleury might have in store for him.

"DD, what the hell happened? Molly says Susan said she's done with you. Things sure looked good for the two of you just a coupla' days ago. How'd that happen?" Ed actually looked pissed. Leave it to Fleury to have figured it out. "You didn't share any of that story about the fantasy lady you've been stuck on, did you?" Dark wasn't surprised. His vacant stare answered Ed's question.

"DD, always figured you so straight you might flip someday, but in all the years we go back you've always been the same guy…guess till now. Jeez, now you're a whack job, aren't you? You've really gone crazy over this, haven't you?"

Dark continued to stare off into space. His face remained somber and then he looked down. "She wants her dog back, Fleur. She was in the woods behind my place on Sunday and tried to get her."

Ed Fleury jumped out of his chair. He couldn't believe Dark was serious about clinging to that crazy lady.

"What? Well give her back her f'ing dog then! It's her dog, isn't it?" He tried to act incredulous. "So there goes your *lady in trouble* story then, doesn't it, huh? She's found *you* and is screwing around your place trying to get her strange dog back and you still think you and her gonna sail off into the sunset someday? Right?...Nut."

Dark had no answer. He actually thought Fleury's words made sense and he got why he was angry. There was a chance Dark and Susan were just growing together and being stuck on an image he probably invented was really screwing him up. He may have, finally, killed his relationship with Susan. Dark stood up to end the berating and turned to face Fleury.

"But Alice and I get along really well. She *is* real, you know. And, Sunday she chose to come back to me." Dark walked away and headed to his meeting.

Under his breathe Fleury muttered, "That is so fucked up."

The meeting turned out to be little more than informational, bringing Lieutenant Davis, from Interagency Support, up to speed assuming that federal and Canadian authorities would soon need to be part of the growing investigation. The more important meeting was now set up for Tuesday he was told. Early, but quickly mounting signs of frustration were contributing to the affinity Dark and Kamp were forming. The Lieutenants were already beginning to worry bureaucracy was impeding planning and could waste valuable time.

Dark called Susan's cell a few times on Sunday, only getting a message. He knew he shouldn't but he called her cell again twice during the day on Monday even though he was aware she was in school. She didn't pick up. He hoped he could convince her to go to dinner over the weekend. Knowing she was almost certainly upset bothered him greatly. He had hurt her. Could he ever explain his confusion?

Getting her to agree to dinner, he hoped, might relieve some of the tension for each of them through the week ahead; certainly at least for Dark, who imagined it was going be a challenging period for him. He thought about just showing up at her place, or even her school, to try to speak with her. Unable to let it rest, mid-day he called Molly to ask if she could help him arrange to apologize to Susan. Molly explained to him how unfair just showing up would be to Susan. She told him she would try to set something up.

———

On the road, in his cruiser, Dark heard from dispatch James Wiley was looking for him. Though he was curious why Wiley was seeking him Dark's initial reaction to hearing of the call was mostly negative. When they last spoke neither was pleased with the other. Now, some days later, Dark was unclear how that happened. Lasting really only a few days, their unexpected, brief, reunion in Vermont seemed to have gone well enough when they were together.

At first, meeting again after so many years, Dark felt Wiley's story about being shot and seeing him with his disability was a living representation of his own worries and fears come true. The story and its timeliness for Dark were quite a jolt. They got along well. Then Wiley took the kids and was back in New York in short order. Disaster struck in the City and it was now clear again to the Lieutenant, approaching Waterbury Barracks, that was when things went sour between them.

He got angry at Wiley for unilaterally making plans to take Jorge, Dark's witness, to a place Dark thought was out of the country. And he knew Wiley was put off by Dark's ignorance of civics and geography. Despite Puerto Rico's commonwealth status Dark didn't like Gonzales potentially out of reach.

Wiley wasn't happy anticipating his own continuing involvement if the kids stayed in the City. A farm in the countryside for the kid actually didn't seem to Wiley like a bad option for a bad situation.

Dark had no idea why Wiley was looking for him. After their recent differences it seemed unlikely he would be calling for anything other than some kind of problem. The Lieutenant decided to try to go easy, hoping they could move on from their recent disagreement.

As soon as Jim Wiley was made aware there was, indeed, a problem he knew what he had to do. He was sick about it and wasn't looking forward to the call and talking with Dark. Partly it was because he too remembered their bad end. But, maybe as disappointing, it seemed to Wiley his involvement in this case just might never end. There was more than a hint of real danger in the Gonzales mess. Wiley, a family man, thought he had removed that kind of risk from his professional life. And there was no advantage, or money, for him in pursuing this case.

Rather than stewing about any awkwardness between them, once he arrived at the Barracks the Lieutenant decided it was best to bite the bullet and speak with Wiley right away. When they connected Wiley's flat tone immediately alerted Dark that either this call was difficult for Wiley or he was unhappy. Turned out to be a bit of both.

"Donald Dark. Guess we're not done with each other for a while yet." The Lieutenant said nothing. "The kid, Gonzales, is gone."

A jolt to Dark. Instantly he felt a rush of frustration tinged with anger. Wiley expected there would be some anger. They would both be disappointed but Dark was the one who would have to deal with the consequences as it impacted the developing case. Dark, intentionally, tried to restrain his response.

"Well, Jim, what exactly do you mean? What do you know about it and where do you think he is?"

Good questions, to which Wiley had little information and so, few answers.

"The kid is apparently nowhere to be found on the farm or in the small town a few miles away. Still not clear if he left on his own or something else happened." He paused and Dark assumed something like a sigh was barely audible. "Before calling I checked with Laurinda's family and was able to call her a little while ago. She's still in San Juan and I don't think she knows anything about where Jorge might be. Before I told her the problem she told me she's had no contact with him at all since she's been on the island.

"So kind of a mess, eh, Don? I have to admit I don't know anyone there in law enforcement but the call I got did come from a police officer the farmer gave my number to. I'd given it to Jorge and told him to give a copy to the farmer. I'm trying to get a number for whoever NYPD uses to liaise with authorities on the island.

"You know, could be nothing or could turn out to be really something. Guess will take some time to get details. I really thought getting him away from his contacts in the City was a good idea. But turns out being in the middle of nowhere may not have been the best location for keeping tabs on the kid, or even, like now, for finding out what's going on."

It was hard for Dark not to think something ominous happened to Gonzales. But Jorge was young and an impulsive guy by his history, so who knew what he might have decided to do instead of working as a farmhand in a rural Puerto Rico.

Without thinking about it Dark managed to say what was on his mind. "Well, that didn't last too long, did it? About a week?"

"Yeah, something like that," came Wiley's weak reply. Dark hadn't meant for his words to sound accusatory.

Distracted, Dark was momentarily confused and briefly messed up again on Puerto Rico.

"Well, if he's still okay and did this on his own he won't be able to get off that island if we quickly get an APB out about him to customs." He caught himself. "I meant he'll probably be stuck in Puerto Rico unless he, or someone helping him, can arrange for a fake ID so he can fly out."

Man, was Dark pissed at himself. He had just done it again. 'What a jerk!' It was so crazy it did ease some of the tension, though. Wiley calmly shot back.

"Remember, Donald, I left him in U.S. territory, not Cuba. If he's okay and wants to come back it's not difficult."

"I'll ask my dad for some geography and U.S. history books so I can stop embarrassing myself, Jim." He paused. "I'm thinking, with what we can assume about whoever is running this drug organization I'm more worried no one is ever gonna see that kid again."

Despite that glum observation Dark and Wiley were getting along better again. No blame was suggested but this was a big, new problem. Wiley told Dark he would continue working to get information from authorities on the island and alert the NYPD and follow along with them.

Wiley verbalized new concern for Laurinda. At that moment neither Wiley or Dark were sure if she was safer in San Juan or back in New York. Wiley said she was asking to go home. They decided nothing should change until local authorities were able to investigate the disappearance for a at least a short period of time.

"So Don, when I told Laurinda I need to hear from her immediately if he shows up or anything comes up about Jorge she surprised me. She said she hopes he's okay but also hopes he doesn't come after her. Said she's glad she broke it off; doesn't ever want to get mixed up with someone like that again."

Wiley's words conveyed how struck he was by the finality expressed by Laurinda about ending her relationship with Jorge. It left both Wiley and Dark wondering if she knew there might be more to Gonzales' story than either of those kids had let on.

"Okay Jim, I hope you will keep us posted as much as you can on this. I know you don't want to lose more hair over this business but we sure can use your help." To Dark that sounded supportive and appreciative.

"Don, why don't you save *going bald* jokes for you and your Lieutenant pal. I said I'd stay on it."

Any sensitivity about Wiley's receding hairline had never previously been observed by Dark, who had no intention of joking with him. Maybe there still was tension between them. Wiley completely misinterpreted Dark's words.

———

- 27 -

Susan opened her door. There was nothing remotely reassuring about the expression on her face. She gave Dark no reason to assume she was glad to see him. It wasn't what he was hoping to see. He knew it took Molly's intervention for this moment to happen. Standing in the doorway Dark's most immediate reaction to Susan's demeanor presaged her agreement to speak with him was as a favor to Molly.

The occasional flurries outside would be the norm for months to come. It was late in the afternoon, cold and overcast, the early onset of dark winter evenings becoming annoyingly routine. Susan had Molly make it clear to Dark he was welcome to come to talk for about an hour or so but that was it. Susan knew he would have to get home to Alice at some point and that would help limit what promised to be a very unhappy encounter for her.

They sat in facing arm chairs in her small living room. It occurred to Dark he didn't know her condo very well, an obvious reflection of the limited time he had spent there during their on-again-off-again relationship over the years. Her whole place was small and felt confining to him. Nothing to be especially impressed with in her unit. A few lamps were on but it still wasn't bright. She nor the surroundings radiated any sense of happiness. It struck him his place probably was not any nicer; only a little larger. Their lives were passing and they each were inhabiting non-descript condo units in small, isolated ten or twenty unit complexes built just off a road, with wide, flat, tire-rutted dirt parking areas and nothing to consider as true landscaping. Places never in anybody's dreams.

After the time and effort it took to be sitting face to face Dark found it difficult to express himself. He knew it was because he was unsure of what it was he hoped for with Susan. He had only a modest awareness of how hurt and angry she was. She spoke almost as soon as they were sitting. Her words made him feel small and callous. The impact of his behavior on another person was more than unfortunate; it was sad, he realized. He truly had no idea. And she told him that.

Resolute in appearance Susan told Dark what was on her mind. Her tone was at times ironic and at other times her anger came through; even as moist eyes accompanied it.

"Donald, I've tried…because I thought I loved you…but it's more than just you. I know that. But I guess maybe I used you to tell myself to put up with things, or maybe to try to stay patient, you know, till a time was bound to come we would find a way to want to be together…forever." A few tears couldn't be stopped.

"Don, have you ever thought about why your sister moved from Vermont when she married? Or my sister too? I love so much about Vermont but it has its limitations. Especially for someone on her own, like I am."

Susan sat back in her chair. It appeared she was remembering certain times in the past.

"You know, Don, when we first started doing some things together your mother called me a few times. She wanted us to get married. Yes, she told me. She said I was perfect for you. But I guess what she felt was I was perfect for her. You and I have never gotten anywhere near that far. After a while I had to ask her to stop calling me; upset me too much. I don't think she really understood. You don't know, knowing she was there, how hard it was for me to go to see you at her house after your injury. But I wanted to see how you were; it sounded terrible.

"And then we started again. And it all seemed almost too good for a time. And I guess it was." She turned in her chair and could not look at him. "Then I foolishly started to dream again. But nothing had changed; had it? I'm dreaming about someone to share breakfast conversation with…and sure, more, and I find out you're doing the same thing…but dreaming, I guess, about that with somebody else.

"Don, that was such a terrible moment for me. I don't know if it showed? We were both sitting there but I never felt so alone before. Such an awful feeling. With you but feeling so alone. Almost like worse than being alone.

"I don't know what you've thought about me all these years. I've made my peace with staying in Vermont. Probably should have left years ago, but it didn't happen. Very few men around as I've become older. I did try, you know. I've been out with some guys but I guess I was pretty stuck on you. I'm embarrassed to say it, because it's not your problem."

Was she saying something like she had been *saving* herself for him? His first reaction was he never encouraged her to feel that way. Didn't matter. He felt badly, even knowing how difficult just speaking those words now must be for her. Their quiet meeting wasn't going well.

Dark was also sad in the moment. None of this was what he hoped to hear and he knew the chance for success in any efforts to repair even whatever it was he and Susan shared before was probably very doubtful. Some of his awareness of the depth of their problem was immediately clear to him. Even though seeing the sadness in her face and listening to her words he felt both love and shame, he knew he and Susan never completely clicked, at least to his satisfaction, and that he remained captivated by thoughts of another person.

Since she was being so direct and serious and it was likely their relationship was over, he decided he could at least ask her about the striking recent change in her responses about futility and risks of his job in the setting of the drug deluge. That subject had become an important concern to him in their relationship. Susan's apparent inability to respond seriously to his worries obviously had bothered him greatly and negatively impacted his feelings about her. Now he was vexed, unable to totally understand or accept as valid her recent, apparently sincere, completely changed attitude about those things.

"Susan, the way you often react to some things I say, often things that are important to me, has been to kind of ignore what I'm saying and tell me not to be concerned. I guess I can't do that. Then, since Ed's brush with death, it's like so much changed…"

"I told you, Don, I get it now about what you do. And maybe dealing with the drugs business is so impossible it's not worth it for good folks like you and Ed to be risking your lives, maybe for nothing…or very little." Susan relaxed in her chair but actually looked reflective again, and definitely communicated the irony in her words.

"So I guess I was in the habit of trying so hard I messed up. Your Mom thought she was helping when she told me you were always *over-thinking* everything. She said all you ever wanted was to be a trooper and go as high in the ranks as possible. She said you needed unwavering support; so I guess I interpreted that to mean uncritical support. I tried. I shouldn't blame your Mom. I loved that you're a trooper, and a smart one. I was happy to do it."

'Oh shit,' Dark thought. It wasn't his mother's fault. He and Susan just didn't know how to take the time to really talk things out. Never working on a relationship in a more than casual way can cut two ways.

They sat in the poorly lit, almost dark room, barely looking at each other; a ticking clock the only audible sound. Susan had spoken openly, certainly telling him more about herself than ever before. Dark was envious she was able to do that. Introspective as he was he wished he could have verbalized more than he did. That meant he left out his true thoughts about Susan over the years they were on and off lovers.

After her words Dark began to get anxious. He was fearful Susan was going to ask him what he thought about their relationship. What would he say to her? It became a discouraging and painful moment for him. Of course it was obvious now, if not before, in a sense he did take her for granted.

 He was pleased she was there when it suited his interest and desire. But he had also decided it was okay to lock her out from the true companionship she craved. He had accomplished defending that in his own mind by determining certain *higher levels* of a relationship were impossible with her. So he accepted what he considered more superficial qualities of her mindset because that suited his perception of her.

Suddenly he wracked his brain trying to recall an instance when he had tried harder to explain his thoughts despite what he deemed a shallow response from her. Or a time he had probed more about her feelings. He couldn't convince himself he had. Dark was more than disappointed in himself. Then he was shocked as a death wish flashed in his brain. He imagined dying in the line of duty and Susan grieving for him. What an infantile asshole he was, he thought.

A terrible day, from start to end.

———

- 28 -

Lieutenant Dark awakened with a sense of urgency. Everything was going to move fast now. He knew that. At the same time, any previous impression he was controlling an investigation, this investigation, was gone now. This was no longer about a trooper's homicide by the side of a deserted country road. The case had exploded.

The significance, or any importance, of a woman unabashedly fabricating a false identity in front of the police remained unexplained and bizarre. The fact that her brief interactions with the Lieutenant and her mystery incidentally set off a longing and obsession for Dark was something he could only attempt to explain to himself. And he wasn't very successful at that. He couldn't shake it off, although, had he really made much of an effort?

With all that was developing he felt the strain from knowing he should share most details of this story with others in the force. Paradoxically, what he talked about with Sergeant Abernathy only served to increase her mystery. That's if Abernathy wasn't making up what he told Dark; just like Wiley's initial fabrication. Who could he trust? Focusing on managing to remain on the case was its own challenge and continued to blind him to his responsibilities. Any thoughts of sharing the complete story of what happened and all he knew about this woman with senior officers was unlikely to end well for Dark. Controversy and a trooper's personal concerns were rarely good news for the force at any level.

Lieutenant Dark was well along on a path to higher levels of command. Well, at least until recently. There was so much sudden activity in the force relating to this case Dark was unsure if his recent frame of mind about policing was known to those above him. Events and the magnitude of the implications of the carfentanil case had rapidly re-ignited his dedication, allowing him to minimize his own uncertainties about his career...for now. Today Dark reasoned his doubts had only been a phase in his career. Was there any basis for him to assume his superiors would not necessarily see that period the same way? The Lieutenant thought not, but he was not aware of recent rumors on the force concerning him. They had not been well received by the leaders of the force.

———————

Abernathy and Dark each had their own reasons for hoping to delay essentially handing everything over to the variety of federal authorities who would be expected to manage a case like this. For Donald Dark even a few days might be enough time to learn more in his pursuit of the woman. Abernathy appeared to have an innate distrust of agents on both sides of the border. Working with Sergeant Abernathy, and even Lieutenant Kamp, seemed promising to Dark. Kamp's evolution had startled but certainly also pleased him. After recent meetings Dark thought they, and Sergeant Haber, could work well together and might be able to make some quick progress. Yet he expected it would be a longshot to get that opportunity.

The Tuesday mid-morning meeting with the brass in a conference room in Waterbury turned out to offer a mixed result. Dark, Kamp, Abernathy, and Haber gravitated to a corner. A few others were also there when the Colonel and Captain strode in briskly. The Colonel sat and the Captain perched himself on the flat wooden table in the front. If this was to be a briefing it was most notable for being brief. Most participants had driven some distance to be there but the Captain was direct and spoke almost exclusively to Dark and the three sitting with him. The Captain was done in only minutes. Right away Dark and Abernathy were disappointed. But they shouldn't have been surprised.

Customs and Border Protection had already been alerted. Whether anyone in CBP was playing a nefarious role in what was going on was not a reasonable concern for the Captain in his role. He reported CBP ran the car's plates, make, and model in their database and had no hits. That meant the Subaru didn't ever cross the border at an established site or was photographed by a stationary camera or drone along the vast stretches of unguarded common border with Canada. Law enforcement knew there still were ways to get a vehicle across unobserved.

But that also raised the possibility of the drug being smuggled into Vermont and then placed in the tires. Or just the tires could have easily crossed the border to be packed with the drug and brought back. Local cross border commerce was continuous and generally not suspicious. Moving two tires to a specialized safe site in Canada seemed to everyone the more likely method. However, even any remote possibility of tires being fitted with the drug in a structure in Vermont became a motivating factor for the VSP to move with all possible haste to uncover such a place…or rule that out. The inherent dangers of such a facility were obvious.

Either way it was clear a farm in Vermont, close to the border, likely was set up to manage a rapid, overnight placement of carfentanil in the Subaru tires. The mule would arrive in the afternoon, hang out, sleep in the bunk house, and head out in the morning, most likely unaware the car had been altered. There were risks but local and state police were well aware of both the undocumented on the farms and the minor trade in marijuana. Each were low priority for them.

The Captain didn't spell out the scope of who was involved in the investigation at that point but he told those with Dark they had to re-double their efforts to locate the farm that was most likely putting the drug or altered tires with the drug in the Subaru. That was what was being requested of the VSP right away. The Colonel said nothing. He and the Captain stood and left the room. Others in the room nodded and left also.

Dark and the three troopers with him positioned their chairs so they could talk, face to face. Dark was notably less disappointed than Sergeant Abernathy. The Sergeant's suspicions about potential involvement of law enforcement on either side of the border left him worried. Dark, though, was pleased his quest was still on; officially sanctioned, he felt. But, immediately, he was in a tough spot.

There was a huge piece missing to help facilitate their investigation. Where was Jorge Gonzales when Dark needed him? As soon as they started talking Jorge Gonzales' absence would come up. Dark's tacit acceptance of his placement and now his disappearance in Puerto Rico was not going to look good.

As quickly and blandly as he could manage, the Lieutenant related the recent details about Gonzales, as he understood them. The take-away was obvious to everyone: Given the probable magnitude of this drug operation Jorge's sudden disappearance likely heralded his death; another homicide in a violent organization's effort to obscure any path to being tracked. With Emanuel Samuel's death, Gonzales's death in Puerto Rico, and who knows who else, personnel in the botched smuggling attempt in the forests of Vermont might all be gone. Logically, the controlling cartel, or whoever, could return to *work* assuming the situation rectified.

"Hey, Lieutenant," Abernathy spoke up reassuringly. "Coupla' days ago looked all the world like you were dealing with a marijuana mule who was in the wrong place at the wrong time. Keeping him locked up probably was never gonna fly anyway." He shifted in his chair. "And you were working with an NYPD detective who might have had a good chance of finding out if the kid had any useful contacts down in the City."

Why did everyone think he was working with an NYPD detective; or working with anyone in New York? Was there any point in explaining, over and over, that wasn't true? Dark quickly decided his imaginary link to the NYPD might be responsible for his continuing role on the case. Even sharing blame for what happened down there might be possible. But he knew he was the one who let events develop the way they did.

Bringing Gonzales out in the field again to the areas of suspicion was the next logical step…if he could be found alive. Absent that they all agreed they would have to go with the kid's sketchy original information; plus observation and suspicion. Haber and Abernathy were given Jorge Gonzales' statement and each sent to pick up an un-marked and spend the remainder of the day driving the roads of that region on the border looking for anything unusual. Lieutenants Kamp and Dark set up an afternoon meeting with a Narcotics Division support staff sergeant who had access to extensive aerial mapping photos from a CBP interdiction field project shared with the VSP several years before.

The best the Lieutenants thought they would be able to plan for was to pick four or five farms from a significant number on or near the border in that area and organize a large scale simultaneous raid. Hopefully one would pay off. Abernathy convinced the officers not to alert any local community police, although most of the areas being searched were so rural the VSP was the only enforcement. Time was important given the events of the last few days.

Lieutenants Dark and Kamp worked hard to use what little they had to plan a complex operation. Their goal was to begin the raids around dawn, no more than forty-eight hours from then. A mid-level emergency clearance was approved by the brass giving authorization to rapidly put four reinforced squads together with men and equipment. That would have to do. It wasn't great and the chances of total failure were considerable. But it would start and be over quickly. A State's Attorney was assigned and judicial access was being set up. Immigration violations would probably get information from those even only peripherally involved.

They quickly determined there were roughly twenty farms within the targeted region. Not having Jorge Gonzales to assist them and not having pushed Gonzales harder when he was in Vermont nagged at Dark as the afternoon passed. Gonzales had driven to the damn farm. Now it made no sense to the Lieutenant the kid didn't know exactly where the farm was. That was bullshit! He kicked himself for not realizing that trying to kill Gonzales suggested more than selling weed was going on.

Where did the lady fit in? Best explanation for taking the kid now looked like planning to meet up with those guys and kill the kid in the woods. Her place in all of this strongly hinted at her being part of the crime. But the story she told the kid and blood in the driver's seat didn't match up with that. Undercover? Certainly could be consistent with the level of the crimes they were now pursuing. How deep would someone have to be to stay that way despite all that was happening now? Her dog? Most likely hers. Would a criminal in deep trouble really try to come back for a dog? Ballsy.

Evidence found in a barn or outbuilding would be good but, more than anything, they needed participants or at least witnesses to the smuggling operation. Lower level players, even with limited knowledge of the scope of the enterprise would be able to direct the police to others; possibly across the border too. And Dark would be able to query about his mystery woman.

———

Disappointment about his handling of Gonzales hung over Dark as the afternoon progressed. He was pissed he hadn't taken some time to think things through when Wiley announced he was taking the kids out of the country. No, he had to remind himself, Puerto Rico is part of the US. Having recently spent extended time doubting himself and his career it was easy for Dark to blame himself for a major screw up. Though frustrated and fatigued he managed to find energy to include anger at Jim Wiley also. He felt Wiley shared in the unnecessary gap this problem brought to the case.

In the midst of a myriad of preparations, and mulling over the recent past, getting a call on his cell from Jim Wiley directly, not through dispatch, struck Dark as quite a coincidence. Any complaints or hostility from Wiley would not be appreciated during these next few days.

"Yes, Jim, What can I do for you?" As neutral as he could be, although it came out more formal than he wished; with an edge. He did not intend to mention what he was planning at that moment and, especially, the role each of them played leading to this difficult day for the VSP.

"Donald…Tried to reach you earlier but, for some reason, the call never went through. So I went ahead and I did what I thought I should. Hope you agree." Wiley's tone was earnest. Dark quickly concluded Jim had a story to tell. Neither spoke like old friends, but they didn't converse completely like professionals either. After a short pause and nothing from Dark Wiley continued.

"So Don, turns out Jorge Gonzales is alive. In fact I'm at LaGuardia right now waiting for a flight to Atlanta where I'm gonna meet an officer from the Puerto Rican State Police who is flying him to the mainland tonight. We'll stay at the airport when he arrives and fly to Burlington early in the morning. Nice of their state police to do that, huh?"

Dark was shocked. Instantly he began castigating himself again, this time for not thinking to contact Wiley or Puerto Rican authorities for follow-up as soon as the importance of the case had mushroomed a few days ago. Finding out what happened to Jorge Gonzales should have been a priority for Dark. Instead he had just assumed the worse. Dark's reaction threw him off in his response to Wiley.

"Alive? Really, that's something, Jim. Some news. Hadn't considered…" It didn't take long for Dark to pull himself together and begin to think about what this meant for the case. "Yes. Yes, we need Gonzales up here right away. As soon as he can be brought here." The Lieutenant's tone softened. "What happened to him in Puerto Rico? He must have run away and been picked up by the police, huh?"

"Not exactly Don. Actually the kid went to the police; kind of turned himself in. He says he was doing okay working on the farm; liked the people and the work. Somethin' for a city kid, huh? Then a guy, white fella, showed up in little town nearby asking about someone who sure sounded like Jorge. Fella offered cash for his whereabouts.

Real early next morning showed up at the farm. Scared the shit out of Jorge knowing someone was looking for him. Took what he could and lit out into the fields. Later in the day says he had a good idea he was being followed. Hid out for a day and today managed to stop a passing police vehicle. An hour later police called me with the number he gave them.

"So Don, there's a wrinkle here, right from the start; just so you know. The police, they think I'm a cop; NYPD. I didn't tell them otherwise. They got a guy bringing Jorge up. Guess that means they're paying for the trip. I'll get him up to you but can't say if anyone might get difficult if a bill or somethin' shows up somewhere sometime at NYPD. Kinda funny anyway, you know." He didn't sound concerned. Neither was Dark.

"Jim, up here, every time your name comes up, I have to tell everyone you're not NYPD anymore. They don't seem to buy it. Seem to like the idea of a link to the NYPD. So it's like they think I'm handling things up here and you're doing that in the City. I think we should just leave it that way. You still have contacts so it might be good, from time to time when you have a chance, to inform someone there about what's going on. I doubt the real story will ever come up but never know."

They quickly discussed transportation for his and Jorge's arrival in the morning. Dark wasn't sure what Wiley would do after Dark took custody of Gonzales. All he told Wiley on that call was an important plan was about to unfold and they were organizing to move on it very soon. Dark said he expected their effort was much more likely to be successful now that they would be able to work with the kid. Thoughts and plans were rushing into his head.

"But, you know, what about the girl, Laurinda, if some potential killer is doing tracking on that island?" The Lieutenant was pleased with himself that something like that pierced his mind. His brain was focusing again. He felt it was a sign he was regaining control. Disparate pieces were becoming manageable in his head again. It was a good feeling.

"I think Laurinda will be okay, Don. Bunch of iron workers and some cops in the family. A squad of them are already after the guy on other end of the island and there's apparently still plenty left to watch Laurinda. Proly still safer there than back in the City for now."

"Okay Jim, hope all goes well. Actually great to hear from you. I better go contact the troopers working with me. A bunch of plans just changed. Oh, and hey, if that guy after Gonzales shows up on your plane or is found on the island, getting him alive could be helpful. Gonna have to work from the bottom up on this one."

"Sure Don. And looking forward to any updates on that mystery woman of yours also."

Was he joking? Or just trying to be polite, or something like that? Dark wasn't sure. But bringing her up in the middle of all that was being talked about and planned seemed out of place to the Lieutenant. Kind of jolted him. He briefly wondered if she and the aura of her *spell* were fading, or less important to him. That also felt good to him. Except she *was* part of this case; not to be completely forgotten or ignored. Right now her trail still remained colder than what had been established about the carfentanil smuggling; and that trail was barely known.

Dark was getting excited. Maybe things would work out. It was late and he had to get home to Alice. He stayed as long as he could at the Barracks contacting the members of his team and support staff enlisted for the raids being planned, now in about thirty-six hours. He reached Kamp but not Haber or Abernathy. Probably still scouting the roads; in the dark now. He would locate and speak with each of them later.

Advising the Captain there might be a major change in plans was difficult for Dark. He thought it did not go well. Uncertainty about how the Captain was thinking about him recently seemed more apparent now after the Lieutenant was forced to explain, in some detail, more about Jorge Gonzales' brief sojourn in Puerto Rico. The need to alter the plans in the search for a farm again, when time was of the essence, bothered the Captain even though it was obvious better information and, hopefully, a more specific location might come with the Gonzales kid directly involved.

With a strategy that required hoping one of four farms would be the site they were seeking the Captain's desire to oversee a well-planned and *surgically* executed raid was shaky from its very inception. Yet, any further changes were all worrisome snags to him, challenging his reliance on the leaders of the effort, but mostly Lieutenant Dark. The large disposition of manpower and resources ultimately were the Captain's responsibility. A dead end raid would be costly in a hundred ways; repercussions long lasting. However, the Captain understood the seriousness and magnitude of what needed to be accomplished, along with the potential for substantial accolades for the VSP…and him, if their efforts were quick and successful.

———————

Tending to Alice was never really a problem. She was a house dog and managed her personal needs outdoors quickly and efficiently. Dark monitored her usual locations where she generally relieved herself, at the fringe of the woods, and made a mental note of where not to tread if he had to enter the forest again, as he had just days before. Given that recent strange episode with someone, probably *the lady*, Dark thought of Alice's accumulating poop somewhere out there almost as a barrier or potential early warning if it was stepped in. Of course perhaps less reliably noticed by a *stepee* in the coming frozen winter. Eventually, Dark knew he'd have to try to clean up as much of it as he could; shit patrol.

Alice was probably going to be easier to leave alone for an extended time than Busted. But he had no idea how the next twenty-four to forty-eight hours might go and a whole day was too long for her. He might wind-up in the field for most of it. He decided he needed to make some plans for Alice. Susan coming into his mind surprised him. He was disappointed he couldn't call her and ask if she would watch Alice for two days. Thinking of her was strange. Susan and Alice had no notable liking for each other, much less any real relationship. His parents were the logical dog-watchers.

He missed Susan. Something was different now. She had made it clear she wasn't going to miss him anymore. The excitement and tension of the evening became entangled with Dark's continuing thoughts of Susan and the likely end of whatever relationship they had. Being alone in his home, Alice his only companion, was discouraging and depressing, especially this night. It reminded him of his mood the last few months. He accepted his loneliness was mostly self-imposed. Sharing worries and concerns about the events of the last weeks with another person would be very different, he assumed.

Knowing he took Susan for granted for some years wasn't an entirely new thought for him. The intensity of their relationship seemed to have picked-up with the unfolding of recent events and time together. He thought about her. And he thought about the mysterious *Alice*. He decided it was probably best any vestige of a relationship with Susan be left as it was for now; at least until that woman was identified and explained.

He called his parents.

While packing things for Alice, who was clearly startled by early evening activity related to her, Sergeant Haber called. Later, just as he arrived back home after dropping Alice off, he heard from Sergeant Abernathy. One feature of their reports was very similar and interested him, in particular. Each had suspicions about one of the farms they had driven by. Not surprisingly those farms were located in isolated areas but both seemed to have a notable level of vehicle traffic while they were being watched by the troopers.

Possibly unusual this time of year when most farm activity, beyond tending to the animals, was already wound down for the winter.

Now that Jorge Gonzales would, hopefully, be with them tomorrow by noon the Lieutenant alerted Kamp, Haber, and Abernathy to be at Waterbury around one o'clock ready to discuss their surveillance and the pending plans. In addition to hearing from the kid that would include an effort at gaining any easily available information about those two farms. The Sergeants' suspicions could be harmlessly explained by friends coming to play cards or any other number of innocuous reasons so Dark decided not to have those properties monitored through the next thirty hours. Jorge Gonzales was their best hope for improving the chances of success of the operation.

He needed to get some rest but was keyed up. A great deal stressed him. Finding nothing would be a disaster. Arresting *foot soldiers* linked to the bigger crime would be very important and justify the effort. But was it too late? The smuggling operation might have been shutdown as soon as Jorge was caught.

And what on earth was the involvement of that woman? She was smart, appeared eminently capable, and, obviously, the myriad of emotions he read into her words and facial expressions continued to sustain his fixation on her. They had barely interacted personally. After that everything he knew about her left him with suspicions about her connection, in some way, to these crimes. And yet, it didn't exactly all fit. Just that hint of uncertainty seemed enough to make him believe he could continue to feel compelled to know her better.

Suppose she was trying to help Gonzales? Some form of law enforcement official? Still possible but becoming less and less likely. The brief look of sadness in her eyes was really all that stayed with him when he thought of her now. If Susan ever duplicated that look would that have made a difference in their relationship? Possibly... no, probably not. So much of *that* Alice was really only a product of his brain; an idealized image which conveniently showed up in the midst of a time ruled by his personal feelings of uncertainty and low spirits. He was slowly figuring that out.

Lying in bed, unable to sleep, for the first time in a long time he wondered how he could have let himself live a lonely life and even wind up in a career he recently wasn't so sure he believed in. Alone in the dark, without even his dog, Dark wrestled with accepting the idea that if this was what depression was then he must have it. A long time coming, he supposed.

The only positive in his life he could come up with at that instant was an unusual but very smart *yip-yip* dog. Really?

Oddly, his actually momentous self-realization that night led Dark to wonder if the events of the coming days were going to be significant in his life. Definitely odd. Eventually, he, restlessly, fell asleep for a few hours. On waking he knew he had confusing dreams; a nasty headache his only conscious remnant.

———

- 29 -

Farming in Vermont virtually always meant or included dairy farming; traditionally, small family ventures frequently passed down for generations. Success, defined by profit, often had little to do with the work ethic of the farmer. Hard work and long hours were a given. Variables like resourcefulness, skill, ingenuity all meant something, but generally only on the margins for income and any hopes for true financial security. Routinely, differences in standard of living were beyond a farmer's control. The price of their cows' milk was set for them, not by them.

National parameters determined milk pricing, often pitting family farms against large agribusiness operations. Banding together in co-ops may be saving many…for the moment. The farming lifecycle included bankers. Often a surprising number of the essential pieces of equipment in those tattered appearing old barns were up to date and remarkably expensive; a major source of a farmer's chronic debt. Whether only that, or usually also seed and fertilizer for fields in the spring that had to be paid for by winter, the banks, like an albatross (or perhaps a vulture parked on a fence), were an omnipresent unseen weight on the farmer.

Beyond the efforts and labor of un-salaried husband, wife, and children farm help was generally unaffordable. Documented and undocumented immigrants were required to meet basic daily operational needs. Long hours *every* day for poor pay eliminated even most Vermonters, a group with significant numbers of unskilled workers used to low wages. And so a culture had grown up around using very low wage Hispanic immigrants; many undocumented. The need was as essential as a bank loan if the farms were to function.

―――――――――

Morning dawned bright and unseasonably warm. The ground hadn't frozen consistently yet so, despite the warmth, there would be no early demonstration of mud season causing tires to sink into dirt roads or bounce from rut to rut. The temperature was almost a mirage anyway. By the time the rest of the working world caught up with early rising farmers and were on their way to their daily responsibilities a freezing wind swooped in from the west and the morning sky began to fill with thick, dark clouds dropping down closer and closer to the ground. Whether winter arrived in fits and starts or all at once ordinarily didn't matter to Vermonters. It was an inevitable, and therefore acceptable, part of the environment.

Precipitation, rain, sleet, or snow generally didn't bother the Lieutenant. Yet Lieutenant Dark watched this front come in with worry. The weather on the ground didn't trouble him, but any possibility Jorge Gonzales' and Jim Wiley's flight might be delayed, or even cancelled, would be a disaster, he thought. Plans were set and being readied to be carried out. Tomorrow, by mid-morning, this had to be over. Time was critical.

Possibly because he was nervous and anxious about so much he found himself, impatiently, watching the clock, waiting for when he knew he could call Ed Fleury. Williston Barracks was to pick up Jim Wiley and Gonzales at the airport as soon as they arrived and bring them to Waterbury. Confirming those details with Fleury was only a marginal reason for calling. Dark hoped passing a few minutes with their usual back and forth would break some of the building tension of the day. He was unable to admit to himself he was also lonely.

"Fleur, I know you're really busy over there this time of morning, but you know I don't give a damn. This weather's got me spooked. Yesterday changing so much for the raids now that the kid is coming back was a struggle. Captain's gonna send some of the squads after *me* if this doesn't work out, I think."

Fleury got it. "Yeah, imagine you convincing him to arrange to send somewhere up to sixteen troopers fishing for the morning… oops, I mean to clean out some barns around morning milking, DD. Oh, who knows, bet some of them are Vermont farm boys who really can help out with the cows…or at least shovel some of the cow patties out of the way and help clean things up. The community service should look good on your record.

"So you say making you a tad high strung, huh? Don' know why you're a bit wired pal. Odds of finding what you're after probably almost nil; wouldn't you say? Chances of failure so great what's the point of worrying? Sure, it's a decent plan with a shot. Maybe like going after a bear with a BB gun. Could work, I suppose."

Dark appreciated his effort but nothing, so far, lightened the air for him. After words like that actually a bit of dread joined his nervousness. Fleury continued. He knew he wasn't where he wanted to be on this to help his friend.

"Well, you know, DD, you and I been stressed with the responsibilities of command for a while now. Things don't go well next day or two, maybe be your chance to be relieved of the pressure for good. Then maybe you'll find more time to track Alice's owner and be able to chat about the pooch."

"Jeez Fleur, nothing funny about anything's come out of your mouth on any of this. All I said was now the weather's on the list of worries too."

That drew a quick response from Fleury. Dark had never heard it before. It was inane enough to break the tension, at least from Fleury's recent words.

"DD. Whether the weather is hot, whether the weather is not, whether the weather, whatever the weather, whether we like it or not… So said my grandpa… So, anyway DD, you and those boys try not to get hit on the head tomorrow, okay?"

"Fine Fleur. We won't lick any wrapper paper either. Just get those guys over here as soon as you can, please."

Not what he was hoping for but at least Fleury left Susan out of his brief recitation of Dark's problems.

———————

The flight turned out to be uneventful. The Lieutenant wondered if Wiley would be upset being brought to Waterbury, located in the middle of the state. Dark had never even asked him if he was planning to take the next flight back to the City. He thought they should talk in person, at least briefly, about what was going on and what Wiley might have gleaned from the kid on their short trip. Arriving at Waterbury Wiley was friendly and appeared to be a man in no hurry.

It may have been warm in Puerto Rico and Atlanta but around mid-November in Vermont it was not. Dark was surprised to hear Wiley had brought the winter coat Gonzales was wearing. A nice gesture. Wiley had a sweater under his ever-present suit coat. Might not be warm enough if he stayed around.

Gonzales was seated in a locked waiting area, in clear view of many people, especially Sergeant Haber. The kid looked like he did the time the Lieutenant saw him wounded, in the hospital. He was scared shitless, again. Wiley and the Lieutenant sat in Dark's small office.

"Had no idea I'd be back here so soon, or maybe ever, Don." There was a slight edge to his words. "We can go over all the shit happened with the kid, but bottom line is he's alive and here. Don't think he knew what he was transporting and never connected his handler's words about losing that Subaru with meaning anything beyond the expense of the car.

"But don't blame you, Don, if you don't completely trust him. He knows the places he dropped off his stuff and where he spent the night. Not sure why he played dumb. Just a feeling, but get an idea the way they got him to stay the overnight included some time with a woman; probably courtesy the assholes.

"Still wasn't easy for him to even hint at that with me. He's okay, and got some brains, but he's a fucked up kid; maybe gonna be in trouble forever, I guess. Made like a buddy with him. Even bought him a beer. I think he gets that it's over with Laurinda now so he was willing to talk some. And he knows the stakes are even higher now so I think he'll talk and do whatever you want him to. Maybe growing up a little."

A hint of a lessening of his tension drifted through Dark's body and it felt good. This was big news. It could have a major impact on the impending raids. If true, conceivably a way to eliminate so much of the uncertainty they were planning for. He would have to hear this from Gonzales but immediately he told Haber to get the word out to Kamp and Abernathy to be at Waterbury as soon as possible.

After he finished with the kid he might have to find the Captain, right away, to discuss the likelihood of another change of plans for the next morning. He also asked Haber to quickly find a large unmarked, something like a Chevy Suburban or Ford Expedition, in the event Dark decided some of them should make a fast trip up north later in the day. It was obvious, if Jorge was cooperative, a quick run close to the border might solve the critical question of which farm should be raided.

Jorge looked terrible. He was frightened and sat bolt upright in his chair, tapping his left foot rapidly on the ground, clearly anxious. "I had no idea, officer; no idea. They never told me any of that. Just weed, that's all I knew about." He looked around nervously. "Now they're gonna hunt me down till they kill me. Oh shit, what am I gonna do?"

Calming the kid down wasn't all that difficult. Telling him, logically he would no longer be of interest to anyone now that the word was out and those people were the ones being hunted, helped. That generally confirmed what Wiley had been telling him and reassured him. But Lieutenant Dark made it very clear to Gonzales his assistance now was his best chance for ever hoping to have a chance to return to a normal life. Any screw up would be disastrous for him. A deadly serious Jorge Gonzales nodded his understanding.

———

The Lieutenant was excited about all that Jorge's presence might add. He decided there was time and still enough light left in the day to make that quick dash with Jorge to scout for *the* property they would be after. Everything would make so much more sense if they were sure where they needed to go. Sergeant Haber was able to procure a big, old, black, unmarked Suburban for their trip. It looked beat up both inside and out, clearly getting close to the end of the line for its useful service life. It would have to do.

Lieutenants Dark and Kamp believed the hastily organized operation for the early morning should not be delayed. There were just too many arrangements in place to even consider an attempt at a reset at this late date. If the actual farm was identified all resources would be directed to that site. Four of the four person Tactical Service Unit teams, members of the Clandestine Laboratory Enforcement Team, plus support, all descending on a small farm at dawn would be quite a sight, that was for sure.

By the time they actually were on their way in the old SUV the day was getting late and Dark realized darkness could hinder his plan for the afternoon. He drove fast, concentrating on the road, while Haber, in the front passenger seat, did the navigating. It was awkward because Gonzales was sitting in the small third row, forced to shout back and forth with Haber since Wiley and Abernathy occupied the second row. When they all tumbled in the seating seemed to make sense but now they realized the shouting was annoying and added needless tension. Wiley was set to return to New York the next afternoon so, with the time frame planned for the operation, he asked to go along to observe the activity. Lieutenant Kamp opted out of the trip to attend to other details.

Even though they were on the road for almost an hour there was little talk. Their goal was clear, but they all worried about their task. If Gonzales wasn't able to positively ID a specific farm the entire trip would be for naught. The Lieutenant tried not to consider that possibility. After confirming the correct farm and quickly determining details about the location they would rush back to Waterbury to meet with the task force commander and team to determine the final details and plans for early the next morning. It would make a huge difference in accomplishing their goal. Dark felt the trip was very important but he remained unsettled because of his uncertainty about Gonzales' truthfulness and reliability. His worry distracted him. Failing now would not portend well for the original plan either.

They knew they were getting close to the likely area and Dark slowed down. The border wasn't far. Following Jorge's directions, turning from one winding dirt road onto a second one Haber commented to the Lieutenant he was sure this was the way he had traveled the day before. He suspected the property he made note of then could very well be where they were headed. Today he never said why.

A decided decline in intensity of sunlight gave early hints of pending twilight. The surrounding fields were flat but some rolling hills were visible, off a distance, away from the road. It was all brown now, just like the spot where Ed Clark was found. Wire fencing blocked off a great deal of the land. Infrequently, a farmhouse and barn came into view set back from the road.

"Lieutenant! Look up ahead!" It was a jolt to everybody and the silence. Suddenly, Jorge was shouting, leaning into the middle row, and pointing. "I remember that red truck… There! That's the place!"

Indeed, barely ahead up the road a red-cabbed flatbed truck with black deck and stake walls was pulling out of a long entrance road from a farm and into the road they were on. It turned south, in their direction. In no time the truck and the Suburban had to slow on the narrow road, finding just enough room for each to pass without one yielding.

Moments beyond passing Jorge screamed to the Lieutenant. "There she is! Sitting on the flatbed! It's her! She's got some kind of rifle!"

Dark slowed to a crawl and turned his head sharply as far as possible. He could see someone with a weapon. He had no idea if it was the lady they were calling Alice. Everyone in the vehicle had turned and was fixed on the truck, which was starting to pick up speed, heading south. There were more people on its flatbed.

The Lieutenant slammed the brakes. Dark had to quickly decide if he should turn around to try to catch up to that truck or keep to the plan for observation only for today. Fleetingly, he also considered driving into the farm immediately to check it out. His vehicle was stopped in the road..

Seemingly from out of nowhere, a sudden jarring impact along the right side of the Suburban made a deafening thud and crushing sound as the vehicle was practically raised from the ground for an instant. Everyone was shaken and glass sprayed throughout the cabin. Wiley shouted out in pain. Dark turned and saw him writhing in great discomfort. Abernathy was leaning over toward Wiley, his own face covered in blood. Then for some seconds it was strangely quiet in the car. But there was commotion outside.

Peering as best he could through a shattered window Dark could see a car. Doors were open and someone was trying to get out. It quickly became clear to him that when he slammed his brakes he was close to the middle of the entrance to the long driveway to that farm. A car coming from the farm, probably at decent speed, must have been coming up that driveway. It might as well have been a mid-air collision the way the two vehicles managed to find each other in that lonely spot, each with a reason to be there at that moment; neither at all aware of the other.

"Haber, call in all the emergency codes! We need immediate medical assistance and max back-up support!"

"Right."

Dark started to open his door so he could go around to Wiley's door and also find out what happened with the crash.

"Pop! Pop!.....Pop!"

The popping sounds of low caliber bullets thudded into the Suburban's right side. Dark slid out and down to his door well to stay low. "Haber! Call in shots fired!." Hearing no response or Haber's voice he looked across the seat. Haber's head was slumped against the passenger window, blood now further obscuring any visibility through the remnants of the shattered glass.

The Lieutenant kept his head at seat level and crawled across the floor to Haber's side and picked up the radio mic. Now *he* added a screaming "shots fired; trooper down!" to the final words from Haber's last communication. He pulled his weapon from his holster.

Dark immediately discarded any idea of attempting to drive away. Even if the vehicle was still operational emergency assistance would arrive long before he would be able to get to any meaningful medical support. Of course that was only if he had been heard. He knew they were in terrible trouble. Surprising words abruptly flashed in his head and remained persistent in his mind: 'Don't forget to reload.' He had two accessible clips beyond the one already loaded, meaning he had twenty-seven bullets. Haber's and Abernathy's weapons might be available if there was time to search for them.

The Lieutenant was sweating and getting a *déjà vu* feeling as he tried to slither out and around his door, hoping to get to the front to use the hood as a shield while he tried to take a measure of his apparent opponents this time. Dark was already well aware this confrontation was going to be more deadly.

Carefully raising his head he was astounded to see he recognized the vehicle that had broadsided them. It was the same green car from a few weeks before. Apparently it bounced off or was able to be driven about eight or ten feet away from the site of impact. Now it was most likely dead where it sat. All four doors were open. He assumed everyone inside was injured or planning to abandon it. Probably all armed.

Quickly out and standing by the front passenger door Dark saw the same young kid who, he remembered, had shot up his unmarked in the forest. The kid, with pistol raised, was apparently the one who had already started shooting in a flash.

Would there have been any point or a requirement for Lieutenant Dark, in such a situation, to identify himself at that moment as a Vermont State Trooper and demand that kid cease firing? And the others lay down any weapons…and lie down themselves, or put their hands high in the air, for good measure? That would be nuts. Men were dying. This thing had to be ended as quickly as possible. The kid's head barely moved and his eyes and Dark's eyes met. Any hesitancy was moot as the kid raised his weapon.

"POW! POW! POW!" As he fired Lieutenant Dark braced his elbows on the hood and aimed as he had been trained over many years. The kid went down.

Suddenly Dark heard the metal frame of the rear cargo doors of the Suburban bark open. Jorge Gonzales was bailing. Did that mean he was with these guys? Didn't seem possible. Probably running for his life… Hoping to anyway.

From the driver's side rear door of the green car a man emerged clearly handling an assault style weapon. Everyone was furious;

certainly those men, but the Lieutenant also. Instantly, Dark and others, who he felt were his responsibility, were in a completely disastrous situation. Everything was bad before there was even a chance for it to deteriorate further. Anything worse would signal the end of all of them.

Bullets were the apparent objects of choice for this close quarters battle. Dark wondered why those guys didn't try to disappear into the fields. He was in no position to go after anyone. Their anger seemed to make them oblivious to any implications of them being fired at. The radio was trying to hail him but there was nothing he could do about it. Even if support was on the way he felt he had no logical ability to stall any further shooting.

This was absolutely another desperate life and death situation. He recognized that and quickly determined it was either him, and those with him, or the murderous crew only a few feet away. If he went down there would be no further defense for the others. Preserving witnesses or participants in the carfentanil case never made it to his mind.

Apparently Gonzales made some progress after sliding out the back and crawling a short distance for his life. Then he made a mistake and stood up when he thought he was far enough away to begin running. The man with the assault weapon turned toward him. The guy stepped beyond his door as he leveled the weapon and pointed it at Gonzales. Foolish.

Those remaining in the car didn't work to use their advantage in numbers and were staying in the vehicle for the moment. The guy outside aiming at Jorge had put himself in the open. Dark simply braced himself again and fired four more rapid shots. The man went down. As he collapsed his weapon managed to fly from his hands, a strange sight, landing in bushes just off the dirt driveway. Then it was quiet.

Dark still had rounds in his first clip but he kept remembering that phrase: 'Don't forget to reload.' So he exchanged clips. He wasn't really certain what would happen next. If there was a chance of a lull he considered trying to quickly check on Haber, Wiley, and Abernathy. Or should he go on the offensive? The calculus hadn't changed enough to hope to wait for back-up. Assistance to the wounded and risk for more potential casualties troubled him.

There were at least two more in that car. Catching his breath for a moment now he recalled a goal of the operation planned for the morning: Arresting one or both of the men still in the car would accomplish a major component of one of the hoped for goals of the raid; someone who could provide information about the people and organization doing the smuggling.

With the apparent pause he decided to quickly go ahead and try to announce who he was and demand those men surrender. He felt he had to try. Before he could shout at them loud, rapid gunfire erupted in a staccato pattern from the side of the road. It was Jorge Gonzales, holding the automatic weapon like a tommy-gun, shooting wildly. The Lieutenant no longer had to guess if it was a truly automatic rifle. Bullets were whizzing everywhere, but mostly hitting the green car. The driver fell out of the car…motionless.

The, hopefully, last person in the car, in the right rear, jumped out. The man was close enough to Dark the terror and anger in his eyes and face were visible. Dark hollered he was Vermont State Police and told him to freeze, drop his weapon, and raise his "fucking" arms. The Lieutenant attracted his attention, but instead of complying the idiot raised his own pistol, readying it to fire at the Lieutenant. By now Dark trusted his aim and had the range down. He hoped to hit a non-vital region but three bullets almost guaranteed one would be fatal. And one was.

Jorge Gonzales emerged from the edge of the bushes holding the automatic rifle at his hip, looking like a seasoned soldier. He walked carefully up to the shot up green car, apparently planning to inspect for any remaining passengers; dead or alive.

Was it over? Everything was quiet. No lights were visible around the area and the road remained deserted. It was cold, windy, and virtually dark now, but Donald Dark was still sweating. Unsure about what exactly just happened he certainly didn't know why. What felt to the Lieutenant like an hour lasted only minutes. Despite the cold wind he thought he could still smell gunpowder.

He walked slowly toward Jorge, reaching his arm out for his weapon. Jorge was motionless, staring at the scene. He was crying.

"You can give me that now, Jorge."

———

- 31 -

In the time of the *old west* local press would have come up with
a name for that shoot-out. In contemporary Vermont, and even
in the national news, that brief, bloody battle near the border did
attract notable attention. The 'straight shooting' young Vermont
State Trooper who, almost singlehandedly, very likely saved himself
and all but one of those travelling with him was a natural hero for
the media. The malignant criminal histories of the four dead men
could only be imagined. The young man of Hispanic origin who
also had an active role in the incident was treated almost as an
afterthought by the media.

In fact, Lieutenant Dark was further praised for his foresight in
bringing the young man along so he could translate if anyone at
the farm they were seeking could not speak English. And that did
happen. Into the night, emergency support of every conceivable
type arrived and parked up the dark, isolated road while police
vehicles, exclusively, swarmed the actual farm. No one beyond
the state police knew the firefight was completely unexpected,
occurring during informal reconnoitering a day before a planned
raid.

Unfortunately, Haber was dead when support arrived, just like
the four men arrayed on the ground around their vehicle. Jim

Wiley was obviously critically injured from the crash. His pallor and limited alertness suggested he might be bleeding internally. He was awake, barely, but could not move. The Lieutenant quickly rummaged around in the rear cargo area in the back of the Suburban and placed a blanket he found over Wiley. He gave a towel that was also there to Abernathy to hold over his bloody right eye. It looked like his bleeding had stopped. Abernathy kept his pain and that he could not see from that eye to himself. Sergeant Abernathy was sitting, stoically, quietly in his seat when help arrived.

Despite the darkness and somewhat uncertain terrain for a night landing a medivac helicopter was able to touch down. One of their team stayed behind so there was room for the Sergeant to return with Wiley to the hospital in Burlington.

Jorge's presence was invaluable again when troopers who carefully occupied the farmhouse and barn called for someone who could translate Spanish. During their search of the property troopers found a body on the steps of the main house and a presumed illegal was alive, hiding in the barn. That young man was terrified and looked like he was almost in shock. Jorge's arrival barely reassured him. He had seen Jorge before.

The story he related to Jorge was terrifying. While he was speaking Jorge interrupted him and pleaded with the troopers to have the Lieutenant brought over to hear what the young man was saying. When he arrived Dark appeared distracted himself, as though he wasn't going to be able to fully concentrate. It was all he could do to listen while images from what he was calling *"the ambush"* continually flooded his mind. Initially quite a struggle for him.

"Officer, it was her; I really think it was."

Over the hour or two that passed after the red cabbed truck and the unmarked slowly moved by each other Donald Dark had given no thought to the woman with a rifle in the back of the truck. In fact, even with its major implications for what had been occupying much of his brain for the last few weeks, he forgot about it. Less of a surprise, but neither, throughout the shooting, had he given a thought to his other preoccupation: his fear of the futility of the life and death risks generated by drugs in his dangerous job. That fixation, which had been so prominent in his mind for a few months, had been fading fast with recent events.

Jorge acknowledged the man sitting in front of him. "Officer, Felix says a tall, slim, Anglo woman walked down the road to the bunkhouse where the workers stay and then to the farmhouse. She was dressed all in black, with a black beret on her head, he says. And she was carrying a long rifle."

Dark was not feeling sharp but an image of Patty Hearst flashed in his head.

"She rushed everybody outside and, in Spanish, told them they had to leave immediately. She said some men would be coming soon to kill all of them. Pointing to the truck, Manuel ran for it and drove it over for everyone to jump on the back."

Jorge seemed to know the questions to ask so Dark and the other troopers just listened to the cadence of his queries in Spanish and translation of the man's animated responses.

"Felix says he drifted away from the others and ran to the side of a small shed attached to the barn. He says he doesn't trust anyone so he was afraid the lady would take them to authorities who would arrest and deport them. He says the farm man came out of the house but when she yelled for him to come he refused. Felix says the man shouted to all of them, in Spanish, he would not leave the herd and he would be okay."

Felix pointed to a body laying on its back, arms and legs oddly extended, straddling several steps on the porch of the house.

"When the men came Felix says he was able to climb to the second floor in the barn where he hoped he would not be found. He could see a man in the green car get out and go up to the farmer. They yelled at each other but he could not know what they were saying. Suddenly, the man from the car, he sounds like the first one you shot Lieutenant, showed a pistol and shot the farmer two times. Then they left, driving fast, heading to the main road."

Donald Dark did not like the way Jorge felt the need to tell him about the killer of the farmer, reminding him that he, Dark, then killed that man. He was sick about everything that had taken place. He fought hard to keep himself together and stay clear about what was happening. Something wasn't right with Felix's story, but what? Unusual for him, Dark talked about it out loud.

"That can't be right, Jorge. Tell Felix something is wrong with what he's telling you. That green car came up the long entrance fast and they were obviously hoping to catch the red truck. They would have caught up to the truck a short distance after the driveway, or down the road." He pointed with a sweep of his arms to demonstrate the direction to the road. "First the green car had to come down that road before, to get to the farm. Something's not right." He looked to the other troopers. "I don't know if we can trust what he's saying."

The expression on Felix's face while Jorge was explaining the Lieutenant's concern showed he understood. "Lieutenant, Felix says there is another way to the farm; over behind the barn. Only a few people know about it. Felix says it's only used by some Anglos who also worked with the farmer sometimes."

By then it was too dark to see anything around the corner of the barn. Shortly, worried about the possibility of some type of activity at the other end of whatever road was there, two heavily armed Tactical team troopers with night vision gear appeared and headed off, slowly, on ATVs to investigate. It was another entrance.

Before they had gone too far those troopers radioed finding a sizable, isolated shed that, when inspected by other troopers, obviously was serving as a garage for the exchange of tires used for smuggling. As of dawn the next day no materials for a drug lab had been found on the farm.

The search for the source of carfentanil in Vermont was over before it officially began.

- 32 -

In a time when so much bad news, especially about drugs, was never-ending, this event near the border had all the earmarks of an interdiction. Other than the police no one knew for sure what had prompted the shootings but it was easy for the media to paint what they did know as one small victory ("possibly very significant") in a never-ending war. Even just knowing the war was being waged actively meant a lot to many people. The man who "was on the ground" and risked his life leading this skirmish was a man worthy of great praise; a symbol of who was needed to work toward the safety of the citizenry; to fight this terrible scourge.

The popular side of this story gained momentum over several days as VSP public information officers offered small bits of information to the public. Without specifying what drug was involved or the nature of the event, it was confirmed that the Vermont State Police, undertaking a major operation, was responsible for making a large dent in the spread of a key deadly drug, part of the rise in the *lethality* of this national crisis.

One reason the police decided, early on, to make such a statement was to quell an instantaneously developing negative public reaction to a fatal gun fight over, presumably, marijuana; well known to be sold to workers at many farms. The average Vermonter had little quarrel with use of weed and would be unlikely to support such a deadly police action to interdict it's sale. Somewhat mysteriously referring to a much greater danger ensured Lieutenant Donald Dark's fame as a trooper battling the worst of the worst; on the front lines, "in the trenches." For this he was widely celebrated for performing his duty, successfully, under tremendous stress and danger.

The days following that incident were troubling and difficult for Lieutenant Donald Dark; almost as problematic as his recent fixation on that woman and his uncertainty about the underpinnings of his career. His sudden rise to unwelcome notoriety elevated the true drama and major impact of the episode for him beyond anything he could ever have imagined. How could he be considered a hero when the men with him suffered terribly? In his own mind he could not escape his great upset about Sergeant Haber, Jim Wiley, and Sergeant Abernathy. How could he have let this happen?

Repeatedly, he admonished himself for being blinded by his quest to know more about that woman or find her, without truly measuring the danger of that effort. The cost for what was accomplished severely tested his more recent acceptance that winning a battle in this war was worth its risks. He had no sense either that the day offered anything more tangible about that woman…except this time there might be reason to think she was not a criminal. He could not make certain sense of her actions.

Once the crash happened, his own actions were directed by his training. There really was no time to second guess much. This time, just as weeks before lying behind a tree on the forest floor, he knew his active engagement would be required if there were shooters and anyone was going to survive. And that's what he did. He was angry at the men he killed. He felt no pleasure or satisfaction in their deaths.

Through it all an undercurrent that ran through his mind afterwards and for some time was his uncertainty: what was he doing there in that situation? How did his life get him to that point? Life and death moments and challenges were coming regularly recently; or so it seemed to Dark. Tough as they were he vacillated a little but mostly was convinced he did what he had to do in those impossible settings once he was in the middle of them.

That first night, before the story and his name were known, Dark went home to his empty condo. Being alone was not great. Alone his mind continually re-hashed the day and, now again, the thoughts he had been living with for weeks. He was exhausted but at first found it difficult to rest or sleep. A recurring image of Susan upset him; another testament to his loneliness. This was a night he probably would have been conversant with Alice but it was too late to stop at his parent's house to pick her up. He had no appetite for speaking with them right now.

He called the hospital one last time and after being assured of the stability of both Wiley and Abernathy got into bed. When he awakened five hours later he was amazed he had fallen right to sleep.

Waking very early in the morning he found himself in a dialog in his mind with Ed Fleury. He was sure he and Ed would agree there was no way for Ed to begin to spin any of what happened to help relax or, certainly, pick on him. But Dark told himself, and believed it, that Fleury was with him in spirit, as strong a supporter as ever. Dark wondered how Susan would react to what happened. He had no idea at that early hour that a society that needs to have heroes was about to enshrine him, at least for a while.

And for the first time since the unfolding of the events of that afternoon he thought about the woman. What was she doing there? Who the hell was she? And then a completely new thought, never before acceptable to his brain, became clear to him. Whoever she was, the things she was doing strongly suggested she was nothing like the image and personality he had insistently created for her. Possibly a remarkable person. Maybe crazy. But, either way, greatly mis-read by Dark.

Little before six he lay in bed, awake, feeling adequately rested. His mind was still a jumble, dizzy from all the events of the day before. On his night table next to him his cell chimed. A text from Edmund Fleury:

So DD, what you been doing with yourself lately? Anything interesting going on?

Dark was wrong. Fleury would try to make lemonade from virtually anything. It was harmless and meant he was thinking about him. Dark smiled and got out of bed to begin his day. It was a terrible time to be alone. Completing his usual chores for Alice would have been nice. He thought spending time at his breakfast table talking with Susan would be even better.

He didn't call the hospital because as soon as he showered and dressed he planned to head there. At the sight of the shooting the Captain asked him for his weapon and told Dark he was on administrative leave while the entire episode was reviewed by the force; standard procedure, and with full pay.

He didn't have to but the Captain indicated to Dark that, with all that happened, the investigation was going to be complicated and Dark might be off duty for some time. The Captain advised him to be patient, try to relax and even try to enjoy the time off. All he asked was for Dark to check in from time to time so interviews and meetings could be arranged as the investigation progressed. The Lieutenant wondered if the Captain's words meant his recent mood and preoccupation with that woman could possibly be part of what he called 'complicated.'

Initially Dark was pleased his sole focus for the time being would be the health of Jim Wiley and Jason Abernathy. Both were seriously injured and recovery would require a protracted period of time. Abernathy's right eye was probably gone. Wiley sustained direct blunt force trauma from the crash, lacerating his liver and fracturing structures in his right hip.

It all happened so fast. Afterwards he thought the event was so sudden there was no other way to have managed any of it. If the injured men or the force placed any blame on Dark it would have to be because *his reading* of events from the time of Gonzales' arrest was the main impetus for the entire operation. Were his motivations purely a reflection of his detective work? Not completely. Dark felt that way, anyway.

Was it an appropriate and well planned action? Had necessary contingencies been anticipated and potential responses structured? Of course not. Dark certainly never thought beyond how helpful finding the farmhouse would be. Should the potential of an ambush have been considered? Vicious, brutal people were on the other side and he knew that. Had he let his guard down? He was fine physically; untouched. Haber was dead and the men in the hospital were seriously maimed. Survivor's guilt, especially given the Lieutenant's recent fragile psyche, would stay with him a long time.

When he was able to remove himself from the emotional component of his reaction to the episode he thought not only about why that lady was there but what impact everyone showing up at the same time might have had. Knowing her *true* story, of course, would help significantly. Obviously, word would eventually get back to whoever was controlling the illicit operation. What that group might know about the woman could greatly affect the impact of their being told she and the state police were at the same place at almost the same time. Dark guessed a lot of people might have been angry that day for a bunch of different reasons. Who knows?

Days later, Ed Fleury told Dark how impressed he and others were with the way he was managing the natural strain from the after action investigations and public acclaim. A surprise to Dark.

———————

- 33 -

Jim Wiley was alive and the Lieutenant was told the doctors
expected him to recover. As he strode down the hallway to the ICU
in his civilian clothes Dark had all his ID's in his hand in case he
was challenged while he was walking. He knew he'd need them
to get in to see Jim despite normal ICU restrictions. None of that
turned out to be a problem, but Donald Dark remained anxious his
entire trip to the unit. He wasn't at all sure how Wiley would look
and he had no idea how the man was reacting to what happened to
him. Wiley was clearly unlucky to have been seriously injured on a
mission that was in no way required of him.

Propped up in bed, a plastic tube in one nostril was draining dark
green material to a suction machine tethered to the wall. With
Oxygen tubing, IV lines, and heart monitoring electrodes as well,
Wiley projected an image of a man requiring intensive care. Some
apparatus expanding and deflating under a blanket, presumably
where his calves were, completed the visual picture of a very sick,
and highly restricted man. He was awake. Wiley offered a wan
smile when he saw Dark talk his way into his cubicle. He was
glad to see a friendly face. The timbre of his voice reassured the
Lieutenant.

"Don, good to see you. You look okay. Are you? Ya know it all happened so suddenly and I was mostly out from the start. The racket from that fuckin' helicopter sure woke me up, though. What the hell happened, Don?"

Wiley didn't know much about how he wound up in his present condition. Despite his appearance Dark felt he was clear enough to be told as much as he wanted. So he offered Wiley a detailed account of much of what was repeating over and over in Dark's head the past twelve hours. Wiley seemed interested but asked few questions, mostly only about Sergeants Haber and Abernathy. The Lieutenant felt he should apologize to the man because of the unfortunate turn of events. He started to say something that included "sorry." Wiley lifted his free arm and waved him off.

"Let's not talk about any of that today, okay?"

Dark was okay with that but an awkwardness remained. There clearly was a lot on Wiley's mind, beyond changing the subject.

"Who can figure out that kid, Jorge, huh? Guess that's why they say you can't really have wars without nineteen and twenty year old's; kids like him. Only ones willing to take those kinds of risks, huh? But listen, Don, I talked with my docs and also Idelia, my wife, before you got here. Gonna be okay, I think, but sounds like gonna take some time. Idelia says she's gonna come up today and stay till I get out of here. Told her that may not be a great idea but she won't listen. Laurinda's mother is moving in to watch the kids. Don, I can't begin to figure anything out up here. Can you help her? I'd really appreciate it if you can."

Dark sat back in his chair. "Jim, I'm on leave while all this gets investigated. I'm glad you asked me about this right away. I need things to do to occupy my mind while this goes on. I'll talk with the docs and hospital people and I'll get your wife to you and help her through this with you. We'll get you home as soon as possible."

Thanks, Don… And Don, please try to remember Puerto Rico is part of the USA. Might not be good for Idelia to think you didn't know; Okay?"

———

The task Jim Wiley set out for Dark was in no way simple. Settling his wife in Burlington, open ended, was a challenge, and getting him back to New York City became a bigger challenge. Even if Wiley's recovery went well his medical issues would limit his ability to travel and require prolonged impaired mobility. Doctors told the Lieutenant Wiley's hip and femur repairs meant he could not bear weight on that leg for at least four weeks.

That meant he needed to be on anti-coagulants to prevent blood clotting from his immobility. The doctors were worried that the blood thinners were a theoretical risk for more bleeding from his just repaired lacerated liver. In sum, they said once the need for acute hospitalization was over Wiley would require time in a rehab unit in Burlington for four to six weeks to be supported and monitored and, over time with therapy, resume independent ambulation.

How could Dark begin to tell this to Wiley, or his wife? ...He decided he wouldn't tell Wiley right away. He went to another ward to see Abernathy, but the Sergeant was leaving for a test and the Lieutenant only had a chance to tell him to "hang in" and he'd plan to come back later. So Dark immediately threw himself into organizing as much support as he could for Wiley and his wife. The tasks weren't easy and were very time consuming, which was the best part for Dark.

First he worked with social service at the hospital and community liaison from the force to set up assistance for Idelia when she arrived. He asked Molly Fleury to arrange to meet with her and take her to dinner, if she could. Then it got really complicated. Dark knew the best solution to a bad situation for the Wileys was to get Jim close to his home as soon as possible while he rehabbed.

Wiley retired with a disability pension and his ties to the NYPD remained strong. His insurance was the same as an active duty policeman. So Dark worked with a thousand names he was referred to over several days. His ear hurt from pressing the phone handle hard to his ear so he could understand all kinds of accents. There was a good level of cooperation and support and he thought rehabilitation in New York instead of Vermont was going to be doable. Dark determined to find a way for him to drive the Wileys from Vermont to a facility near them in the City.

During this intensive effort the Lieutenant was also being interviewed and debriefed by administration in the force. He met with, among others, Internal Affairs, Safety, and also was required to see a mental health provider since there was a shooting with deaths. The Psychologist irritated Dark by only asking questions; barely making any comments. Once the man said something like "well everyone has doubts" and that was about it. The Lieutenant answered his queries about the violence reliably, but wasn't completely truthful about his feelings concerning his career and personal adjustment.

The Captain said it all would take some time. The final step would require the Lieutenant to meet with several of the top brass after they received all the reports. Especially from the Captain, but also along the way during most of the sessions, Dark was strongly advised to avoid the media and let Public Information, from the force, handle that. The Lieutenant strongly agreed. His name was out there and anyone he came in contact with who knew who he was was annoyingly flattering. His parents were higher than a kite and only very unhappily honored his insistence they stay quiet.

Then, once more, it got complicated and, in an instant, all the carefully and laboriously organized plans for Jim Wiley were up in the air. The docs weren't sure it was safe for Jim to travel in a car for the six or more hours it would take to get to the City. Another two days on the phone, with completely different people, led to the solution. The New York State Police arranged for New York State Air Ambulance transport to send a plane from Albany to Burlington and then New York. It turned out the NY State Trooper, Regardi, who was a captain when Wiley and Dark briefly interacted with him in the case seven years before, was now a major and he made it happen. Amazing.

Dark rushed to the hospital later in the afternoon to tell Wiley and his wife what had been worked out. Rather than wait for the elevator he took the steps in the stairwell, two at a time, and then strode, briskly, to the room. He barely paused to knock at the partially closed door and walked in. He could hear light, friendly conversation, even some laughing, as he essentially burst in with his intention to deliver good news. Instantly, he was knocked off his game. Besides Jim and his wife there were two other people there.

Molly was sitting in the room and Susan was with her.

––––––––

Susan may have had an idea he might show up but it's highly unlikely such a thought had occurred to Dark. Caught off guard he looked awkward and stammered as tried to tell his story. Everyone else in the room seemed relaxed but Susan's presence flustered him. She had been in his thoughts and he wished they still shared enough of a relationship for him to have spoken with her during this period. Dark missed her and standing there felt her loss acutely.

He was no longer as spellbound by that mystery woman, but the woman continued to puzzle him and he was far from thinking he could just forget her; certainly not what on earth her role was in all that had happened. But seeing Susan, and the minutes he stayed in the room, generated a warmth he longed for and would never associate with that lady. Susan's support and being close to her flooded his mind and was all he could think about. Had he lost her forever?

Tall and thin, with remnants of an adolescent's gangly features, Donald Dark stood in the middle of the room, dwarfing the others who were all sitting in chairs, including Wiley. He could not have felt in a more unwanted spotlight. Susan got up, walked to him, and hugged him modestly, like any old concerned friend would. She told him she was very glad he was all right. Then she sat again. He had no idea what to make of that. He quickly decided there might be a reason to hope. He was far from sure, though.

Dark was so focused on his reaction to seeing Susan he was uncomfortable staying in the room after he delivered his news. Later, after that chance meeting, Dark called Susan twice but she never responded to his messages. He saw her again, a few days later, at a small gathering in a hospital meeting room for a kind of celebration of the Wiley's pending flight back to New York the following morning.

Dark and Wiley never did have any serious discussion about that terrible day in the Suburban. There was every indication they were parting as friends, though. Probably the most striking talk at their last meeting in Vermont was about Jorge Gonzales, who was in the room also.

Gonzales' misdemeanor case in Vermont was, effectively, dropped. He, too, was returning to the City. There was a plan for him to become a sort of gofer for Wiley and his business during Wiley's period of acute immobility. It turned out Jorge learned to take direction well and developed a notable intensity about his work that impressed Wiley and his associates.

That late afternoon Susan and Donald said scarcely more than hello to each other. The Lieutenant, again, assumed he was more uncomfortable in the room than anyone else. Staff and others, including Susan, had developed a friendship from their efforts to support Idelia and Jim Wiley. Dark couldn't shake feeling he remained almost an outsider there. He decided it was because Susan had moved on from him. It forced him to try to come to terms with something he had never truly considered would happen.

––––––––––

Dark requested and received permission to go for three days to visit his sister and her family in Massachusetts. He wanted to try to break a cycle, recognizing he was feeling low again. He hoped that also would aid his effort to avoid or at least minimize his sudden, unwanted fame which, truly, only disconcerted him. He took Alice with him.

The visit was a revelation. Dark was dismayed to realize he knew Ed Fleury's kids better than his own young niece and nephew. He teased Fleury about his *nuclear family* but realized he had never given much thought to what that meant, or could mean. It wasn't that Dark also felt like a total outlier in his own family. No, they all got along well. It was an observation, though, that repeatedly hammered at him during the time he spent with them.

His sister, Mary, and his brother-in-law, Joe, gave every indication of being devoted to each other. More than that though, Dark saw their life with their kids energized and pleased them. Being a family was so important and satisfying to them. The interplay among them fascinated him as kids and parents constantly struggled to make sense of each other.

Their small suburban house was toasty warm in the November chill. It was an environment he thought most anyone would want to come home to. It set his brain off. What had he been doing?

Anyone who has raised a family knows significant challenges and difficulties are unavoidable and may seem endless for years. Dark's idealized perception of his sister's family served his need at that time as he struggled with his confusion about so many things. Neither Mary or Joe queried him about the headlines his mother insisted on calling them about. The kids were five and seven so it was obvious to all the less they knew the better.

He took a long walk with Joe, the brother-in-law he knew only from a few regular holiday visits, and they talked about everything but police work. Like with a doctor, so often people tend to constantly want to question professionals with important, challenging jobs about their work. In social settings the general public certainly frequently steer discussions with state troopers to the dramas inherent in policing. Dark had been okay with that for a long time, but not lately.

They talked about Joe's job as a businessman. But mostly it was Donald Dark who peppered his brother-in-law with questions about the kids and raising a family. It was clear to Joe that Dark, ever so subtly, was also asking him about dynamics of being married and the impact of kids on a marriage. It gave Mary and Joe quite a lot to talk about after Donald left.

Dark wanted to believe he felt like a fool. He had been dealing with his uncertainty and confusion long enough though to know nothing was going to quickly banish what was going on in his head. And besides, by his age inertia and the challenges of change often appeared to limit an adult's ability to alter the trajectory of a life or a career path.

Alice was a hit with the kids and played her role as a friendly dog very well. The trip down, and especially on the ride back, Dark worried he projected a relationship between a man and his dog that highlighted his attachment to Alice, and his loneliness. On the return trip Alice migrated from the back seat to shotgun. She seemed quite comfortable there. Her ear motions looked to Dark to be an uncanny reflection of the discourse going on in his own mind. Was this all there was going to be for him?

Driving back to Vermont Dark definitely was not surprised to find himself brooding about many things. He remembered Jim Wiley was making a good living using skills he learned and honed as a policeman, but now in a non-violent setting …And then he thought some more about his sister and her family. That nuclear family of hers was missing only one thing…a dog.

When he returned and checked in with headquarters there was word the Captain wanted him to connect with Sergeant Abernathy and meet with an officer at the Northeast Customs and Border Protection (CBP) Regional Headquarters near Massena, in Upstate New York. It was a long day trip. Interestingly, Massena was also no more than a few miles from the Akwesasne Reservation, famous to Lieutenant Dark as the presumed origin of the letter sent to him by *the lady.*

———————

- 34 -

"Well, you never talked to me. Who knows how much of that bloodbath might have been avoided, Lieutenant?"

Captain Harold Magee, CBP Chief Intelligence Officer for the Northeastern border region, had a firm frown that wasn't going anywhere while he talked with Donald Dark and Jason Abernathy. Lieutenant Dark had just briefed the Captain about his VSP activity from the time of Trooper Clark's homicide to portions of the shoot-out and after.

"Granted, there are some pieces you figured out that we hadn't completely put together yet, but really Lieutenant, what the fuck do you think we do here? You know, we work closely with the Canadians, too.

"We sure know more than you do about that lady you're talking about. She's the worse kind of *good guy* there is: a vigilante. People who take the law into their own hands are generally a lawman's worse nightmare. You know that. You want to know her story, why didn't you ask me?"

In addition to his anger the Captain's manner readily displayed his disappointment. It was quickly obvious to the troopers this man was trying, very hard, to do his job. In this case he was filled with knowledge about narcotics smuggling that the Vermont troopers knew nothing about. He didn't label their effort amateur, but he was angry they had never informed his division.

"Believe lady's real name is English; Lori English. Grew up on a border farm here in Upstate New York, close to the Mohawk Akwesasne Res down the road. A few years ago her father got involved with guys bringing drugs across, maybe fentanyl by then. Have no idea if parents were willing or unwilling parts of that. Daughter was living in Syracuse an probably had nothing to do with any of it…but who knows for sure.

"Parents were murdered and my guess is she and, maybe, a brother came back to the farm, hired some folks to run it, and made it seem like they were gonna try to make a go of it… Small family farm? Make a life and some money there? Shit! Those days are long over." His ironic words and tone suggested he had personal knowledge on that topic.

"Think it's clear now that was all just a front to be close to border smuggling and seek out the parent's killers. But this lady had bigger ideas also, I guess. She started looking for the bigger players; just like we are. So she was seen from time to time at the Res. Indians there move back and forth like there is no border. Anyway, that Res is actually on both sides of the border, you know. Word is she got an Indian boyfriend and he and a few others were game to shake up some of the local cartel bigshots. Revenge most likely, but you never know, always a chance, slim we think, her plan's been to put them out of business so she could do the same thing.

"Crazy, but smart. They have really put some fear into the head honchos; not only by killing some of them, but by destroying their merchandise. Those fuckers managed to blow up most of a small container ship on the Seaway as it was getting close to Montreal. Jesus, even though the actual size of shit, we assume carfentanil, being brought in wasn't enough to fill anywhere near a tenth of a single small shipping container, blew up half the ship! And then, about six weeks ago a place and some people in the woods in

Sherbrooke, close to the Vermont border, were blown to kingdom come. Probably some kinda lab. We thought that would put the cartel out of business for a while.

"Guess not. Your story means stuff may be continuing to get to someone who still has a setup for getting it across the border. I doubt there's anyone those fuckers running the cartel want dead more than her and whoever's left with her.

"So maybe she's left the cover of the Indians and is looking for the latest source for this shit." For the first time his face showed a hint of some emotion. "She must really be something. Imagine her messing with state police that way. Showing up one day pretending to be a lawyer and the next day not even acknowledging that or that she cut that really long hair that she used to confuse people about being an Indian. Course doing that could mean she's in trouble too."

Dark's head kept drooping down farther as he listened. The story he was being told certainly was complicated, but his own endlessly recurring take on what her story might have been could not have seemed anymore naïve or childish now no matter how he might try to spin it. This woman was living a life of intense focus and constant, unbelievable danger. She was extremely organized and committed to a goal. Whatever she once was she had morphed into a hardened killer herself, apparently remaining committed to wiping cartel resources and personnel from the map.

Probably not a lady who would be interested in a leisurely jog followed by dinner and a movie on cable TV. In fifty ways he was out of her league. Their very brief moment sharing frustration likely was an expression of a valid part of each of their personalities. But so what? People wind up traveling in different worlds and that's just the way it's going to be. Fixations, or obsessions, have more to do with the psyche of the 'obsessor' than any likely reality.

Searching for happiness or fulfilment in a self-created fantasy? Even if Dark and this woman did actually share something the countless levels of distance between them could never be plausibly penetrated for any happy solution. Dark should have known this. Of course, he probably did know it even as he wished otherwise. Someday this woman was going to end up dead or in prison; that was it.

They all sat quietly for a few moments. After hearing all the Captain said Dark's words startled both the Captain and Sergeant.

"Captain, I have this woman's dog. I think she wants it back. Any suggestions?"

"There's a tavern and grill near here, Lieutenant. Why don't we go over there; maybe get a bite and a beer. Long trip back."

Jason Abernathy hadn't said more than two words during the meeting with the Captain. It was logical for him to be there with the Lieutenant but there was something about him that put Dark on guard.

They travelled in Dark's cruiser but neither was in uniform; Abernathy maybe never again. The Lieutenant was still on leave. When Dark picked him up at the Williston Barracks both Dark and Ed Fleury noted the Sergeant was dressed less than casual as he tossed an athletic bag in the back seat of the cruiser. He didn't say much on the ride though they talked a little about sports. There was no reason for Dark to think Abernathy's words of support in the hospital had changed. There was no hint of rancor expressed. But he did seem somewhat distracted, not the more upbeat type of personality he had presented in the past. Dark thought, 'who could blame him?'

The Lieutenant also noted that Abernathy comfortably directed him on the roads of this rural border region in New York. The tavern they wound up at was not an especially appealing looking place. Few people were inside in mid-afternoon. The Sergeant led them to a table in a corner, away from others. Dark was trying to decide if he could order a beer since he was driving his cruiser but was off duty. Abernathy began to speak as soon as they sat and Dark quickly decided he needed a beer.

"With all due respect, sir, you have no idea what you're doing." That got the Lieutenant's full attention. "This is war. You know, in war you gotta expect casualties, and sometimes no one takes any prisoners. It's violent and that's the way it's meant to be. You've figured out some of it: after a time it's more like kill or be killed instead of why. Even all the money, which is always the beginning, can fall to second place, you know.

"That Captain was right and you know it. Nothing much accomplished in that gun fight. Hoods like those guys are available everywhere. Kill one, two more get recruited. Weapons and money to buy them grow on trees. Gotta cut off all of a Hydra's heads to kill it to begin to even make a dent. If I just work within the VSP it's never gonna happen. Ever."

His words stunned the Lieutenant. How many layers of any of this was *Abernathy* involved in, Dark wondered? 'Shit! This is something.' He quickly figured where Abernathy was heading as he continued.

"You're trying to put yourself in the middle of the small potatoes part of these crimes, Lieutenant. Eventually it may get you killed. Not sure what the extent of your deal with Lori English is but I think you're off base there too. I don't think you are looking to fight a real war, Lieutenant. In real wars people do terrible things. It's ruthless. There are casualties; you could lose an eye. But the war goes on. Understand?

"Neither the cartels or the police agencies want the people to know how much progress renegades are making, even if it's still small. Rules and regulations stifle effective interdiction operations, and law officers can be bought. The future is beyond you or me or Lori but some hurts don't go away.

"Your work found stuff that could kill maybe a thousand people. We have destroyed a hundred times more and have eliminated enablers and leaders from the US and Canada to China."

This rapid education of VSP Major Crime Investigator Lieutenant Donald Dark meant the lives of Dark and Sergeant Jason

Abernathy were about to change forever. With the loss of an eye Abernathy's time on the VSP was coming to an end. It was clear any anger about his major injury would be focused on those he was at war with. He would transition to a new phase. There was no sense of looking back in him.

By telling all this to Lieutenant Dark Abernathy almost assured Dark's career would be altered also. Abernathy was surprised Dark offered a bit of a challenge.

"Abernathy, haven't you and whoever you are with ever thought about how stepping up the violence only breeds more; that people act and shoot more quickly and easily in situations like open warfare?"

"You don't get it Lieutenant. By spreading this poison how much more viciously could one human go after the lives of thousands of others…only for money? Killing from a distance. Keep your hands clean while you kill. You know, like air force pilots who kill with bombs from high in the sky.

"Probably can't change the world, Lieutenant, but awfully hard to sit by and watch family and friends perish because of drugs and weapons. Just trying to bring some of that excitement to the lives of the people who profit from doing it."

Abernathy's words and intensity had an immediate impact on the Lieutenant. It was a lot to begin to absorb quickly. He guessed that after that Captain's insights Abernathy assumed it was only a matter of time before Dark figured him out. Telling this to the Lieutenant offered a challenge to Dark. What was he going to tell his superiors about the Sergeant? Abernathy anticipated that.

"Lieutenant, I tried to be patient and work with the VSP. I liked it and I been treated pretty well; given opportunities. It just isn't going anywhere in this war." He glanced around and, looking down, in a low voice, said "Big things are coming up, Lieutenant; big things." He sat up again, leaned back and his mood lightened.

"I think some vision is coming back. Might even be usable in time. But the injury reminded me anything can happen at any time. It's time for me to move on."

Dark realized he was so affected by what Abernathy was saying he was breathing more deeply. He would have to think over what he was going to tell anyone.

The Sergeant changed his tone and turned to, what for him, was more business.

"So Lieutenant, about Lori English. Don't know her too well, and that might surprise you. Hear she's hard to know. I don't know what her deal is with that dog but can believe it might be important to her. I can try to find out if she wants it back if you want me to. Things like that can be worked out."

What an important day this was turning out to be. After weeks of his confusing obsession and all the negative and bad things it contributed to in his life Dark had more than enough motivation to resolve any outstanding components if it could be pulled off. He was ashamed it took others to drive him away from a fixation he clearly had created himself. So what if he and this woman shared some things? How mis-guided he was didn't matter. The effects on his life were terrible. Again, he wondered how he could have let himself be swallowed up in such a mess?

Dark considered all the many inputs, from shared sorrow about the dangers of the unwinnable, therefore futile, battling of drugs and the devastating impact of guns, to imagined physical attraction. All of those pieces actually only served to intensify his discouragement and loneliness, yet still allowed him to spurn a woman who loved him. What a fuck-up!

"I've had some ideas about the dog. You know, this woman came to my place and tried to get Alice, ...the dog, to come back to her. So she may really want her and it's hers. I think it would be good to know what she wants to do now. I don't mind keeping her but she can have her if someone figures a way to get her."

No one spoke for a few minutes. A long time had passed while they were at that table in the corner. Looking around now there were people beginning to filter in for an early dinner hour. They stood up and stretched, paid their bills, and bundled up to walk outside. Standing by the cruiser in a chill wind and darkening skies Sergeant Abernathy said his last words to Lieutenant Donald Dark.

"It'll be a kind of code, Lieutenant, but you'll figure it out. It will tell you what she wants to do about the dog. Will try to get it to you soon…before you leave the force too." Abernathy removed his bag from the back seat and shook the Lieutenant's hand. "Good luck to you, sir."

Dark made no response to the Sergeant's provacative words. "Good luck to you too, Sergeant."

Abernathy walked down the road to where the Res was located nearby.

———

- 35 -

The day of the Lieutenant's important meeting with his superiors finally arrived. The disappearance of Sergeant Abernathy was still very fresh. He decided Captain Bushey barely said a word about the Sergeant to try to shield Dark from any perception of personal responsibility or possible sense of guilt from his involvement in the obvious final chapter in the Sergeant's once promising career in the VSP. It was just as well. Dark was willing to report CBP intelligence concerning apparent vigilante activity in the drug war, and he did. However, he still hadn't accepted that he knew for sure what Abernathy had done. Was he truly gone? Did the brass know? Not being positive, Dark wasn't comfortable being the one to inform the force about what he *might* know about the Sergeant's disappearance. So he didn't.

Walking into the Colonel's office for his meeting to review his various meetings and personal reaction to the shoot-out with the Directors of the force struck him as unlikely to be nearly as challenging as he had assumed the session might be only a few weeks before. Despite Abernathy's prediction that Dark's days as a state trooper were over also, the Lieutenant did not now anticipate going in that direction if it remained his decision.

During the many post-action interviews and meetings he endured prior to this meeting to determine if he'd be allowed to return to active duty Dark believed he had fooled the psychologist and others more easily than he thought he would be able to. Dark assumed the required session with Captain Bushey and the Colonel, the head of the force, would be his final hurdle in getting back to work. As he sat there with them and the Colonel started speaking he quickly felt as though his brain was on a roller coaster. Then his thoughts began to race.

It didn't begin well. There was a period of time in that meeting Dark figured he was finished. His superiors were trying to be supportive but it was quickly clear some on force believed he had lost his nerve and probably was or, hopefully, *had been*, suffering from depression. The Colonel got right to it.

"No, not just the post-action interviews. There's been talk about you by some of the officers for a while… I assume you know that Dark. They say you've always been kind of a quiet guy and some say they haven't been comfortable with the way you've come across to them, especially lately. A few said they wonder if you've lost your nerve or lost interest in what we are trying to do on the force, Lieutenant."

As he talked the Colonel was staring directly at Dark. He always spoke in a formal way, tending to be heard as sounding stern. But not then. His tone was neutral, no sign of anger, disgust, or, even for that matter, of great concern. Dark knew to look straight back at him, but it was a moment of disappointment. He assumed the likely impact on others from his recent period of notable doubt about many things.

That, especially, included his weird fixation on someone which he had turned into a devotion that had become almost untenable even to him (…almost, that is). And also periods of extreme, job related, dangerous life and death activity confounded by worries of the futility of those risks. The Lieutenant hoped he was moving beyond much of that. He had been feeling pleased at the promise of his return to the satisfaction he once knew as a state police investigator.

He and Sergeant Abernathy were drawing different conclusions from major battles of the past few weeks.

Dark wouldn't challenge any of his peers questioning his commitment recently. If that meant he was no longer regarded as reliable for the force, he knew immediately, he would not argue with the Colonel. He also knew if that was the case, even if he managed to find a way to continue on the force, his career as a leader would, effectively, be over. Wondering whether that was about to happen, thoughts of how he might still hope to rendezvous with that lady passed through his active mind.

The Lieutenant sat quietly, not sure if the Colonel or Captain Bushey wanted, or expected, him to say something at that moment. Getting back to work, a routine, was appealing to him and he actually thought the force might at least respect his recent exploits. Although Dark understood many of his decisions and activities during the last weeks could be viewed more critically if certain force protocols for assessing behaviors were considered, he was not sure, through it all, if he had actually done anything wrong or outside of the regs. He realized, though, even just the act of repeatedly pulling the trigger of his weapon made him responsible for the deaths of a bunch of people, and that's what reputations are made of. That type of reputation, for the force, could be a definite liability.

But, in the view of the force there was a fundamental bottom line in the thinking about Lieutenant Dark. It formed the core of decision-making about him. Dark probably never really thought about how significantly his recent history affected the perspective of the force that ultimately determined his future on the VSP. Indeed, almost before many of the meetings it was generally already decided relieving him could be more problematic than retaining him. For one, Dark's solid, impressive, if not demonstrably successful, actions under fire, on several occasions, convinced them he was all right and they thought it was reasonable for him to return to active duty.

Further, the leaders of the force were also well aware the general public felt his actions in the firefight were cool-headed and heroic. Any idea of permanently relieving someone who was a hero to the public was fraught with problems for the force. No one in any of the sessions even broached the more complex concerns about what was actually accomplished to justify the carnage. And the force remained significantly undermanned. If Dark was okay with returning to active duty he was needed.

The Colonel and Captain didn't look grim; there wasn't a sense of anyone hanging crepe in the room. The Colonel stood and started to move to the door as he spoke. Now he wanted to sound friendly.

"So Lieutenant, one thing for sure, you do got a bunch of buddies on the force. Sonsabitches see nothing but good for you and your future on the force. Jeez Bushey, way they talked about him our jobs may be none too secure, you know.

"Dark, some good friends on the force can make for a better law enforcement team. That Lieutenant Fleury is a character but he manages people and he's good at it. And Lieutenant Steve Kamp's another good guy who's gonna leave a mark on this place. You're lucky to have them as good friends. I sat with each of them and those guys didn't want ta stop talkin' about how impressive it's been working with you. Spoke real highly 'bout you.

"You been through a lot, Lieutenant. I hope you're goin' back on duty for all the right reasons."

"Yes sir. I believe I am."

————

'Steve Kamp?' Driving home and thinking about Steve Kamp Dark was astounded. For an hour he was completely distracted; couldn't stop thinking about Kamp and their fractured history. Dark's gradual realization and acceptance of a role he must have played in the maturation of Kamp's outlook and career in Narcotics amazed him. That obvious affirmation of Dark's ability to impact on others was slow to gain his acceptance, but it did. It became a moment of profound clarity for Dark. He was a leader and, apparently, inspired others. His judgement was good.

Just like the world we live in his career was filled with ambiguities, he thought. In fact, he ruminated, to allow yourself to be ruled by doubt was too easy. Donald Dark guessed he would always have some struggles with doubts. However, he now accepted the return of a path to self-confidence and respect for his own abilities; some, perhaps, unique. He regained a perspective that allowed him to experience a sense of personal accomplishment as a professional and for society. That included positively impacting others on the force. 'Yes,' he quipped to himself, he 'was a force on the force.'

————————

"DD, why are you so sure that Abernathy isn't bullshitting you? Maybe's he's gone over to the other side; or always was, you know. His story sounds pretty shaky to me. Would be something, though. Assholes at CBP don't really know shit."

Dark started to wave his arm to blow off Fleury. But Fleury continued.

"You don't know if that Sergeant, or even that lady, aren't on the other side. You know wars can go on between gangs too. Pretty common in the cities they say. How you know all your contacts with that lady weren't her just trying to protect her investments in this thing?

"Bud, I think she played you like a drum right from the start. Maybe easy to figure you out from those sparkles that showed up in your eyes every time you looked at her, huh?"

"A fiddle, Fleur, a fiddle. You *beat* on a drum." Dark thought that might break the direction Fleury was going in. But Fleury didn't hesitate. He continued on.

"Yeah, first she blows those fuckers and their stuff up and then takes their territory. Think that's gonna start a war? And sure, then it got messy when we got in the middle of it. Huh? And then that Sergeant does his part and tells you to get out of this business. Fits?"

Dark dropped his arm. Leave it to Fleury to find a way to further complicate things. He stopped to think about what Fleury said and consider some of it. Possible? Plausible?

"Ah. More bullshit from the master bullshiter," Dark responded. "That's what I think, pal." But the damage was done. Certainly possible, which would mean he was played by Abernathy also…big time. Not too plausible though. The Lieutenant could check-up on the Sergeant if he did decide to go ahead and spill everything to his superiors. Messy to do that though; especially for Dark now. And Abernathy and the VSP also. At Dark's request Fleury agreed to keep that discussion between the two of them for the time being.

- 36 -

Returning to active duty was not difficult for the Lieutenant. Actually, he was eager to get back to a routine and looked forward to new assignments. Stuck in the back of his head Abernathy's comment that he was done with the force played on Dark's mind. The moment and setting when Abernathy said that it made some sense to him. But lately he was much less certain. All that had happened and his time away from work made him more openly reflective about his mood over the prior year and, especially, the fixations he had developed as part of that.

His own raw emotion and obsessions were finally something he was able to begin to place in a context where he felt he could understand them, and himself, better. He hoped so anyway. He had functioned, completing his job responsibilities at least adequately, he thought. But he knew his personal life was certainly a bummer; obviously lonely for most of the year, and probably more. Was it finally becoming easier for him to begin to accept how much of his existence was being ruled by loneliness?

And yet...being honest with himself, while he thought more longingly about his loss of Susan, that mysterious woman and his ill-defined passion for her continued to occupy a place in his mind.

Now, more than ever, it was clear to him it would be best if that obsession would vanish. He wished for that to happen. But…

––––––––––

Perhaps a sign of lingering concern about Lieutenant Dark's conduct over those last months he was *asked* to be on duty, extended hours actually, over the Thursday and Friday of the Thanksgiving holiday, coming just two days after his return. His recent leave made scheduling him with the duty appear reasonable to Dark, and likely his fellow members of the force also. His parents went to his sister's in Massachusetts. Dark graciously declined Molly and Ed's invitation to join, even for a brief time, the ever ongoing excitement of a house with four kids. So his only personal responsibility was managing a quick run home to take care of Alice in the middle of two twelve plus hour shifts. Dark enjoyed being busy those days. He felt refreshed and energized, knowing he had useful skills to apply to his work. There were no thoughts of futility.

––––––––––

Donald Dark never told his superiors what Sergeant Jason Abernathy said to him or why Abernathy walked away toward the Res late that afternoon in New York. The force reacted to the Sergeant's disappearance with worry and anger. Abernathy appeared to have turned, in many of their minds anyway, into a role model who had failed *them*. For some, the worst view of Abernathy's actions confirmed a stereotypic, prejudiced image of the poor reliability of Native Americans…if, of course, he wasn't dead.

Abernathy's outstanding record the few years he was on the force no doubt amplified the concern of some troopers and officers. Lieutenant Kamp was completely blindsided by Abernathy's sudden disappearance and told Dark he was planning to closely monitor the ensuing investigation.

The lieutenant wrestled with himself about why he continued to offer incomplete information about Abernathy's apparent actions and the potentially serious implications of Abernathy's words. But he knew, despite it all, he did not want, in any way, to inhibit his hope Abernathy would provide a link to the woman he was unable to completely remove from his thoughts.

———

Searching for some sort of a code or signal from Jason Abernathy was a minor distraction during his first week back on duty. Quickly, Dark was very busy. He liked that. He wasn't sure if drug related felonies were being directed away from him or the large number of other major crimes assigned to him just made him wonder about that. Settling into a routine at work and with Alice at home was far from what he wanted in life but he found being back in a regular schedule at work was reassuring.

Who knew what Jason Abernathy really meant or could know when he told Dark something would happen soon about Alice and the woman; presumably this Lori English? Maybe Abernathy contacted her and she said to forget it and this was all over. Dark could understand that but he was hoping for a more definitive resolution to this business. At the same time, being with Alice so consistently since she first showed up led to a clear bonding for each of them by now. He was still embarrassed to tell people she was his dog, but admitted to himself he cared about her.

Alice was a part of a truly fucked up time in his life that he was hoping and trying to put behind him. If returning her to Lori English was a necessary piece for putting this whole episode in his past he told himself he would do it. So he kept looking for something, but he didn't know what.

———

When communication came it was nothing like what he had imagined he had to be alert for. An envelope postmarked the Akwesasne Res, with no return address, arrived in his mail slot in Waterbury. He was pleased no one in the office brought it to his attention or commented on it. The Lieutenant put it in his pocket, planning to open it later, when he was home. Dusting it for prints or any type of analysis, he knew, was a waste of time.

As soon as he found that letter he was unable to get it, and all it would imply, out of his mind. Reacting that way frustrated and worried him. He thought he was managing to move on from his difficult period, and that woman. Maybe not. So he closed his door, sat, and opened the letter.

Any worry a challenging or cryptic code would need to be cracked faded instantly. The note on the piece of typing paper inside was handwritten, and clear enough.

Soccer field at Mt. Harding H S
Path up hill to clearing behind football field
3:30 PM Saturday
Bring dog

The school was in a hilly, rural area about fifteen minutes north of Waterbury. He guessed the soccer and football seasons were over for the year and the fields would be deserted that time of day. He wondered how dark it would be? It would get dark quickly anyway. Reading the note late in the day, Thursday, meant he had ample time to mull over as many angles of the situation as he would let himself dream up. Dark tried not to but sensed danger, although he was not sure why.

This lady obviously wanted her dog back and he could get that. So what was he worried about? At home in the evening his thoughts drifted to what *he* wanted from the meeting beyond returning Alice. He wasn't sure but it was enough to bother him. Could he, possibly, still be hoping for some kind of extraordinary relationship with this woman; that their shared world view and attraction to each other would surmount the thousand reasons that was not logical, or remotely possible? He didn't think so…but he wondered.

———

- 37 -

He slept fitfully that night. In the morning he woke feeling mostly unburdened by the complications of their story and was pleased to feel more resolute. The goal of the meeting was to return Alice to her rightful owner and then they each would hit the road. It would be nice to judge his reaction to chatting with her again but that would be the end of it…he hoped. Before he left for duty he managed to find the rhinestone collar that was on Alice when she was found with him. He tossed it on a counter, intending to put it on her on Saturday.

During the day Friday the Lieutenant found himself heading to the Williston Barracks to interview a trooper. After a brief back and forth with himself he decided it would be prudent to at least let Ed Fleury know where and when he was going to be on Saturday. Fleury might actually say something helpful about what was planned. Nevertheless that also meant Fleury would get an opportunity to jab at him about such a peculiar setting. That was not appealing at the moment but he would put up with it.

"Jeez, DD, I dunno. That's out in the middle of nowhere when there's no school stuff going on. Pretty guaranteed to be deserted that time of day. And it'll be dark before you're through, you know."

"Yeah, I know. But this lady is probably wanted, you know, although that CBP Captain never really said that. I'm not gonna call him, that's for sure." He was pleased Fleury seemed to be taking the upcoming event seriously.

"You know, DD, that lady might bring people, or who knows what, with her. Could be a set up. Who knows. She did some weird things down here. Remember? Unpredictable."

"That's for sure."

Then Fleury began rattling on. But Dark could tell he was also thinking.

"You think lady will know it's her dog without that chichi collar she came with? You know all those *papi-yonders*, or whatever, all look alike. And we got tons of them up here, you know."

Now Dark knew it was time to go and stood up.

"Wait, DD. Wait a minute. Don't you think we should arrange some back-up, at least waiting down the hill on the football field; within earshot of the field above?"

At the door, Dark stopped and spoke.

"Nah, don't need it Fleur. The less fuss in the force about all this the better, I think. Just giving the lady her dog back. Really nothing else possibly to consider. Should be quick... And I got Alice's rhinestone collar out; ready to go. So there won't be any chance of mistaken identity. Call you when I get home."

While he was talking with Ed Fleury Dark decided he would remember to go to the meeting armed.

———

Thanksgiving week and this week after were still notably dry. There was virtually no snow on the ground other than man-made at the ski areas. But it was cold and the days were more gray and blustery than sunny. Precipitation that would stick would come, in large amounts. It was still only a question of when.

Doing little until late in the day on Saturday meant getting through a long, tense time. He was nervous. Losing Alice was unappealing and upsetting but he hoped returning her would be a key to ending an unfortunate saga of his own making that he no longer wanted to be bound by. He needed to do this for his own future.

Just days before Lori English's letter arrived he bought an insulated neon yellow Gortex jacket for Alice to protect her from the wet and cold and from aggressive Vermont hunters. XS was still a little big.

Later in the afternoon, at the right time, he placed her rhinestone collar and bundled her up. They were on their way.

———————

- 38 -

The school parking lot and lower field were deserted so he drove his cruiser across the field to the edge of the woods where there was a trail. No signs of lighting for the field. He assumed the same would be true for the soccer field. Daylight would be a challenge if the exchange didn't go quickly. On trees capable of dropping leaves, even the oaks, most leaves were down. As they entered and walked the hilly path to the upper field Dark had a sense of the barren landscape where Trooper Ed Clark was murdered. The terrain looked a bit forbidding in the darkening day. Yet the path was only about twenty or thirty yards up a gentle grade. It was protected from the cold wind on the field, but there was a soft whistle from the surrounding fir trees. Much darker walking the footpath, but lighter up ahead.

Only neon clad Alice, in his arms, stood out when they entered the quiet and deserted clearing that was the soccer field. Forest bordered all four sides. As he suspected, the field was unimproved beyond two long, low benches marking sideline boundaries. The Lieutenant decided to walk toward the mid-field markings but hugged near the sideline, staying only about ten yards from the dark, surrounding forest.

After going only a few more feet into the clearing he heard the woman before he saw her. He was surprised how sure he was he recognized her voice. Then she showed herself, standing alone, at the edge of the woods, about twenty yards from him. In the dimming light he doubted either of them could make out much of the other's features at that distance. As he had during the past few weeks, he relied on the few images from his memory to picture her.

Alice remained nestled in his arms. He was in the open; exposed. The woman was not. Staying where she was she got right to it. She spoke loudly and the tenor of her tone was unmistakable.

"You really pissed me off, *Lieutenant.*" She made the word 'Lieutenant' sound like a joke. "For a time I couldn't stop thinking about you. Sitting there with that kid I suddenly got a feeling you and I looked at the whole insane world the same way. Couldn't get you out of my mind." She paused, as though some of that was, briefly, fresh for her once more. Then her tone hardened again and her words were pure anger.

"Then you followed me. I couldn't believe it. Can you imagine. In the beginning I told myself you were doing it because you were interested in me. Oh right; sure…I guess not for those reasons, huh? It was obvious you were on to me. But you didn't want to kill me, like those scum. No, you wanted to arrest me cause that's what troopers do. Right? I bet the moment you saw me you knew the Border Protection people wanted me… I thought I had pulled it off but you were just stringing me along. Except hadn't counted on you getting into my head. It's been a disaster ever since.

"I had to get out of there and I couldn't find my dog. Of all people you wind up with her. Guess we were fated to keep meeting then. That's not good…for me anyway."

As she continued she raised and lowered her voice but her anger never diminished.

"You know, you really never did anything, *TROOPER!* Really! …But you kept showing up and screwing things up. Made everybody's work harder. Even those shits you killed at that farm were blamed on me."

He couldn't see her well. She had moved behind some rocks at the edge of the trees. It would be completely dark in a short time. There were light flurries but, all of a sudden, no wind. He heard her perfectly. He sensed the anger but also fear in her voice. Dark wondered if she was really alone. Alice stayed silent and still, wrapped in her neon yellow jacket. Even before the woman spoke again he started to drift away from the open area moving closer toward the protection of the edge of the woods.

There was no longer any doubt in his mind she was dangerous. Whatever she was doing, whichever side she was on, obviously nothing was going well for her. Holding him responsible for her difficulties or failures suggested he was in a very bad position standing out on that field.

Dark wished he could know, for sure, which side she was on. His mind briefly wandered back to their first meeting. Turns out that short, fateful interaction messed them both up; maybe her even more than he. Imagine. They both were playing dangerous games when he followed her. Maybe hers was more dangerous. But so what? What was going on, right in front of him now on that field, had the makings of another life and death moment for the Lieutenant.

He didn't know what to think about the things she was talking about. It made no sense to him. If she meant some of what she was saying it was mind-boggling. So he asked her about the episode he did know something about. He shouted out and, reflexively, pulled Alice closer to him.

"Why did you spend hours in the woods outside my condo trying to get the dog?"

Dark truly thought she wanted the dog. He didn't want to give Alice back but there was no point prolonging any potential for further dangerous contact with this woman. A fresh start meant putting all this behind him. He should let her take Alice. Doing that would be one more piece of his disturbing life that would be left behind. Over.

"You asshole, you still think this is about the dog! What an idiot! You can't have three sides fighting a war, you jerk. *Nobody's* gonna get out of that alive."

Why did it matter to him if her underlying motives were altruistic or criminal? Would he react any differently in this setting if he knew? She sounded truly menacing. So it was him she was after that time outside his condo. He finally was closer to understanding her.

"You didn't even come into the woods when I had the dog, you bastard. Two times she broke away and ran back toward you. I should have come out of those trees after you right then... You! You were sleeping with a lady while I was freezing in the cold. Fat chance you were dreaming about me while you were doing it, huh? Should have ended it then. Right then."

She must have moved just beyond the border of the forest and now was completely out of his view as she was speaking. After a short pause he heard her voice again; more softly. "Pointless, I guess."

While she was talking he wondered how difficult it could have been for her to hang on to Alice? Maybe Alice had some moves he wasn't aware of. Regardless, it was becoming obvious now, this woman held him responsible for a lot. Dark guessed very little had been going well for her for a while. The truth of any relationship, real or fantasized, for these two was rapidly becoming self-evident to Donald Dark.

Starting weeks before, for a ridiculously long time until very recently, Dark dreamed of the moment they would come face to face again and declare their innately obvious true love for each other. She, on the other hand, after a short time, apparently only wanted to kill him.

He hadn't, remotely, considered such a motivation for that prospect and was at a loss over what he should or might do. Getting to his weapon would be awkward with Alice shivering in his arms. And he couldn't see trying to shoot her for acting threatening. That wasn't right and would haunt him…no, for Donald Dark, paralyze him, for the rest of his life. He quickly decided waiting around to respond if and when she shot at him was also a poor strategy. What was a Vermont State Trooper supposed to do?

"Lori English, or a woman who is called Lori English, I'm Major Crime Investigator Lieutenant Donald Dark of the Vermont State Police and I'm arresting you on suspicion of felony smuggling. I'm asking you to place any weapons you might have on the ground, put your hands high in the air, and walk out into the clearing where I can see you…" And then he lied and added "…better." Dark and Alice moved to partial cover by a tree and didn't move.

It became eerily quiet. Nothing. No words or sounds from her. Dark believed this woman was very dangerous and he was reluctant to move toward her last location. Any idea she had withdrawn into the woods and was leaving was not going to be a satisfactory resolution for him. Worry she might come back at any time, maybe even over years, was unacceptable. He had been ready to say they should each walk away, her with the dog, and end it. But they never got to anything like that.

With some hesitation he slowly began a distressing walk to the area where she had been standing. Putting Alice down would make any potential action much easier but he was reluctant to do that. The first few steps, exposing himself on the open field, were the most harrowing and, he assumed, the most dangerous.

Still nothing; not a stirring or sound. He stopped where he had last seen her, at the edge of the woods. He was sweating and assumed Alice was also.

"Shit!. She's gone." To no one. "Damn!"

Like so many times before, so much danger and yet nothing important was accomplished. He still didn't really know who she was or what she was doing. Well, that was not entirely true. Odds were, like Fleury said, she was trying to put some piece of the cartel out of business so she could run her own enterprise. Shit, the drugs on that boat in the Seaway probably were removed before they blew it up. Small amounts of that commodity fueled big prices. A smuggler's dream. But he didn't know if any of that was true. Not at all.

Dark figured she was a lot like him; unable to clear her mind of her preoccupation. Trouble for him for an awfully long time. He guessed Fleury's badgering him to do this with back-up probably would have been a better plan and they might have her. Dark knew why he nixed that: he was dying to have even a brief chance to speak with her again; alone. He hoped to confirm, once and for all, he was beyond her forever. Hours before he had actually laughed to himself when a similar use of 'dying' passed through his mind anticipating their meeting.

As he cautiously stepped farther into the darkening woods his confidence began to fade. Once again he reminded himself this had always had been a fool's errand. He and Alice slowly advanced about twenty yards. Nothing. If she had planned to shoot him she had ample time. Enough. Walking backwards, he slowly re-traced the steps he had taken into the woods until he reached the clearing again.

———

- 39 -

They walked the thin, modestly downhill path through the thicket of woods to the lower field and his cruiser. He tried to keep his ears sharp for trouble and assumed Alice was doing the same. The only sounds were his own footsteps on the firm ground. He was discouraged and disappointed. Ultimately, his mood morphed to anger; at himself, and her. All this had accomplished nothing. Maybe worse.

Reaching the clearing Dark was surprised to see a vehicle next to his. It was dark now so he had to cautiously move closer before he realized it was another state police cruiser. Immediately, he figured it was Ed Fleury, the only person who knew what he was doing and where he was. All illumination was off but the engine was running. The driver's window was open, presumably so he could listen for sounds or shots, just like Dark.

For the first time in hours Dark felt himself begin to relax, although he remained upset. A period of resignation was beginning. He opened Ed's passenger door and started to slide Alice and himself in. When the courtesy lights went on he noticed Fleury had his service weapon tucked next to him on the front seat and a long rifle in a canvas case stretched across the back seat.

Most notable was the comforting warmth being generated by the cruiser's heater. He thought he could feel Alice sigh as they sat. Donald Dark took a breath also and they all rested, silently, for a minute or two.

"Fleur, any idea if we're in one of the towns where it's illegal to leave a vehicle idling?"

Fleury had determined to let Dark take his time relating what he chose to say about whatever happened at the soccer field. He kept his gaze and ears on the forest as Dark and Alice got in and said nothing at first. After Dark's words he turned to him.

"Are you going to give me a citation, Trooper? …Guess that means you plannin' to stay on the force now, Trooper?"

Dark hadn't thought about it as much recently but he probably was. He was comfortable being back and, like for many others, it was all he knew.

"Well, buddy, glad you're back from that isolated field. Cold out there and I was close to deciding I better put a headlamp on and go out there and find you…Was about to call for back-up before I headed out. Always a good idea, you know."

As soon as Fleury finished Dark spoke, with some intensity. "It was a disaster, Fleur. Nothing like what I thought it would be. Maybe the only thing that lady and I really have in common is we're both crazy." From looking forward, into space, he turned to face Fleury. "Ed, please try to keep your reaction to yourself on this one, okay? Turns out this lady became obsessed with me. Like I was with her. Only I think I've slowly realized I made up so much of her and have gotten over her. She's decided I'm responsible for a whole lot of a string of bad luck for her and I think she wanted to kill me.

"She wants me dead and didn't give a shit about Alice. Really sounded crazy. No one died up there that I know of. That may not be good Fleur. Lady made it clear she's after me. Don't know if I can live that way. She's obviously resourceful. Can you imagine never knowing when you, your dog, or someone you care about could become her victim?" Verbalizing his frustration and fear made it that much more real for him. Dark's upset and sense of despair momentarily increased.

Ed Fleury didn't have a sympathetic expression on his face. Alice glanced at Dark, stood up, stretched, then jumped over the front seat to the back and lay on top of the rifle bag. She was with Ed Fleury.

"DD, now you gonna tell me you never gonna drive on a two lane road again because all these asshole young people, worse than drunks, are out there playing with their damn phones while barreling down the road, ready to kill you? That's danger pal. But it's the world we live in. This lady? Shit. If she wanted you dead why didn't I hear any gunfire up there? Bet there was time for her to say her piece and then try to blow you away...or never say anything and blow you away as soon as you walked onto that field. You know, like the ambush you're telling me you have to worry about for the rest of your life. Come on pal, a little too f'ing dramatic don't you think?"

Alice stood, looked over disapprovingly at Dark, and settled again. Dark freely admitted to himself he was all wound up. Fleury's words made sense. The Lieutenant, like every law officer, had been threatened many times. Just never affected him like this. He had to get in better control of himself. After a minute Donald Dark reached his right arm across the front seat and waited for Ed to respond and raise his. Then he shook Ed Fleury's hand.

"Thanks for the back-up, Fleur. Appreciate it. Guess that's what we do for each other, eh? Come on, Alice, let's go home." It was dark and a strange place. Alice wasn't about to find her way on the ground. She hopped into the front seat and into Dark's arms. It seemed natural to each of them.

But they didn't go home.

———

Driving more slowly than usual Donald Dark quickly was lost in his thoughts as he navigated the dark, winding back country roads toward his home. He was struck by a subtle, but noticeable, lightening of his mood. Then it seemed to build within him. He was excited to sense at least a beginning of an end to a long troubling time.

Those brief, bizarre minutes with that woman were essential. Talking with Fleury after that was a hard knock on the head he sorely needed. Lately, Dark realized he was living as though he considered himself almost a bystander in the pageant of his own life. The stresses and dangers of his job were in no way a fiction but, as Fleury said, you can't live your life in constant worry. Any idea his own fiction about that woman could be helpful to him was nonsense. He sure learned that.

Rather abruptly he became consumed with thoughts of Susan. He desperately wanted to speak with her. He headed toward her condo and was overtaken by a flood of thoughts of them together; forever. Images of happiness and hope came to him in a torrent. Dark envisioned them hugging each other so tightly in an embrace it almost hurt. He had to be with her.

He needed to tell her so much. They should have kids. And they would name the first child after Haber; Dennis…or…Denise if it was a girl. Dark was sure Susan was now the key to a life that would allow him to feel comfortable with himself and others.

In his increasingly exuberant state he was certain it was all over now. He just knew it; believed so. The burden of his pursuit of that woman had ended. They would not seek each other again.

He wasn't sure why but he didn't call Susan until he was parked outside her condo. As her phone began to ring he realized it was inconsiderate of him not to have given her an opportunity to 'freshen up,' as women say, before she might see him. And he forgot it was Saturday night. Those mistakes could thwart his hope of talking with her.

Her voice suggested the call caught her off guard. Initially, she was non-committal about speaking then. Immediately, Dark was pissed at himself. But then she did agree.

"Listen, Don, I have a special book group tonight. Have to be at the restaurant in half an hour. Give me a minute and I'll sit with you in your car for a few minutes."

"That's great, Susan. I appreciate it." He felt a wave of disappointment, quickly realizing the only opportunity he was going to have to talk would be rushed. What should he say to her? He kept his engine running ('fuck the environment,' he thought) and asked Alice to get in the back.

Susan didn't appear to act distracted or in a rush as she slid into his front seat. She, briefly, had a start as she entered and noticed a moving fluorescent appearing object on the back seat. She quickly figured it out. Nor did she lean into Dark with a kiss. She kept a distance and her expression, if anything, was somber. Yet she wasn't completely formal either.

"Nice to see you, Don. I imagine you've been busy now that you've returned to active duty. Everything working out okay for Jim Wiley in the City?"

Dark stared at her. Even after a week teaching little brats she appeared energized, dressed casually for an evening with friends. He thought she looked radiant. Moisture developed around his eyes. He was surprised. He was much more emotional than he had realized. He took a breath and battled to pace his racing thoughts.

"Susan, we know each other too well for me to disturb you without warning to suddenly tell you I'm sorry for so much and expect that's all that's needed. You know lots of things have been complicated for me for a while. Most of it has been kind of crazy and the last weeks have been *really* crazy; especially today. Today I, foolishly, probably put my life on the line just to prove to myself the mistakes I've been making. And I did.

"Looking back it all has become painful, Susan. I know it's been painful for you too, Susan. Your words were so upsetting to hear, but made a big difference for me. I can't explain why I've made your life… our life…so difficult. So much has happened in a short time, Susan, and now I feel like I understand myself and the world around me better. Except for one thing, Susan. And that's us. Too many years have passed. Maybe babies have been delayed. But…"

Susan was watching him the entire time he spoke. She felt a confusion she thought, perhaps hoped, she had banished. She spoke slowly and softly, but determinedly. "Don, I'm not sure I can let the past go so easily. Maybe not as easily as you hope you can. Honestly, I don't know if I can trust you, Don." Her last words didn't exactly express her intended thought. She wanted to say more and briefly opened her mouth but stopped herself, deciding that might be too upsetting for her.

He got it. But he was not of a mind, after all that had happened, to give up on himself…and them, again. "I think I understand, Susan." Though it was more likely a part of him had believed she would always be there, waiting for him to figure himself out. Now, he told himself, it all made sense to him. They *must* be together. No one spoke and they sat quietly for a time, neither sure what should come next.

Dark knew he wanted them to at least keep talking every day. "Susan, I told the Wileys I would go down to New York to visit them the end of next week. Please think about coming with me. Play hooky from school and let's spend some time together, out of Vermont." Words continued to flow rapidly from Donald Dark. Susan assumed his racing speech must be a reflection of what was going on in his mind. It was nothing she had ever seen from him before.

"Let me try to show you what kind of an idiot I can be devoting myself to you instead of the years we've spent together that I've worried about me. And Alice loves you too. I miss being with you, so much."

Sitting in his cruiser, struck by how intensely serious he appeared as he spoke, Susan didn't know what to make of Donald Dark. The very unusual way he was acting almost frightened her. Was this truly the moment she had constantly, longingly dreamed of until only very recently? She wondered if Donald's dramatically out of character behavior was a reasonable reaction to his emotional stress over the last few months, even if much of that was self-imposed? Or was this seeming difference in his personality some kind of a sign of more trouble ahead?

For a long time Susan hoped joining together in their mutual loneliness would benefit each of them. She concluded the attempt would be a worthy try for both. Though, with the latest events, she was starting to wonder if he was more needy than she. Until recently Susan thought only changing Alice's name might be enough for her.

Despite Donald Dark's recent terribly hurtful treatment of her she found herself unable to remain resolute in her determination to stay away. He was the only man Susan ever loved. She gambled with herself Donald would never hurt her that way again. Impulsively, Susan leaned across to him and they hugged…tightly, as Dark had hoped. Susan realized he was crying. It surprised her.

THE END